Praise for Vlad

"I had been waiting for this story and just loved Vlad. I read this in one sitting, just could not put it down." —*Malisa, GoodReads*

"First, holy crap, this book was awesome. Vlad is a dark, mysterious, basically tortured soul…I love Patricia's take on the vampire genre and to add in sexy bikers in the mix…hell yes." —*Krys, GoodReads*

"Fabulous read…Vlad holds your full attention from the very beginning until the very end! 5 stars!" —*Sherry, GoodReads*

"If you're looking for a good book to curl up with and a new Book Boyfriend, I highly recommend Vlad and the entire Sons of Sangue Series." —*Desiree, GoodReads*

"Vlad's story didn't disappoint. I found it wonderful and loved his and Janelle's chemistry and their journey to love." — *Merianne, Goodreads*

"The shock and awe within the pages had my jaw dropping. WOW!! Holy Hot Hunky Biters!!" —*Trudy, Goodreads*

"I devoured this book in 3 hours. That should say how much I liked this book." —*Karen, SiKReviews*

Other Books by Patricia A. Rasey:

Viper: Sons of Sangue (#1)
Hawk: Sons of Sangue (#2)
Gypsy: Sons of Sangue (#3)
Rogue: Sons of Sangue (#4)
Draven: Sons of Sangue (#4.5)
Preacher: Sons of Sangue (special edition)
Xander: Sons of Sangue (#5)
Ryder: Sons of Sangue (#6)
Wolf: Sons of Sangue (#7)
Love You to Pieces
Deadly Obsession
The Hour Before Dawn
Kiss of Deceit
Eyes of Betrayal
Façade

Novellas:

Spirit Me Away
Heat Wave
Fear the Dark
Sanitarium

Vlad
Sons of Sangue

Patricia A. Rasey

Patricia A. Rasey
patricia@patriciarasey.com
www.PatriciaRasey.com

Publisher's Note: This is a work of fiction. Names, characters, places, and incidents are a product of the author's imagination. Locales and public names are sometimes used for atmospheric purposes. Any resemblance to actual people, living or dead, or to businesses, companies, events, institutions, or locales is completely coincidental.

Book Layout ©2013 BookDesignTemplates.com

Ordering Information:
Quantity sales. Special discounts are available on quantity purchases by corporations, associations, and others. For details, contact the email address above.

Vlad: Sons of Sangue / Patricia A. Rasey – 1st ed.
ISBN-13: 979-8-6174190-7-0

Dedication

To those of you waiting for VLAD—
This one's for you!

To my editor, thank you for the fast
turnaround on my edits! I owe you!

Acknowledgements

Thank you to my cover artist, Frauke Spanuth, from Croco Designs for creating the Sons of Sangue covers. I am always grateful! Vlad's cover is one of the best!

THE MATTRESS DIPPED AS THE SIX-FOOT-FOUR MAN standing next to her bed placed one knee beside her hip and looked down upon her. The sheer size of him made Janelle draw in a sharp breath. Eyes black-as-coal, irises nearly swallowing the sclera, set deep beneath his prominent brow. His unnaturally high cheekbones spoke of something inhuman. Bluish-black hair floated about his shoulders like Dracula's cape, cloaking some of his facial features in shadows.

Oddly, she wasn't frightened.

He stepped back and shucked his leathers, wearing no boxers or briefs. His overly large erection jutted from his abdomen, a small bead of moisture decorating the tip. *Good Lord*, the man's stance spoke of his intention to impale her.

Janelle licked her lips, her mouth suddenly dry as the Sahara. Her gaze slowly traveled over his muscular chest and abdomen, then followed the descending trail of hair to his swollen cock.

Wetness pooled between her thighs, dampening her panties. This man was certainly fuckable, but Janelle was never one to crawl into bed just for a good lay. And yet, her hands moved of their own accord.

Reaching for the hem of her threadbare tank top, she discovered it already missing. In fact, her flannel shorts were nowhere to be found either and yet she couldn't remember removing either of them. Even though winter had long set in, she was far from cold, even with her thick down comforter pooled at her feet, leaving her nearly bare for his appraisal. The heat rising from her could have easily melted the icicles hanging from the eaves outside her opened window.

The man moved back onto the bed, capturing both her wrists in one large hand, drawing them over her head. His heated gaze held hers captive as firmly as his grip on her hands. He crawled between her thighs, easily spreading them. Sliding his free hand beneath the silk of her panties, he rent the fabric, tossing them aside. The head of his cock nudged her opening, finding her wet and bringing a satisfied smile to his full red lips, nestled amongst the dark growth of his close-shorn beard. She couldn't help but find his lips pleasing. Until he parted them, revealing a set of large, razor-sharp fangs.

A scream seized her throat as his cock breached her opening. Pushing forward, he fully seated himself inside her. Lowering his head, he snaked out his overlong tongue, licking a path up her neck to just below her ear. Fangs penetrated her skin with a soft pop, sinking deep into her throat.

A gasp left her lips. Janelle sat up abruptly, trying to draw a breath, her hand covering her neck. *Dear Lord.* That vision had been all too real. Her heart beat laboriously; her pulse roared. As he sank fangs deep, drawing from her throat, she hadn't been afraid but had almost climaxed upon penetration.

Glancing around the room, she found herself alone. Her gauzy curtains fluttered in the cool winter breeze from the gaping window she couldn't recall opening.

How the hell?

More importantly, why was she completely naked with her night clothes strewn across the floor?

Janelle got up from the bed, noting her panties were still in one piece. She quickly dressed, then padded across the carpeted floor to pull the window closed and secured the lock.

A shadow of a large man disappeared into the shrubbery at the far end of the lot her cabin sat on, a cabin few knew about. Janelle blinked to clear the vision. Surely, the man was a remnant of her dream. Pulling the curtain closed, she turned and headed back for the bed and yanked the comforter to her chin.

Vampires weren't real.

But Vlad Tepes the man was real, and her vision had just conjured him up.

CHAPTER ONE

V LAD TEPES CIRCLED THE SMALL AREA IN FRONT OF THE altar. Two humans lay near his feet, legs and arms askew. Large holes gaped from the carotid which once pumped their blood. Very little had spilled onto the red carpet beneath them, telling him what he already feared. This was the work of his bastard brother.

Waste not want not.

Or at least that's what he thought went through his brother Mircea's minuscule mind as he'd attacked these poor mortals. Normally, Vlad might have agreed but not when it came to a human life.

Never take more than needed.

A vampire did not need to drain a human to sustain life. Which was the exact reason Mircea needed to be stopped. His brother had lost his damn mind. This was the second such occurrence from the reckless fool. The first happened months ago, when Mircea and his sidekick Nina took the lives of four Mexican cartel soldiers. Vlad hadn't been overly concerned with those killings, as he'd thought the world had been done a favor.

But this time?

Christ Almighty. The Lord himself would likely want penance. These two spent humans lay at the altar of a Catholic church, one of the largest in Eugene, Oregon. The man at Vlad's feet wore a blood-stained collar, labeling him a priest, the woman a nun's habit. These two didn't deserve his brother's rage or revenge against Vlad. They were innocent, for God's sake.

Mircea had sent him a text only moments ago as to where to find his latest carnage. Vlad wasted little time in arriving, though he had falsely hoped it was nothing more than Mircea's shenanigans. If Vlad was a gambling man, he'd bet law enforcement had already been dispatched. Mircea no doubt hoped Vlad would be standing over the bodies upon their arrival.

Janelle Ferrari came to mind.

Fuck, that woman had wet dream written all over her. She'd been on the earlier case; one he had successfully convinced her was the work of a rival cartel and not the work of a blood-thirsty vampire. The case remained unsolved. This crime scene, though, wouldn't involve the DEA, Drug Enforcement Administration, and would be left to the locals. Too bad. He wouldn't have minded running into the stunning brunette again.

His mind traveled back a couple of months, when he had followed the special agent to a little hideaway in the woods. Like a thief, he had snuck in through her bedroom window while she slept. But instead of searching her cabin for files on her previous case concerning the dead cartel soldiers as intended, he'd stood rooted to the floor. She dreamt, moaning like she was in the throes of passion. Hell, he could still recall her scent and her naked image had been burned into his corneas. Vlad, jealous of her fantasies, had slipped back through the window before she woke.

He shook his damn head. Getting women into his bed had been as easy as a snap of his fingers. Never had he needed to crawl through a window unannounced, nor stand over their sleeping form like a pervert of the worst kind, wishing he'd been invited into the bed she had stretched out upon.

So what made her different?

Vlad was pretty sure should he suggest they get horizontal she'd shoot him down faster than a gossip spreading juicy news. Janelle Ferrari was now and forever off limits. He should've known from the get-go she spelled trouble when he had been unable to hypnotize her.

Sirens in the distance, in all probability headed his way, caught his attention and brought him back to the calamity at his feet. It would do no good to remove the poor humans from the scene as he didn't have time to clean up after his brother. He hoped Mircea was smart enough not to leave behind DNA, or Vlad would be taxed with making the evidence disappear.

Mircea needed to be found and stopped before the fool exposed the reality of vampires. Humans would never understand or see them as equal. Vlad had seen human nature at its worst. There would be no stopping them from eliminating the threat until the last of his kin breathed their final breath.

Vlad's acute hearing picked up squealing tires, car doors being slammed, and feet pounding the cement as they thundered up the church steps. Using speed undetected by the human eye, he turned and exited through the rear of the church before any law enforcement could circle the building. He didn't stop until he was safely miles away from the bloody corpses.

Pulling out his cell, he tapped a quick message to his brother.

You killed for the last time.

Little dots appeared on the screen before Mircea's reply appeared.

Says you. Oh, and don't bother using this number again. This phone will be destroyed following this conversation.

Lord, he wanted to throw his own phone against the nearest thick oak and watch it shatter into pieces. His anger would do him no good.

Why the priest and nun?

Gritting his teeth, he impatiently waited for his brother's reply, a reply that did not come. He supposed the phone had already been crushed beyond use and tossed away. His question would go unanswered.

Why the hell would Mircea go after two so undeserving?

When he found his brother, he planned to beat that very answer out of him. Right before he ripped his head clean from his shoulders. For now, there was nothing more he could do.

He needed to look up his grandsons and make them aware of Mircea's latest devastation. Hopefully, Mircea had momentarily shelved the hunt of Kane and Kaleb Tepes, giving them some needed time to find the son of a bitch. Vlad wasn't foolish enough to let his guard down, though, not where his kin was concerned. Mircea had made the threat to take his grandsons out and Vlad knew his brother too well to hope he had given up on that quest. Mircea's antics were no doubt done in hopes to flush them out.

It appeared Vlad would be spending a lot more time in Oregon, at least until he could find his brother and stop him from taking any more innocent lives.

THE WORK CELL ON HER DESK chirped, illuminating the screen with the name *Eugene PD*. Janelle couldn't help but wonder if Detective Barker and his team of investigators had turned up a lead regarding a past case concerning the murders of Joseph Flores and three other cartel members.

Something about the incident hadn't set quite right with her, even if conceivably it appeared to be the actions of a rival cartel quarreling over territory. All evidence indicated that to be the case. And yet, she hadn't been able to let it go. Her conscience warred against the obvious choice of suspects. To date, Janelle hadn't found one scrap of evidence linking the case to one of the rivaling Mexican cartels. In fact, if her informants were to be believed, she had been told to look outside the box on this one.

Grabbing the cell, she slid her thumb across the screen and put it on speakerphone. "Special Agent Ferrari."

"This is Detective Barker."

Wonderful. She could barely stand the man. Barker had an ego the size of Mount Rainier and an exclusive membership to the man club, meaning he didn't believe women could do his job. He barely tolerated her on a good day, which meant the phone call must be of some importance. Janelle supposed it was better than a house call. Could she possibly hope for a break in the case?

"What can I do for you, Detective?"

"We have a new case that might be of some interest, as much as it pains me to say. The chief asked me to contact you regarding it."

Janelle shifted in her seat. This had to be good if Detective Barker was following orders from Chief Jennings concerning her. No way in hell Barker would call her on his own.

She hadn't heard of any new developments concerning any cases within Eugene the DEA needed to look into. "Want to fill me in?"

Detective Barker cleared his throat. "We have nothing new to report on the Joseph Flores case and his three minions. As far as I'm concerned, it's a dead-end. Let the cartel kill each other and do the world a favor."

Figures the ass would give up easily.

"About four hours ago, we got a call of a double homicide over on the corner of Cross and Main. The city's oldest Catholic church occupies damn near the entire block."

"The case, Barker." It was hard not to get annoyed with the blowhard. "I assume it has something to do with the Flores case or you wouldn't be calling me."

"Right." Janelle could hear the chief's robust voice in the background, no doubt issuing orders. *Him* she liked. "We have a dead priest and nun on our hands."

"And this would interest the DEA why?"

"Normally, I wouldn't have bothered calling you. But this isn't a normal murder, Special Agent. No gunshot wound, no stab marks."

Her breath caught in her throat, recalling too easily the Flores case and what was left of the men's throats. "Are you saying it's the same MO?"

"Possibly, though the choice of victims this time makes no sense. Where the last scene was brutal and we had blood all over the goddamn place, here it appears the blood was drained from the bodies via neck wounds, leaving very little to soak into the carpet beneath them."

"The victims killed elsewhere and dumped there?" she suggested.

"The fixed lividity suggests otherwise."

"You said these weren't knife wounds."

"No, Special Agent Ferrari. It appears someone tore out the throats of the victims, using God knows what, and then drained them. Which is reminiscent of the Flores case in that the victims were left devoid of blood."

She swore beneath her breath. "Do you still believe this is the work of a rival cartel? If so, what purpose would they have for killing a priest and nun?"

"We don't know that to be a fact yet. We're trying to make a connection, see if the church was involved in any illegal activities we may not have known about."

"The crime scene processed? What about the bodies?"

"The bodies are at the morgue. We did process the scene but we're leaving it closed off to the public until you guys sign off on the case. We figured you might want to nosey around."

Janelle smiled. "But you're hoping we'll sign off."

"I would never wish these cases to go unsolved."

"No, but you wouldn't want your case to be taken over by the DEA either."

Barker laughed, the sound deep and gravelly. "I assure you, Special Agent Ferrari, I couldn't care less what you do. Chief Jennings said to contact you and that's what I'm doing."

"I assure you that you have no need to worry about your case, Barker. I'll check with my boss, Captain Melchor, but I'm sure he'll want me to come by and take a look. If I find nothing connecting this case with the previous one, it will be all yours."

"I appreciate that. When can we expect you?"

"Within the hour. Don't let anyone else in the church until my team arrives."

"I wouldn't think of it."

Janelle hung up the phone and leaned back in her chair. The detective was a wise ass. She almost dreaded heading to Eugene. This case though? It intrigued her. Which, of course, brought up the one man she had hoped to wipe from her radar, Vlad Tepes. Janelle wasn't sure why these cases conjured up the man, or stirred her visions, which were premonitions of future events, but she intended to find out. He had shown up at her office inquiring about the Flores case. Could he possibly be interested in this one as well? If so, what was the man's angle?

She had given Vlad her card when she stopped by the Sons of Sangue clubhouse months ago, and yet he had not called as asked, enlightening her on his interest in the case.

Ever since Vlad's strange visit to her office and her following erotic dreams of him, not to mention the vision of a tall man slinking into the forest at the back of the cabin's lot, her psychic visions had gone silent.

Maybe it had been her apparent obsession with the man that had quieted them. Something about him stirred her sexually in ways she hadn't been accustomed to since becoming a special agent. Typically, her work fulfilled her. The fact she craved a dangerous man like Vlad alone should have her steering clear. Instead, he intrigued her, preoccupied her thoughts. Vlad was a distraction she couldn't afford, regardless that he'd had her libido working overtime.

CHAPTER TWO

THE SUN BEAT DOWN ON THE BACK OF VLAD'S NECK. THANK-
fully, the whole vampires can't go out in sunlight was
more fiction than truth. Worse case, he'd sunburn quicker
than most and his eyes were more sensitive to the bright light.
Nothing a good pair of sunglasses and SPF 50 wouldn't correct. He exited his newly purchased 2019 Aston Martin DB11
convertible in a sleek magnetic silver. Granted he had paid a
pretty penny for the vehicle, but he couldn't be seen driving
any old sedan. Vlad had been a Romanian ruler and needed
a vehicle worthy of one. In the past, he hadn't used normal
forms of transportation, hadn't seen the need.

His feet had always gotten him where he desired, except
for when the need arose to continent hop. Using planes had
become a necessity to take him where his legs couldn't. Unlike fictional vampires, he couldn't simply turn into a bat and
fly. A ridiculous notion at best. Besides, if he could
shapeshift, he'd pick something majestic like a bald eagle, or
cool like a sleek black panther.

Now that he was going to be spending more time than
usual in the United States, Vlad needed to embrace tradi-
tional methods of traveling or draw unwanted attention.

His reasoning to remain in the States was due to Mircea's
latest antics and had nothing at all to do with the special

agent plaguing his thoughts. *Ludicrous.* Not once had Vlad allowed a woman beneath his skin or into his musings, at least not in the last few centuries. Janelle Ferrari was merely a remarkable and intelligent young woman, one he had not been able to hypnotize, and thus had piqued his interest.

Several motorcycles lined the lot near the door of the Sons of Sangue clubhouse, which along with their vampire scent, told Vlad several of his grandsons' friends were also in attendance. Even though it was cold enough to freeze a witch's tits, these boys still traveled on two wheels when snow wasn't piling up on the asphalt, no doubt making the contraptions downright treacherous.

Driving his Aston Martin, he'd at least stay warm.

Vlad headed for the entrance. Kane and Kaleb had been given a heads-up on his impending arrival. The Sons of Sangue met and carried out their business within the four walls of the small, white-sided building. He supposed there was no sense in advertising their clubhouse with a flashier exterior. Better to keep the riffraff and wannabes at bay. Vlad, though, preferred his laid-back beach lifestyle and much roomier Spanish-style home on a remote island just off of Belize to anything the States had to offer, that was until Mircea decided to fuck everything up and forced him to leave behind the island life yet again.

If not for his brother, then he would have never met Janelle.

Something else he had his brother to thank for, though he wasn't sure if that was a good thing. Before he reached the door, it swung inward and stopped his musings cold. Good, he had wasted enough time and thought on the alluring special agent. He needed to focus on the matter at hand without distractions and she was definitely a distraction.

Kaleb stepped through the doorway, a large smile pasted upon his face. They may have had their differences in the past, but there was no denying the unbreakable bond of love they shared. He'd give up his own immortality before he allowed Mircea to harm a hair on his grandsons' heads.

"Grandpa." Kaleb's eyes twinkled in merriment, the big male knowing full well Vlad only allowed the nickname when it came from his grandsons' mates, Suzi and Cara. For being over five centuries old, Vlad looked nothing like an elderly grandfather, and preferred not to be referred to as such. "Good to see you."

Vlad wasn't one to chatter. "Vlad to you, dear boy. Where's Kane?"

Kaleb chuckled and stepped back, allowing him to pass through into the small dwelling. Kaleb was large in his own right, but Vlad had a few inches on both his grandsons and had to duck beneath the doorframe.

A few of the Sons of Sangue members gathered about the living area. All the better. Kane and Kaleb's brethren needed to be a party to Mircea's insanity, since this might also affect them. If Vlad didn't find and stop Mircea soon, it could be the downfall and end to all vampires' existence. Racism ran rampant through society, despite humans' best effort at maintaining peace. If humans found out about vampires, their fear of the unknown alone would dictate their desire to hunt down and eliminate them.

"Shall we gather in the meeting room?" Kane rose from one of the sitting area sofas, clapping Vlad on the shoulder. "I asked everyone who could make it to be here. I think we all need to be on the lookout for your crazy-ass brother. The bigger our numbers, the better odds we have of catching him before he does more damage."

"Afraid he's already struck again, Kane," Vlad grumbled. "He's murdered two innocents this time."

"You have proof it was him?" Kaleb asked.

Vlad nodded. "Smug son of a bitch messaged me, told me where to find his latest crimes against humanity. He also alerted the authorities, maybe hoping they'd catch me red-handed instead, or that I wouldn't have time to clean up his fucking mess."

Kane offered Vlad a seat, which he declined. Vlad was too keyed up to sit. "He took out a priest and a nun."

"Fuck me," Ryder said from his position near the front picture window.

"He's trying to fuck us all, apparently, but me in particular." Vlad clenched his teeth hard enough that had he been human, they would have shattered.

"What do you need us to do?" Alexander stood and walked to the bar area where they all now gathered.

Grayson took down a couple of bottles of Gentleman Jack and several tumblers, pouring two fingers' worth for everyone. "I think this is a call for whiskey."

Alexander held out his hand. "None for me."

"Still a pussy I see, Xander." Grayson chuckled, handing Alexander a can of Sprite.

"Fuck you, Gypsy."

"Sorry, Xander, I'd rather be fucking my mate. Tamera has you beat in that department. Everyone else drinking?"

Several moments later they all stood around the bar, sipping the amber liquid. Vlad tipped back the last of his, the whiskey warming him from throat to gut. He normally preferred a glass of vino, but this certainly did in a pinch. At least it was a smooth whiskey with hints of vanilla and caramel. Very tasty.

"We need to hunt down Mircea and take him out." Vlad set down his glass, which Grayson quickly refilled. "I don't want any of you acting recklessly. Don't get me wrong, he needs to be our top priority. All club business needs to be set aside until he's dealt with. When you go looking, do so in pairs and take a primordial with you. All the blood Mircea's consuming is going to make him stronger. Don't take him lightly. He's probably waiting for one of you to fuck up. Right now he's taking out mortals, but don't think for a moment, given a chance, he won't take your head."

"I'm assuming that's what his intentions are anyway," Kane said. "He's trying to flush us out. So if any of you encounter him, don't play the hero. Kaleb, Vlad, Ryder, or I must be along for the confrontation. Even with our primordial blood, he won't be easy to take down. I don't want to lose any more men. If you see Mircea, you need to call one of us. We may also call on Draven and Brea's primordial strength if need be."

"I'll get the prospects scouring Eugene, asking questions, see what they can find out about the priest and nun, maybe see if there's a reason Mircea chose them." A muscle ticked in Kaleb's jaw, evidence of his underlying rage. "This son of a bitch has used up eight of his nine lives. Time to take the ninth."

Vlad growled. "This is my mess. I created the bastard, gave him his immortality. In all my years, I've never regretted anything more."

"You aren't in this alone, Grandpa. This became our mess when he came into our territory."

"Vlad," he corrected Kaleb again. The last thing he needed was this gang of bikers referring to him as an old man. He'd show them old, by God. He glanced around the room, looking at each member. "I appreciate you having my back, but I don't want to be the reason he takes any of your heads. Be smart and follow Kane and Kaleb's lead."

Vlad rattled off his cell number. "Store it in your phones. If any of you come across Mircea, I better be the first number you dial."

"No offense, Vlad," Kane got his attention, "but if I find him first, I'm taking him out. You won't stop me this time. The bastard won't slip away a second time."

"You have my blessing. Remember, though, you have my primordial DNA running through your veins, but he's consuming large amounts of blood. He'll be gaining in strength."

"Are you saying we should all follow suit and bulk up on blood? I can find some degenerates."

"I don't want more dead humans on our hands, Kaleb. It's not who we are, even if our choices are those who don't deserve to breathe air. Keep up your strength by drinking daily, but don't harm the blood donor. Mircea won't stand a chance against our numbers if he's traveling alone. I don't care how much fucking blood he's drinking."

Kane narrowed his gaze, taking in the men sitting around the room. "We could use more numbers. I can call in the Washington chapter. I'm sure Gunner, Smoke, Axel and the boys will be willing to lend a hand."

"That might be wise, Kane." Vlad picked up his glass and downed the contents, the whiskey warming his gut much like the sweet essence of blood, though not nearly as tasty. "I'm betting Mircea is aware of your men to the north. We don't need them unmindful of the situation. They'll need to be filled in on what my brother's been up to."

"I'll make the call," Kane said. "I volunteer to head to Washington. They'll need a primordial should trouble arise."

"Cara needs you here, Viper. She's got two buns in that oven, not far from her due date, and needs your protection. I'll go."

"Thanks, Hawk. I appreciate that, but I can handle—"

"Fuck that. I'll head for Washington." Ryder braced his hands on the bar. "I owe Gunner for taking a bullet for me. Gabby and Adriana can keep each other company while I'm gone."

Kane rubbed the whiskers on his chin. "Ryder is right, he might be the best choice. Maybe you should think about making Gabby a mate before you leave. You don't want to leave her vulnerable."

He shook his head. "Not before she's ready. Besides, there isn't enough time for me to help her through the change, let alone teach her the ropes. I won't force this on her because of Mircea. She'll be fine with all of you here to watch over them. And I'll be fine going on my own as I have all the confidence in Gunner and his men. I'll be in good company."

"I'll have the women keep a close eye on Gabby and Adriana," Anton said. "And maybe with India ready to pop, Xander should sit this one out too. Help keep an eye on the women."

Alexander ran a hand through his hair. "India may be due any day, but fuck I don't want to let you guys down. You need numbers."

"I agree with Rogue," Kane said. "Besides, I think you would do better keeping an eye out for Gabby and Adriana as well. As president, I make the decisions. I'm sure Ryder would appreciate your help watching Gabby."

"Your mates—"

"Shouldn't all be in one place at a time. This isn't negotiable, Xander. You'll take India and go over to Gabby and Ryder's new place." Kane chuckled. "Enjoy the peace while you've got it, bro. Once that baby comes, there won't be much of that to be found. The rest of the mates I want here or at the Blood 'n' Rave. They shouldn't be going about town on their own either."

Kaleb smiled. "Listen to you, Viper. You have twins on the way. I can't wait to see how you handle that when Cara decides she's going back to work. I don't see her giving up the detective job any time soon."

"With good reason, Hawk. We need someone in there who has our back, especially once Joe Hernandez takes over as sheriff. He's running unopposed. Who better to keep an eye on him than his old partner?"

"You guys sound as if you have this handled, not to mention it's wise to keep a close eye on your mates. No telling what Mircea might do." Vlad had plenty of confidence in Kane's men, the ensuing chatter proving as much. The room bustled with excitement for the impending hunt.

The idea Mircea might target the women had Vlad thinking of someone else. Should his brother discover his infatuation with Janelle Ferrari, Mircea might use her to get to him.

"Not to be rude, but there's a special agent I think I need to pay a visit to."

"You never are one to stay long."

"There's really no point in being idle, Kane. Not when I have business."

"Like this special agent. She the same one from the last case, the murdered cartel members?" Kaleb whistled. "She certainly was a hot little number."

"One and the same. I do suppose she's easy on the eyes." Vlad grimaced, downplaying his interest. Janelle was hot …

sexy, arousing… "I need to see if the DEA will be looking into this recent case, if they think there's a connection."

Kane's brows drew together. "Why would you think the DEA would be involved?"

"The victims were all drained from neck wounds. The latest case from the church wasn't near as messy as the four dead drug runners, which had gained the DEA's attention. I don't want the special agent connecting the dots between their deaths of these two cases and helping the locals to do the same."

"You handle the special agent and I'll handle things here," Kane said. "If you need me to get Cara involved on the law side—"

"I got this." Vlad sure in the hell hoped he did. "But thank you for the offer. I'll be in touch."

Kane walked him to the door and opened it. "Sweet ride. When the hell did you start driving?"

"Thanks. I just got her."

"She?"

"Anything smooth as butter with sleek lines and sexy curves is a she."

Kane chuckled. "I suppose you're correct. When are you going to let me teach you how to ride a motorcycle? Two wheels are so much better than four."

Vlad chuckled. "Maybe once the weather clears up."

"I'll remind you."

"I have no doubt you will." Vlad's face sobered. "You guys take Mircea seriously. You boys are all I have now that Mircea's gone certifiable."

"We'll watch our backs. Besides, I have a couple little Tepeses to bring into this world."

"And I'll be looking forward to meeting them."

Vlad strode through the door and headed for his sleek new vehicle, definitely a she. Maybe he'd take the special agent for a ride. A smile slipped up his cheeks.

Pun intended.

CHAPTER THREE

J ANELLE STUCK THE KEY INTO THE HOLE AND LOCKED THE door of her office. It had been a long day and her boss, Captain Robbie Melchor, was being a complete dick about the Flores case having no viable suspects. There wasn't one shred of evidence connecting the recent murders of the priest and nun in Eugene to the Flores case, but she could feel it in her bones it was the same UNSUB, unknown subject. Captain Melchor wasn't buying it and she had no grounds, other than her inkling, to prove otherwise.

What a time for her visions to go silent.

And all thanks to the man, Vlad Tepes, who bore the same name as an ancient ruler who impaled his enemies, erecting the stakes into the ground to serve as a warning. If she could figure out why her visions had suddenly dried up following his odd visit to her office a few months ago, she might be able to figure out how to restore them. Having had them all her life, it was as though a part of her had gone missing.

Not that they'd give her the name of the faceless person responsible for either crime, but they often steered her in the right direction. Janelle had witnessed a lot of bad in the world. Nothing should surprise her. But this latest case, killing two who had pledged their life to God? What the hell had they done to deserve their brutal deaths?

She took in a deep breath, stepped onto the elevator, pushed the button for the parking garage, then leaned against the mirrored back wall and exhaled. It was Friday, and thankfully, she had a two-day reprieve from the office. Her grip tightened on the handle of her briefcase, which held the files from the Flores case along with today's. She'd be able to work from home and blessedly not have to deal with a boss, who at times, could be a sexist jerk.

What was it with some of the men in law enforcement, anyway? Thinking women couldn't do their jobs. Janelle had worked damn hard, twice as hard as any man in her office, just to prove them wrong. The workload of cases she had solved and the criminals she had brought down spoke for themselves.

Captain Melchor was an egocentric, handsome asshole who went to the gym every morning before work, giving him a body most women drooled over. And he was one hell of a womanizer. When she had first graduated from the academy and came to work in the Oregon office, he had tried to take her to dinner. Of course, Janelle had declined. Dating her boss would be detrimental to the path she had set for herself. She wasn't about to start her career by sleeping with him.

After a few years on the job, she had come to realize Robbie Melchor hit on a good share of the pretty women in the office. Most had declined his invites. But those who hadn't? If the rumor mill could be trusted, Robbie could be physically and verbally abusive and had supposedly raped an old girlfriend. Though those who were close to Robbie quickly squashed the latter tales, saying they were nothing but the rumblings of a spurned ex.

The elevator dinged and the doors slid open on the parking level. Keys in hand, she walked across the concrete to her waiting Chevrolet Tahoe. The clack of her heels echoed in the nearly empty garage. She pushed the button on her fob. The Tahoe's lights illuminated the darkened space and the doors unlocked.

Frank's Place, the local tavern just around the corner, would be hopping on a Friday night. Maybe she'd stop in for a beer and wings before heading home. Many of her co-workers would likely still be there. Opening the back door, she tossed in her briefcase before shutting it when a set of headlights rounded the corner of a cement barrier at the end of the row. The lights, positioned lower to the ground, appeared to belong to a sports car. As the vehicle approached, it slowed to a crawl before stopping next to her, effectively blocking her Tahoe from leaving. Since the parking garage had security access, allowing only those who worked in the building to enter, Janelle wasn't alarmed.

Because she hadn't identified the car, her hand went on autopilot anyway and shadowed her issued Glock holstered at her waist. The tinted window silently slid down, revealing a man Janelle recognized, but wasn't all too happy to see.

"What can I do for you, Captain Melchor?"

The dashboard lights illuminated his white smile, his upper face remaining in shadows. "A drink?"

"I was just about to head home."

"Ah, come on, Janelle, surely you can spare an hour. What were you going to do? Go home and open that brief-case you just tossed into your backseat? You can't work all the time."

Janelle took in a deep breath and sighed. Even if she declined, she knew he'd follow her to Frank's, call her a liar, and invade her space anyway.

"I suppose I can spare the time for *a* drink." She held up her pointer finger. "One drink."

"We can talk about this morning's findings. Or," he paused, "we can just enjoy each other's company."

No way in hell would she be enjoying Captain Melchor's company, but she supposed it would be rude not to try. "New car?"

His smile widened as he patted the dashboard. "Just picked it up this week."

"Nice."

"Hop in, I can give you a ride to Frank's. I'll bring you back later."

No way in hell. "I'll meet you at Frank's in five."

Robbie gave her a wink before he slid up the window, revved the engine just enough for effect, then spun off toward the end of the row of vacant spaces and disappeared around the column at the end. Janelle groaned. So much for her peaceful night. Turning to reach for the handle of her Tahoe, she squealed.

A wall of muscle and darkly mysterious man stepped from the shadows. Long hair caped broad shoulders, while the shadow of a short-cropped black beard encompassed a stunning smile. Hell, his lips alone spoke of all things sinful. What she wouldn't do for one night with this man and those lips. Not to mention his body, which was seriously harder than her sexist boss she was supposed to meet in five.

Janelle's hand fluttered to her chest. "You scared the hell out of me."

"I'm sorry, it wasn't my intention."

"If it wasn't your intention, then why hide behind my Tahoe only to jump out when I turned around?"

"I beg your pardon. I didn't jump. I merely walked. And I wasn't hiding." One of his dark brows inched upward. "I was waiting for you out of plain sight so you wouldn't have to answer about my appearance to the man who was obviously hitting on you."

"How did you get in here?" Janelle looked around the garage. "This place has the best security."

Vlad chuckled. "I assure you, Special Agent Ferrari, there isn't any place that can keep me out if I want to get in bad enough."

"Last time you visited, the security cameras had somehow been scrambled. I suppose we would find the same should I look at the garage feed later?"

"Of course. Simple parlor trick."

"Then you must show me how sometime."

His eyes crinkled in merriment. "Not many know the trick and I'd prefer to keep it that way."

"You're a magician then?"

The humor fled his eyes as he shook his black silky mane. Janelle bet it would be as velvety to the touch as the man from her dreams. Which of course, she didn't need to be thinking about when said object of her fantasies stood just inches from her, close enough that she could detect the wood and amber undertones of his cologne.

"I assure you I'm not a magician."

Taking in another deep breath, Janelle tired of the verbal circles they danced. "What do you want, Mr. Tepes?"

He chuckled again. "You can drop the mister. There isn't anything proper about me or my thoughts. In fact, we could go back to your place, slip into something more comfortable, like your sheets, then later we can talk about today's findings."

Janelle's brows knit together as her temper flared. "Are you for real? Do those lines actually work for you?"

"I assume it's the getting naked part that is getting you all up in arms."

"All up in arms? What century are you from?"

He turned his palms up. "Take your pick, Special Agent Ferrari."

"Look, no. Getting naked with you is not going to happen. Not now, not ever." Too bad her libido wasn't getting the message. Even as angry as she was, her damn sexual urges were taking notice of the seriously hot strange-as-he-may-be man and his suggestions. "And you sure in the hell aren't getting details on today's case. Why does it even interest you?

And more importantly, why do I feel this relates to the last time you came knocking at my office?"

"Too bad about not getting naked. It could have been quite pleasurable." Arrogant much? Janelle rolled her eyes, but he stopped her from telling him exactly where he could go with his raised finger. "Even as much as I'd enjoy a little carnal embrace, I am more interested in the case. If you'd care to point me in the direction of your home, we can talk about this privately."

Vlad Tepes was nuttier than she already assumed if he thought she'd show him where she lived. Finding out where he lived, though, might be of benefit. Going to his house alone could be foolhardy at best, but something told her this man wouldn't take what wasn't given.

"If you want to meet up, then we can go to your place."

Vlad seemed to contemplate her suggestion. "If that's your wish. Although, my home is over 3,500 miles away. I'm guessing that's not where you were intending. I am currently renting a suite if you would like to meet for cocktails there."

This man further confounded her. What the hell was he doing in Oregon? And why the interest in her case files? Janelle wouldn't get the answers unless she took him up on the offer of cocktails. She'd need to text Captain Melchor and let him know something came up, because nothing was going to stop her from getting to the bottom of Vlad's intentions. She needed to figure out his angle. He didn't look like a vigilante, but then they never did hang a sign over their head that said, "Sociopath here," with an arrow pointing down. It might help catch them a whole lot faster if they did, though, she thought with a chuckle.

"Where is your suite located?"

Vlad rattled off the specifics, which she quickly typed into her phone. When she glanced up to tell him she'd be by shortly, he was gone. Vanished. Janelle glanced around the garage, seeing no sight of human life at all. He might not be a magician, but he certainly had the disappearing act down to a science. No one vanished into thin air.

She drew in her lower lip and thought about her foolish choice to meet him in his place … alone. If the man was a murderer, then she was giving him every opportunity to take her life. She'd keep her guard up. Drawing in a deep breath, she opened the door to her Tahoe, climbed in and started the engine. She'd need to stop by Frankie's first to tell Melchor something had come up.

Nothing was going to stand between her and getting her answers. Not even an insanely sexy man and his ability to confound her.

VLAD'S GAZE LANDED ON THE ornate bronze clock that nearly covered the square footage of the herringbone-textured papered wall, complementing the theme of the rented penthouse. It was small by his standards but would do while he was in the States. The California King in one of the two bedrooms, however, fit his size quite nicely. Not to mention, he was fond of the antique oak four-poster bed. He could easily envision putting to use the four wooden posts. Wine silk draped the four corners of the canopy, long enough to wrap around a pair of wrists and ankles.

Vlad couldn't help but think about the special agent bound.

Speaking of, what was taking her so long? His rented penthouse was but a short sprint from the parking garage, ten miles at most. Janelle Ferrari should have been here by now and he wasn't accustomed to being kept waiting. The more the second-hand on the clock ticked away, the more his annoyance grew.

A bottle of Napa Valley Reserve Cabernet Sauvignon sat uncorked on the table with a pair of stemless glasses beside it. He had promised her drinks, hoping she enjoyed a dark red. If not, then he'd have the lobby's restaurant bring up something more to her liking.

A quick glance back at the clock told him a half hour had passed since he had left her standing next to her Tahoe. Maybe she had changed her mind and met up with the man from the parking garage. Jealousy burned in his gut, an unfamiliar emotion and one he had no right to feel. After all, he barely knew the special agent.

Damn his egotistical hide for thinking she'd do as requested when he should have suggested hitching a ride. At least then he would've been able to keep a better eye on her.

He ran a hand through his overlong hair, brushing the strays from his eyes. Agitation streamed through him like flood waters over a dam. It was possible he had scared her off with his sexual innuendos, though he hadn't missed the rise in her desire. As a vampire, he could scent it on her as easily as a lion to prey. He affected her, that much he knew for certain.

Besides, what woman didn't love him?

Vlad had likely been too pushy about the cases, no doubt making her apprehensive. Of course, she would be overly protective of the details. She got paid to keep her mouth shut. Vlad needed to be more subtle in steering her focus away from the neck wounds which caused the victims' deaths. Thanks to Mircea, Vlad was taxed with keeping the authorities in the dark about vampires and minimizing the risk of exposing them. He had managed to keep the secret for centuries and his brother was about to fuck that up. Over the years, Vlad had witnessed humankind at its worst. There was no hope the vampire population would survive if the truth got out.

Vampires would be hunted and killed, if not out of fear, then for sport.

Vlad's nostrils flared but a second before his sonic hearing picked up the ding of the elevator arriving on the top floor. The penthouse ensured his privacy, keeping nosy neighbors and tourists from poking about his business.

Striding to the door, he opened it before Janelle had the chance to knock, causing her to jump. She was more fidgety than an addict in a room full of confiscated drugs.

"How did you—"

"I heard the ding of the elevator."

"Of course, you did." Janelle white-knuckled her grip on the briefcase, telling him she wasn't exactly on board with sharing whatever she had inside. Nudging past him, she walked into the room, her gaze sweeping the elaborate surroundings. "You said suite."

"Penthouse … suite, what's the difference?"

"I was expecting a smaller room comped by a corporation of some sort, not the entire top floor."

"I'm not owned by a corporation, nor do I own one, if that's what you're wondering. I'm much more of a loner." Vlad grinned, gave her his back and headed for the table. "Can I interest you in a glass of wine, Special Agent?"

"Please call me Janelle. No need for formality. And yes, I'd love a glass. Thank you."

"I have a Cabernet Sauvignon uncorked, unless you would prefer something else. I can call down to the restaurant…"

"No, that's fine. I prefer my wine dry."

Janelle followed him to the table where she set the briefcase on a chair next to the table and took the proffered glass. She took a sip, nodded her approval, then looked at him.

"Why didn't you call? I gave you my card months ago regarding the Flores case, and yet you never used it." She set her glass on the table and crossed her arms beneath her breasts, drawing his gaze to the delectable cleavage spilling over her snug black top. "Now, we have a case with similarities and you show up in the parking garage where I work.

Why? What is it about these two cases that have you snooping around? I'm not here to share with you anything about the case … or for that matter, anything physical. What I want to know is what the hell is your interest in all this? And to make sure you aren't the subject I'm hunting. Are you responsible for these murders? I swear—"

One of his brows arched. "You think I did this? What possible motive would I have? I didn't even know the victims."

"How do I know you're telling the truth?"

"I guess you'll have to take my word. Besides, I haven't been in a Catholic church in years, so what purpose would I have for killing a priest and a nun?"

Her gaze turned hard as steel. "I never told you who the latest victims were."

Vlad raised a hand. "Relax. I didn't do it. Christ, it's all over the damn news already."

"Why the interest?"

He chuckled. "You're the one with supposed visions. You tell me."

"For some reason, my visions have taken leave and I'm not sure why. This past winter I thought I saw a man in the backyard of my cabin who looked suspiciously like you. You wouldn't know anything about that, would you?"

His face heated and he never got embarrassed or made excuses for his actions. His white lie would suit him better. "I have no clue what you're talking about."

Janelle studied his face and Vlad hoped she didn't see the untruth. Explain to her why he stood over her naked form and watched her in the throes of what appeared to be a hot dream? Not likely. Nor was he about to admit the fact he had gone back to the penthouse and jerked off in the shower to the image of her burned in his memory.

"I do hope that's the truth, Vlad. I'd hate to think you're some sort of creeper."

Which is exactly what she was making him feel like, fortifying his reason to stay away until now. Janelle Ferrari was temptation at its finest and the last person he needed to get tangled up with.

"I can't help but wonder if you're the reason my visions have stopped."

"Why on earth would you think I had something to do with that?"

"Because I haven't had one since your odd visit to my office."

Luck was indeed on his side. Should her visions return, they could very well expose the truths about the existence of vampires.

"Well, that does indeed suck they have gone silent, Special Agent... Janelle." He twirled the deep red liquid in the glass. "But I'm sure that has nothing to do with my visit or me."

CHAPTER FOUR

JANELLE COULDN'T HELP BUT NOTE THE SLIGHT REDDENING OF his cheeks, or the way Vlad avoided eye contact when she had mentioned the man in her backyard. He didn't look like the type who made excuses for his actions, nor was he someone who was easily rattled. But bring up the man who disappeared through her hedges and he looked downright uncomfortable. Her gut told her Vlad had been her intruder.

Why go to the bother of spying on her?

It wasn't as if he didn't have her phone number. She had handed it to him months ago when she confronted him at the Sons of Sangue clubhouse. So why not use it instead of sneaking in through her window? A locked one at that. Just the thought of him standing over her nude form sent shivers up her spine. Christ, the thought alone should scare the living hell out of her, not turn her on.

And yet, here she stood, wondering how good he was in the sack.

She was beyond pathetic.

Vlad didn't appear guilty of anything more than breaking and entering as well as trespassing, at least that's what her intuition was telling her. Not that he didn't look capable of inflicting harm. On the contrary, he looked menacing. She'd need to stay on his good side. Otherwise, she didn't stand a chance in hell of getting any answers.

If her instincts failed her and he was guilty of murder times six, then she'd just stepped into the lion's den. With the sheer size of him, he could easily overpower her; no amount of training or weapons would save her.

This man wanted something and apparently he wouldn't stop until he got it.

"Well if not you, Vlad, then who? Who broke into my home?"

Vlad shrugged and took a sip from his glass, likely trying to hide the actual truth. The bastard. "I wouldn't have the slightest clue. Maybe you should think about upping your security. One can't be too careful these days."

"No, one can't." Janelle narrowed her gaze. "What exactly do you want to know about this latest case? Because, let's face it, it's why you looked me up again. What is it you want, Vlad? What's your interest and why do I feel like these two cases are connected?"

He ran a hand down the scruff on his chin, the sexy sound filling the silence hanging between them. His deep dark gaze went blacker if that were possible, nearly swallowing the whites of his eyes.

"Call it curiosity."

This time Janelle laughed. "You show up twice now and you think I'm going to take that answer? Tell me why I shouldn't haul your ass downtown for questioning of these murders. Or better yet, book you for them."

"Because I didn't do it."

"Then you know who did." It was no longer a question. Janelle was getting the feeling that was his exact reasoning for his interest in this whole scenario. "Who is it? Save me the fucking trouble."

"Even if I knew, I wouldn't tell you. You're the special agent, that's what you get paid to find out."

"If you're harboring a fugitive or hampering an investigation, I'll make sure you go down. The DEA doesn't take that lightly. If you know something, then you need to tell me."

"How about you do your fucking job, Special Agent Ferrari, and stop trying to pin this shit on me. That's Laziness 101. If you think I know the guilty person, then fucking prove it."

He slammed his glass on the table, shattering it. A small bead of blood welled to the surface of his hand where a shard had cut him. He ignored the tiny wound. "I'm only here to find out what you know."

"Why? So you can get to the bastard first?" Her tone rose, matching his in intensity. She was good and pissed. "If you want to know what I have, then you damn well better be prepared to tell me why these cases are so important to you. And I swear to God if you know who is responsible, then you better turn him in, or I'll see you go away for a good long time."

"You could try, but there isn't a prison system on this planet capable of keeping me."

"Is that a threat?"

"Think of it what you want. I didn't murder these victims. And as far as knowing who did? Let me just say you'd best catch him before I do. Your punishment will be less severe than mine. Now if you'll excuse me, I've grown tired of this."

Her mouth rounded. Was he seriously kicking her out after he demanded she come all the way over here? Well, technically it wasn't that far. She had stopped long enough at Frank's to let Captain Melchor know she wouldn't be staying for that drink.

"You haven't gotten what you wanted. So why bother asking me here?"

"Because it's fucking obvious you aren't willing to share. That goes both ways, Special Agent Ferrari. If I find the culprit, don't expect me to have you on quick dial."

He grabbed a paper napkin from the table and blotted at the small amount of blood running from the cut on his hand, careful to turn the red fluid marring the white inside the paper before stuffing it into his pocket rather than throwing it in the receptacle sitting no more than three feet away. Funny, she couldn't detect the wound where the blood had welled to the surface.

Vlad busied himself, scooping the shards of glass into his palm before carrying them to the sink at the side of the room and dumping them into it. Turning on the water, he seemed to be washing the blood off before then depositing them into the trash.

Strange.

Continuing about his business, he ignored her altogether. A long black hair caught her attention, next to where she had placed her briefcase. Janelle recalled finding one just like it at the church crime scene. While he was still preoccupied, she snagged it and slipped it into a small snack-size bag and tucked it away.

Janelle cleared her throat and gained his attention. "I'm still here."

"That much is fucking obvious," he grumbled, his tone deep and ominous. He pointed to the penthouse exit. "I've already dismissed you. The door is that way."

"You're an asshole."

He grinned, the humor missing from his gaze. "So I've been told."

Janelle wasn't about to be dismissed so easily. "What exactly were you hoping to get from me?"

"The neck wounds…" He looked at her strangely, as if he could read her very soul.

Janelle shook her head, her thoughts scrambling, the same as when he had come to her office months ago. Refusing to be bamboozled by his parlor tricks, as he called them, she glanced away, her thoughts immediately clearing.

"What about the wounds?" Janelle glanced around the room, looking anywhere but at him. "They were similar to the Flores case, but not as messy. If you saw a news report earlier on who the victims were, then you've already guessed as much or you wouldn't be here."

"Look at me."

She shook her head. "I don't know how you're doing what you are, but you aren't getting back inside my head."

"What do you think made the wounds? A jagged knife?"

"I'm not the coroner. He'll be able to tell us that when we get the autopsy report."

Vlad stuffed his hands deep into his pockets and rocked back on his heels. "Maybe that's who I should be talking to. I've been thinking this through all wrong and allowing my desire to get in the way."

"Meaning?"

"Meaning my attraction to you is clouding my judgment. Now if you'll excuse me, Special Agent Ferrari, I have somewhere I need to be."

Vlad picked up her briefcase and handed it to her. Placing a hand in the small of her back, he ushered her toward the exit. His palm heated her flesh as easily as if he had touched her bare skin. Janelle couldn't believe the audacity of this man. First, he demanded she come, and now he couldn't get rid of her fast enough.

Vlad opened the door. "Thank you for coming by, Janelle."

"You haven't seen the last of me." Janelle grit her teeth, holding her anger in check. "I'm sure I'll be looking you up in the near future."

A genuine smile parted his full lips. "Certainly. And I'll look forward to seeing you again. Hopefully, next time will be more pleasant. Good day, Special Agent."

She stepped through the exit, the door closing behind her. Janelle wasn't letting him off the hook so easily. She'd wait in her car for him to leave and then she'd find out exactly where he intended to go.

Vlad desired her, just as she did him. There was no doubt in her mind by the way he looked at her. So why the hot and cold treatment? The harder she probed him about the murders, the more closed off he became—nervous even, which shocked the hell out of her. She'd bet not much spooked the man.

If she didn't know better, this darkly powerful man was afraid she was getting close to the truth and was trying to dodge her. But why? Janelle's gut told her Vlad was protecting a big secret, if not someone who was close to him.

CHAPTER FIVE

JANELLE FOLLOWED HIS ASTON MARTIN AT A DISTANCE, WEAVing in and out of traffic. She may have thought she was being sly, but Vlad had been well aware of the tail. Hell, she had been following him since Friday. No way in hell Vlad was going to tail Mircea with Janelle riding his back. Other than visiting Kane and Kaleb at the clubhouse, following her visit to his penthouse, he hadn't given her much to pursue since he had to wait for the coroner's office to open on Monday.

A smile crossed his face. Why not have a little fun? Being Monday, she had to have known where he was headed. Had she asked, he would have gladly given her a lift, saving her the trouble of trying to be stealthy, not to mention wasting her entire weekend.

Sitting in close quarters of the Aston, scenting her jasmine fragrance, would have tugged at his southern region and made the driving a bit uncomfortable, but it certainly would've made it more pleasant. Any time spent in her company was a delight, even if it meant walking around at half-mast. Vlad wanted Janelle and it didn't take much for his dick to stand up and salute. Seeing her again only proved his need to stay away unless duty called, regardless of how much he enjoyed her company. Janelle Ferrari spelled trouble, no two ways about it.

Passing the Lane County office building where the morgue was located, Vlad watched in the rear view mirror as she slid her Tahoe into an angled parking lot about a block back. Vlad's grin widened as he gassed the Aston Martin and sped past the entrance, his GPS letting him know his need to turn around. Too bad he hadn't been closer to her so he could've seen the look on her face when she realized she had been made.

At the light, he turned left and sped down the city block before taking the next corner right and doing a quick U-turn. The Aston Martin now faced the intersection as Janelle passed. Her mouth dropped, then snapped closed just as quickly before she waved her middle finger.

Vlad chuckled, giving her a wink.

Stepping on the clutch, he put the car into first gear, then took off like a shot in the opposite direction. A glance in the mirror reflected her three-point turn. Vlad waited patiently at the intersection. The window to her SUV slid down as she pulled up next to him.

"Nice seeing you again so soon, Special Agent. Next time, ask. I'd be happy to give you a lift."

The slight rise of the corner of her lips gave away the fact she wasn't pissed at his mischievousness. "Jerk."

Vlad pointed to the parking garage ahead. "Why not follow me and we can visit the coroner together?"

"Bad idea."

"Why?"

"Because you shouldn't be anywhere near this case and I won't be the one responsible for giving you clearance."

"I'm going in there regardless of whether you follow. And … I won't need your clearance."

"Seriously?" Her brow arched. "This I have to see."

Vlad stepped on the gas, popped the clutch, then did a quick turn into the garage. The Aston Martin was a blast to drive. The sports car had some serious get up and go. Inside, he found a parking spot, then waited for the special agent to arrive.

Janelle pulled up beside him, parked and exited her vehicle, a saucy smile on her stunning face. She didn't need the aid of makeup, wearing little blush, eyeliner, and mascara to enhance her God-given natural beauty. "Show off."

Vlad chuckled and held out his hand. "Ladies first."

She shook her head. "I want to see how you manage to get all the way to the morgue without security clearance. I'm betting you won't get past the first floor."

"Which floor is the morgue on?"

"It's in the basement."

Vlad winked again, knowing she'd never figure out his strategies. "Got it."

He walked far enough ahead so they didn't appear to be together, should the security cameras or anyone in the parking garage take note. Stepping into the elevator, he held the door, then pressed the button for the lobby since there wasn't one for the lower level. The lobby must contain an entirely different elevator that led to the morgue.

The doors whooshed open onto the main level. Vlad's eyes heated, his vampire genetics transforming them to obsidian. He turned his head, looked at the lobby camera and reached out a hand. Energy flowed through him, tingling the center of his palm, scrambling the security footage and all lines that ran to it. Vlad stepped from the car, leaving Janelle to trail behind as if they were strangers. There was a good chance those who worked in the building might know her, or at the very least recognize her. Janelle made it clear she shouldn't be seen with him, not if she considered him a suspect.

Absurd.

If he were to kill a human, Vlad certainly wouldn't be leaving a trail behind like his idiotic brother. Besides, no one other than her would even remember him being in the building.

A young gentleman with hair cropped close to the side and left overlong on top to drape over the other ear, manned the lobby desk. He wore a lanyard about his neck, dangling a card with the name Robert printed in black. Vlad figured it doubled as an access card, giving the man clearance to other areas of the building. Even so, he bet that didn't include the morgue. Vlad stopped at the curved desk and leaned forward.

"Can I help—"

The young man's eyes quickly glazed over as he looked into Vlad's marble-like gaze. Vlad requested access to the basement, making sure Robert wouldn't remember him or the inquiry. Robert quickly typed into the computer, placed a card into a slot, then pulled it out and handed it to Vlad.

His well-manicured right hand pointed down the long hall. "The elevators are at the end by the staff entrance."

"Thank you, my good man." Vlad's smile widened. "Oh, and no need to alert anyone to the scrambled feed of the cameras. Just a glitch that will correct itself."

His blank gaze lifted from the monitors and toward the front of the building. "It sure is a beautiful day."

"Not a rain cloud in the sky." Vlad walked down the long hall, hearing footsteps hustling behind him in an attempt to catch up. He didn't need to look back to know who they belonged to.

"How did you do that?" Janelle whispered when she came within hearing distance.

"No worries about being seen, Special Agent. I took care of the cameras."

"You didn't answer my question."

"No, I did not."

Arriving at a larger elevator, he slipped the card he had been given into the slot. The doors immediately slid open and the car, one big enough to roll a gurney into, was thankfully empty. Vlad held out his arm for Janelle to proceed him. They stood side-by-side as the doors closed. Janelle pushed the B, and the car started its descent. He smiled at her in the reflection on the polished metal across from them. Her lips remained tight, her expression making it obvious she was not amused he was keeping his secrets.

"What if the coroner sees us?"

Vlad shrugged. "Easy. The coroner won't remember us being here anymore than Robert will."

"Hypnosis?"

"Yes, but more powerful than four-flushers with parlor tricks, I assure you."

Janelle looked queerly at him as the doors slid open. "Four-flushers?"

"Fakes."

Vlad didn't bother to further explain as he stepped into the cold clinical room. A short, stout man with a balding pate and wearing a white lab coat, approached. Dr. Schultz was stitched in blue above the pocket.

He turned to Janelle and ignored him altogether. "Special Agent Ferrari, did you forget something?"

Vlad's gaze heated once again, before he drew the coroner's attention and purposely kept his back to Janelle. Dr. Schultz's eyes glazed when Vlad told him to answer all questions and do as he was told.

Janelle stepped around Vlad, looking from the doctor to him. He quickly downcast his gaze until the heat subsided.

"How are you doing that?"

Satisfied his eyes had returned to their normal state, he looked at Janelle. "It's not something I can teach."

"Why?"

"Let's just say it's a part of me."

"Well, it certainly would come in handy with my job. Imagine the confessions I'd get. You wouldn't care to tag along with me, would you?"

He chuckled. "Oh, I'm sure that would not be a good idea."

"Why are we here?" she asked, ignoring his reply. He supposed she probably agreed more so than not.

"To find out what you wouldn't share."

"What do these cases have to do with you and why are you so damn interested? Tell me why I shouldn't have you arrested for breaching security at the least?"

"Because we have the same goal in mind, Janelle. I want to find the killer just as much as you do."

"You know who it is." She narrowed her gaze, anger flaring in it. "Why aren't you telling me? This perp needs to be stopped."

"Because it's not that fucking simple. The person responsible for these crimes cannot be stopped by you or law enforcement's inadequate methods."

"I bet a bullet from my gun would drop this son of a bitch."

"Maybe, maybe not."

"You aren't going to tell me, are you?"

He shook his head. "It's for your safety. I'm not afraid of what you could do to this person. I'm afraid of what he would do to you."

"I'll dog you, not give you a moment's peace. I will tail you every day if I have to." She gritted her teeth and pointed a finger at him. "I'll be your goddamn shadow."

Just fucking great. Why the hell couldn't he just hypnotize her like everyone else? "You realize you'll be putting your life in jeopardy. I can't allow that."

"You don't have a choice."

Vlad looked at the coroner, who stood there in an unresponsive state. "*Women*."

He neither smiled nor laughed, his face a blank slate. "What can I do for you, Mister...?"

"My name is not important since you *won't* remember me being here. For starters, how did the nun and priest die?"

"There were teeth marks surrounding the wounds, from what appeared to be elongated canines. Bite wounds surrounded the—"

"No. Hear me now. That's not what killed the nun and priest."

The coroner's brow pinched. "It wasn't?"

"Jagged wounds, consistent with a serrated blade."

"Of course."

"They both died by the same knife."

Dr. Schultz nodded his affirmation.

Vlad looked at Janelle and smiled.

Her mouth dropped. "You can't come in here and alter the case and its findings. This is highly illegal. Take that back."

"No."

"Yes." She jammed her fists against her hips. "Or I'll take you in."

"Trust me on this, Janelle. I want to catch this person as much as you do."

"You're asking me to trust you when your actions prove otherwise."

"Not on this. I'd never do something that would harm you or your career."

"And yet here we are."

"*You* followed me. Look, I'm trying to find your perp. But we have to do this my way."

Her jaw tightened. "Why?"

"Just throw me a bone this one time." Vlad ran a knuckle down her downy soft cheek. "I need you to trust me."

Janelle looked as if she were about to argue, but instead gave him a nod. Vlad looked back at the man. "Your findings show this had nothing in common with the Flores case and the four dead men from last month. Completely isolated cases."

"Two unrelated cases," he agreed.

"Good. I'd say my job is done here."

Without waiting on Janelle, Vlad headed for the elevator. Janelle's hurried footsteps pounded the tile behind him in her effort to catch up. Entering the car, they rode in silence to the lobby where Vlad aimed his palm at the camera to unscramble the feed just before he exited the staff door and headed for the stairs leading up to the second floor where he had parked.

Janelle broke the silence. "I have to take you in."

"Excuse me?" Vlad stopped on the step and turned back, looking down on her.

"It's my job. You broke the law back there." She pulled out a pair of handcuffs. "Turn around, Mr. Tepes."

"So much for trust." He chuckled, grabbed the tiny handcuffs dangling from her fingers and mangled them within his grip, rendering the stainless-steel cuffs unusable.

Her wine-colored lips rounded. He could easily picture them circling his dick. Had she been anyone else, he might have made the suggestion. "How?"

"I told you there wasn't a prison system that could keep me. You think a simple pair of cuffs would work?"

Her pulse beat heavy at the hallow point of her throat, calling Vlad like a moth to flame. Damn, it was all he could do not take the ambrosia he scented rushing through her veins. He gripped her chin, forcing her to look him in the eyes.

Her breath hitched and she backed from his touch. "What are you?"

"I'm human. Just like you."

"No human could have done that."

He laughed. "I lift a lot of weights."

Even though he saw the question in her eyes, she thankfully didn't press the issue—for now. "You can't keep interfering with these cases. You're breaking the law."

"And you're slowing me down, Janelle." His anger slowly simmered and heated his gaze. Vlad bit back the vampire from surfacing.

"From what?"

"From finding my brother." He growled. "You either let me do what I came here for, or you're going to have a lot more dead bodies on your hands. You think I'm dangerous and need to be jailed? You haven't met Mircea. He's the one you're looking for, damn it. Not me. And trust me, he's not nearly as fucking nice."

CHAPTER SIX

V LAD HAD LEFT JANELLE STANDING BESIDE HER SUV IN THE parking garage and drove away as if he hadn't given her critical information—namely, the identity of the unknown subject she had been hunting. If her instincts were correct, Vlad's brother was the same perp from the Flores case, although he hadn't exactly come out and said as much.

Stunned didn't begin to explain the emotion coursing through her as she had watched his car disappear around one of the concrete barriers. Lord, it was the man's brother, no less.

They had exchanged phone numbers before he had hopped into his sports car and driven away like he had not a care in the world. He had entrusted Janelle with information that would put his brother away for a good long time, more likely than not the rest of his natural-born life. Did Vlad think she was incapable of tracking, arresting, and detaining his brother? Janelle was damn good at her job. She had a great percentage rate of solved cases. Or was Vlad's confidence in his belief that he'd catch his sibling long before she did?

Janelle was betting on the latter.

They had a similar goal in mind … catch and stop Mircea before more innocent lives were lost. Their outcome no doubt differed, but the perp was one and the same. Vlad seemed more than happy to exchange cell numbers, telling her not to hesitate to use it should she find herself in trouble. In fact, he had said she might want to put the number in her favorites for quick reference.

Bottom line, Mircea was dangerous and she'd do well to remember that.

Not that she didn't believe Vlad, but he underestimated her as well. She had probably dealt with and brought down criminals just as lethal, if not more so. Janelle was betting she was more equipped to stop the man than Vlad. Although seemingly ruthless, Vlad didn't appear to pack a weapon. After seeing what he could do to a pair of government-issued handcuffs, though, Janelle was pretty sure he didn't need one. But a bullet could stop anyone, including Vlad's brother. Should she encounter the man, she wouldn't hesitate to draw her Glock and use it. Vlad may think he'd aid in helping find Mircea, but Janelle would be the one to bring him down by any force necessary, even if it meant killing him.

One bullet to the T-zone would drop him like a sack of bricks.

Janelle had earned an award for excellent marksmanship when she had gone through the academy. She didn't miss. Mircea wasn't about to be an exception.

After Vlad had left, she returned to the city building, checking with those working if they had seen a very tall, long black-haired man. He was certainly hard to miss. None of the employees, including Robert, remembered seeing anyone by that description. Checking the camera footage produced nothing but static as she suspected, leaving her to go back to her office to do a little research.

When she hadn't been tailing Vlad, she had tried searching for Mircea. Janelle had come up empty-handed. No fingerprints, no DNA, no records of any kind, meaning the man had no earlier brushes with the law or ties to the military.

The only person she had found on a Google search was Mircea II of Wallachia, oldest brother to none other than Vlad Tepes. Two ancient rulers who had been dead for centuries. Janelle couldn't help but wonder if this wasn't some weird type of cosplay. Surely, no mother was cruel enough to have named her sons after Romanian tyrants, especially one with the reputation of impaling his enemies.

Captain Melchor walked into her office unannounced and drew her from her musings. Janelle had left the door open, allowing co-workers to freely walk through. She hated a closed, sterile office. It always made her feel a bit claustrophobic.

Today, she would have preferred the privacy, which would also force the visitor to politely knock. Nothing was ever polite about today's present company.

Closing her laptop with a snap, she placed her forearms over the sleek metal and clasped her hands. "What can I do for you, Captain?"

"I would have liked a drink with you Friday to discuss this latest case of yours, but I understand when things come up." He shrugged. "It was after hours. Perhaps a rain check."

Janelle offered him a smile she did not feel. "Perhaps."

His gaze dropped to her folded hands, then to the small baggie lying on the desk beside the laptop. *Shit.* "Evidence?"

He took a seat in one of the chairs flanking her desk and grabbed the small bag containing one of Vlad's hairs. Janelle had meant to check the hair against the one found at the church crime scene but had wanted to do so under the table. *Not that she was in the habit of hiding evidence.* If she found Vlad guilty of anything, she'd take him down just as surely as she would his brother.

"Is this similar to—"

"Someone broke into my cabin a few months back," she said abruptly, attempting to deflect his attention.

"And you found this?" One of Melchor's brow inched up.

"Yes."

"Were you at home?"

Janelle wasn't about to tell him she had been nude at the time, but she couldn't help wonder why he showed no concern over her wellbeing. "I was asleep."

"The hair—it's quite similar to the color and length of your own. Surely this isn't the only evidence you have that someone broke in. Anything taken?"

She shook her head. "I woke up in the middle of the night, freezing. Cold air blew through the opened window, one I knew was closed before I went to sleep. That hair was stuck to the window latch."

"And you never saw the intruder?"

"No."

Robbie thankfully bought the story and laid the bag back on her desk. "You've since installed security out there?"

"I don't stay out there often, but yes, my property now has cameras around the perimeter." Janelle thought of Vlad's ability to scramble the footage and knew her security wouldn't help where he was concerned. She hoped his brother didn't possess the same skills. "Is there something I can do for you, Captain?"

"I wanted your opinion on the Flores case and this latest one at the Catholic church."

"Of course."

"I just got off the phone with the coroner. Dr. Schultz no longer believes they are related. When I talked to him on Friday, he believed it was a big possibility. What's your take on his sudden flip-flop?"

"I spoke to him earlier. He told me the same thing."

Robbie rubbed his palms on his clean-pressed slacks. "You were at the morgue?"

"I was. I wanted to see if there was anything I might've missed on Friday."

"And you believe his new findings?"

"That the neck wounds were caused by a serrated blade?" Janelle swallowed, finding it hard to hold her boss's eye contact. "I'm no doctor, but I found no reason to disbelieve him either."

"The Flores case? Their neck wounds were consistent with bite marks."

"Yes. And we still believe it to be the work of a rival cartel."

Although, she no longer thought that to be the case thanks to Vlad. But she certainly wasn't ready to share that information, not with her boss. Until she had more evidence pointing to Mircea, more than just Vlad's word to go on, she'd stick with her earlier findings. Which, of course, was nothing. They couldn't prove or disprove the theory that another cartel took out the four soldiers.

Robbie placed an elbow on the arm of the chair, his forefinger now resting on his chin. His gaze narrowed. "To me? It all smells too easy. If Flores or the LaPaz cartel pissed off someone, then I highly doubt they'd go in and chew off their damn necks. More than likely, they'd just go in there with guns and mow them down."

"I can't say I haven't thought the same thing. But these men are brutal and like sending messages, like cutting off heads and stripping their innards, leaving them laid out on public streets for all to see. It's not highly improbable they could be capable of this kind of brutality."

"Maybe not." His gaze went back to the baggie on her desk before standing back up. "Let me know if anything comes of that. I hate to think one of my special agents is being harassed."

"I will," she said, tugging her lower lip with her teeth. Just great, her story to cover up her real reason for the hair just became her boss's new interest. "I'm sure it's nothing."

He took a couple of steps toward the door before turning around. "How long ago did that happen? You mentioned it was cold."

"A couple of months ago."

"Why wait so long to bring that in?"

And there was the hole in her story. She should have known Robbie was far too smart to take her word outright. She shrugged. "I was busy on other cases. I actually forgot about it until I ran across the baggie again over the weekend."

Robbie shoved his hands deep into his pockets and looked at her long and hard. He knew about the similar hair at the church crime scene. There was no doubt in her mind now. So why the hell wasn't he calling her out?

"There's a press meeting at three. I expect you to have your facts straight. Meet me in my office an hour before so we can prepare what we release to them."

He turned and left the room, his shoulders stiff and spine straight. A shiver ran down her own spine. Never had she lied to her boss before. Now having done so, she was seeing a dark contrary side to Robbie Melchor. A side she didn't like being on.

FEET DANGLED A FOOT OFF THE ground, legs flailing, trying to wound Vlad anywhere the man's boney knees could make contact. Too bad for the *nenorocitule*, motherfucker. Vlad's leg muscles might as well have been made of stone for all he felt. Anger coursed through him, hot and swift. His blood ran like molten lava, making the vampire in him even more lethal. This son of a bitch wouldn't make sunrise, no matter what truths he spewed.

"I'll ask you again. Who the fuck are you?" Vlad clamped his teeth, his fangs sinking into his lower lip. The metallic taste of his own blood filled his mouth and fueled his ire.

The vampire in his grip gasped for oxygen. Had he been one of Kane's or Kaleb's, the son of a bitch would have already mentioned that particular fact. No, this sniveling coward came from his brother. He could smell Mircea's blood flowing through his veins. Newly made, the weakling had not a prayer in the world going up against a seasoned vampire, let alone the eldest.

Vlad smiled, the grin no doubt feral. "Who made you?"

"Your brother." The vampire wheezed as the hand wrapping his throat tightened. "I was sent to the city to find you."

"And yet I came across you, trying to drain a human. Have you no fucking manners?"

"Manners?" he squeaked. "I'm a vampire. It's what I do. And I'll take what the fuck I want."

Vlad squeezed, stopping just shy of separating his head from his damn shoulders. "Number one rule of vampirism. We take no more than needed. We don't harm what feeds us, you fucking idiot."

Moments ago, the pungent odor of fresh blood had tickled Vlad's nostrils. He had combed the streets, looking for the cause. This piece of crap was in a garbage-littered back alley, in the process of draining a bartender from some dive bar. After sealing the wounds and hypnotizing the human, Vlad had sent the weakened man stumbling on his way. Another few moments and the bartender would've been another casualty in Eugene, leaving Vlad to wipe up yet another cat-astrophic mess.

Vlad growled, the sound echoing back at him. He loos-ened his grip a fraction. "How many more?"

The reed-thin man's brows drew together over his narrow, crooked nose. "How many what?"

"How many vampires has my idiot brother created?"

The vampire attempted to swallow, his legs continuing to flail, his fingers clawing at Vlad's hand. "Let go and I'll talk."

Vlad was no fool. He wasn't about to allow the man an opportunity to break loose, resulting in him having to give chase. Lowering him to his feet, Vlad kept his grip on the man's throat. "Talk."

He pressed his lips tight.

The *nenorocitule* thought he had the upper hand. Vlad would show him exactly who commandeered the conversa-tion. Dropping his hold around the neck, he quickly switched to a forearm, twisting it behind the man's back, dislocating his shoulder. An ear-piercing squeal was his reward.

"I asked you a question."

The vampire hissed but said nothing. *Imbecile.*

Another twist and Vlad broke his wrist, earning him an-other high-pitched screech.

"How. Many?"

"Mircea made it clear I'm not to answer any of your ques-tions. He promised death if I tell you anything."

"I'll kill you if you don't. And trust me, I won't be nearly as merciful. You'll wish for death before the Grim Reaper ever comes to collect. How. Fucking. Many?"

The vampire grimaced as Vlad twisted his forearm until nothing more was left than splintered bones. "At least twenty of us, if he hasn't already created more. Now let me go."

Vlad dropped his forearm in favor of the other. "Where is he?"

"I don't know." The vampire yipped when pressure was added. "I'm telling you the truth, damn it. Mircea finds us."

Vlad growled, mere centimeters from his ear. "How?"

"A cell. My right pocket. We all have one."

Vlad reached into the vampire's pocket and withdrew the phone. He aimed it at the man so the face recognition unlocked it, then swiped his thumb across the screen. With his free hand, he scrolled through the received calls, all of them coming from an unknown caller. There were no stored numbers. Mircea was becoming adept, which made catching him problematic.

Son of a bitch.

No matter, Vlad would prevail. He pocketed the cell. The next time Mircea called this vampire, he'd damn well get his brother.

"Let go. You promised."

Vlad smiled, another grin he did not feel. "I don't believe I promised anything."

"You said you would kill me if I didn't tell you what I know."

"That I did say." Vlad released his arms, grabbed his neck and twisted his head clean off his shoulders. "But I never promised I'd let you go."

Draping the vampire's bloody corpse over his shoulder, head dangling from his fingers, Vlad sprinted unseen for the woods beyond the city. Mircea's man would be another casualty, just another missing person buried far into the forest, becoming carrion for the critters.

CHAPTER SEVEN

J ANELLE PLACED HER CELL SOFTLY ON HER DESK, HER HAND lingering on the smooth screen, and stared at the closed door in her office. Her fingers tapped the Gorilla glass. Her pulse throbbed in her ears as she contemplated the phone call and the DNA results from Vlad's hair follicle.

Dumbfounded.

Complete and utterly speechless.

She hadn't even thanked the technician, just simply ended the call. The temperature of the room seemed to drop ten degrees as a chill took up residence in her veins.

Dear Lord.

Running her hands across her biceps, she attempted to warm the glacial ice freezing her to the core.

What in the world?

The lab had confirmed her belief. Vlad Tepes had been at the church where the last two dead bodies had been discovered. The DNA on the hair found at the scene matched the one she had taken from the penthouse a few days ago. Of course, Vlad hadn't denied being there, nor had he confirmed it.

Was she to take him at his word? That his brother was the culprit?

71

Vlad's disclosure could simply be his need to cover his acts of violence and bloodshed by throwing his brother under the proverbial bus. Besides, she had no proof other than Vlad's word that this brother even existed.

Forced air from the ceiling vents rustled her unbound hair, tickling her cheek. She tucked the strays behind her ear and released a quivery breath. Though Vlad had never given her an overt reason not to trust him, was she allowing his good looks to sway her common sense? Janelle was positive he had been the one to break into her cabin, making him aware of her vacationing spot, where she worked, and what she drove. No doubt he knew of her apartment in the city as well.

That alone should scare the living hell out of her.

Add this unsettling call from the lab and she was a bit terror-stricken.

The tech had inquired about the origination of the hair strand she had given them, due to the fact the genetic code didn't appear wholly human. The technician explained, in terms Janelle didn't quite understand, that while the chromosomes had some human properties, it wasn't entirely of the human species, making it something they had never encountered. He had called it a medical mystery, unique, and possibly from a species they didn't know existed.

After convincing them to keep their findings on the down-low for the sake of the open case, she had answered the tech's inquiry by sticking with the story she had given her boss. The hair had been found at her cabin following a break-in. Of course, there *had* been a break-in, but it wasn't where the hair had originated.

Vlad had her falsifying stories not only to her superior but to the lab whose only job was aiding in uncovering the facts and helping to solve crimes. Janelle had never been one to break the rules, not even for the sake of a case. As a matter of fact, she went above and beyond to prove she was just as good as any man in the field. Never had she allowed her heart or emotions to get tangled up in the mix … until now.

And damn the man for getting beneath her skin.

Janelle sucked in a breath. If Vlad Tepes wasn't mortal, then what? Her gaze flitted back to the phone. Had the DNA or the results been compromised? Her beliefs centered on the here and now, what could be proven by scientific evidence. Never had she believed in anything paranormal.

Even her visions had centered on what could be explained, nothing supernatural in nature. *That was until Vlad.* Hadn't she seen fangs on him in her visions? Evidence of vampirism in him before her gift had gone silent?

What. The. Fuck?

Janelle turned to her laptop and flipped it open. Quickly entering her password, she opened Google and began once again searching on Vlad Tepes's name. Not that his namesake's history wasn't interesting. Vampirism was a well-known part of the folklore since the ruler had practiced drinking his victims' blood. But nothing of this century came up. It was as if Vlad had just materialized.

She scrolled through several sites, reading countless tales of old Vlad's history, including that of his castle, Poenari Fortress. It appeared his one-time home now lay in ruins. It was also where his first wife had jumped from the balcony to her death in the river far below to avoid capture by the Turks.

The poor Romanian ruler. What a way to lose one's spouse.

Studying the image on the screen, she could see a slight resemblance in the eyes and stubborn set of his jaw. A distant relative at best, but her Vlad was far more attractive.

Her Vlad?

Had she lost her damn mind, feeling he was anything to her? Her cell rang, causing her to jump. Janelle quickly closed her laptop as if the caller could see what she had been researching. Taking in another shaky breath, she noted the caller's name with a smile.

Thankful for the interruption, Janelle slid her finger across the glass and pressed the speaker button. "Hey, Rocky. What's up, girlfriend?"

"What are you doing later?" The warm husky sound of her voice filled the room. "Please don't tell me you're still working. Pssst...dull girl."

Janelle glanced at the round clock on the wall. Most of her co-workers had probably gone home for the day. She shook her head with a chuckle. Rocky knew her too well. They had been friends since high school, keeping in close touch through the years. When Janelle went to the academy and entered into law enforcement, Rocky began to strut the runways around the world. She had become an in-demand model and lived half her life in New York City.

Rocky's father had come from Spain at the age of seventeen as an exchange student, living with a nice German family, where he had met her mother. They had quickly fallen in love. According to her father, it was love at first sight. When his senior year ended and he returned to Spain, he made it his mission to return to the States and marry Rocky's mother, making their courtship one for romance novels. Rocky's exotic beauty came from a mix of their heritages. Currently, she lived in a warehouse flat in downtown Eugene, overlooking the city.

Janelle sighed, not in the mood for the party scene. "What do you have in mind?"

Rocky tsk-tsked, no doubt hearing her reluctance. "When's the last time you went out?"

Had it not been for her pit stop at Vlad's penthouse, she would have gone out Friday. "Don't judge me. I go to Frank's Tavern on occasion."

"With your stick-up-their-asses co-workers?" Rocky groaned. "Go home, put on something sexy, and meet me at the Blood 'n' Rave."

"You can't be serious? I've never stepped foot in there. It isn't my type of scene."

"You don't have a type, unless it's filled with law enforcement people. It's a bar, Janelle. You go, you drink, you have fun. Besides, I hear some sexy bikers hang out at the Rave."

Rocky purred. "You know I've always had a thing for bad boys."

"Which is why you always end up with a broken heart."

"At least I take chances. When's the last time you dated?"

Janelle didn't bother with an answer because Rocky already knew it had been some time.

"Come on, Janelle. Loosen up. What will it hurt to humor me this one time?"

"This one time?" She laughed. "We always do what you want."

"That's because you don't know how to have fun."

Janelle could hear the smile in her friend's voice. And, like any other time, she couldn't bring herself to decline. It was the middle of the week, so what could it hurt? She doubted the bar would be packed or over-loud.

"Just so you know, I don't own anything sexy."

Rocky clapped her hands, the sound carrying through the speaker. "That means you're going."

"Give me an hour and I'll meet you there."

"Janelle?" Rocky stopped her from hanging up.

"Yes?"

"A pair of skinny jeans, platform wedges, and that off-the-shoulder sweater I bought you for Christmas will work."

"It's short and my belly shows."

"Exactly. Your stomach is flat, so why would you care? Live a little. Wear it or you'll hurt my feelings."

Rocky ended the call, not giving her time to argue. Her best friend had infectious energy. Suddenly, Janelle looked forward to a night out. Maybe a few cocktails and dancing were exactly what she needed to forget her present conundrum with a hair—and the man—that wasn't quite human. Tomorrow would be soon enough to deal with Vlad Tepes and his secrets.

BRIGHT COLORED BEAMS OF light crisscrossed the otherwise darkened room. Industrial music blared from the speakers, the heavy beat thumping against her chest, making it nearly impossible to carry on a conversation without having to shout into Rocky's ears.

Janelle already detested the atmosphere and she hadn't gotten beyond the front door. No wonder the soft drone of conversation at Frank's Tavern was her preference. Either Rocky had spent too much time in New York City or Janelle's job made her the stick in the mud her best friend already thought her to be.

Several patrons, more than she would have guessed for a weeknight, sat at tables drinking sodas and cocktails, while others crowded the dance floor. Ravers bobbed and hopped in time with the industrial beat provided by the DJ. Glow light sticks, bracelets, and necklaces dangled from their necks and wrists.

Janelle circled the large tiled floor in search of a table stuck in a darkened corner, away from the mammoth speakers flanking the floor. While Rocky adored the attention, Janelle preferred the anonymity provided by the shadows in the corners of the room.

Just as she was about to choose a table the farthest from the dancers, Rocky grabbed her hand and damn near skipped toward the rear of the club, towing her along. Rocky pulled out a chair and sat at a table not far from a second bar, one not visible from the entrance. Being this far back and away from the massive speakers, at least the music was at a more tolerable level where they could converse without shouting.

A man with longish brown hair stood behind the bar, a Gothic top hat perched on his head. A pair of round spectacles sat low on his nose, making Janelle believe they were either readers or just there for the effect. Four large men wearing motorcycle cuts with the words "Sons of Sangue" on the top rocker stood on the opposite side of the bar, conversing with the bartender. Open bottles of Gentleman Jack and shot glasses littered the wooden top separating them. If the bottom rockers were any indication, two of the men were from Oregon, while the other two came from the state of Washington.

Janelle had been at the Oregon Sons of Sangue club-house once when she had been hunting down Vlad, following his odd visit to her office when he attempted to convince her the cartel had been responsible for the Flores murders. Her visions had told her where to find him, but none of these men looked familiar. While Vlad wasn't one of the bikers, her research proved his possible relatives, Kane and Kaleb Tepes, headed the dangerous group. Kane had been the one she met. The four men at the bar weren't quite as big as Vlad or Kane, but they were menacing nonetheless.

Rocky was keeping an eye on the rear bar and its inhabitants from her position at the table. Even though their presence was intimidating, Janelle could see why they would pique her best friend's interest. Her taste in men tended to run along the same type Janelle tracked as suspects. These bikers were no different. She'd bet one, if not all, had outstanding warrants of some kind.

The one closest to them looked as if he could walk the runway with Rocky. His jet-black hair was cut short along the sides, left a bit longer on top. High cheekbones and a strong jaw made him even more appealing. Tattoos peeked above the collar of his shirt, appearing to be three crosses, making her wonder at the meaning.

The second man from Oregon was taller and looked to be heavier muscled. His lighter colored brown hair was left somewhat longer to curl over the collar of his vest. The third and tallest man from Washington had dark blond curls, much like that of a surfer, while the fourth, maybe of American Indian descent, had deep brown, shoulder-length straight hair.

Janelle did a slight nod of her head in the bikers' direction. "I take it they're the reason we're here?"

"We're here for the cocktails and to get you to stop thinking about work, even if for a nanosecond." Rocky's smile lit her gaze. "But you have to admit they're pretty easy on the eyes."

A woman wearing cutoff shorts and a low-cut, V-neck T-shirt with the club's logo emblazoned across her ample breasts stopped at their table. A leather cord encircled her neck, a small vial containing an unknown red fluid and a single red bead dangled from it between her cleavage. Janelle couldn't help wondering what the vial contained, hopefully not what it appeared to be. Odd to say the least.

With a pop of the gum she chewed, the young woman asked, "What can I get for you?"

Rocky ordered a cosmopolitan while Janelle stuck with her usual of vodka, seltzer, and lime. The barmaid snapped her gum again, then trotted off to the main bar. Janelle couldn't help but note no one used the bar where the Sons stood. Not even the waitresses, who took their orders to the one near the front entrance, even though this one was closer.

Her gaze traveled the room. The same strange necklace wrapped the necks of most of the barmaids and some of the patrons. Maybe a new fashion statement Janelle wasn't aware of. Then again, being a special agent didn't give her much time to stay up on the latest styles.

The blond, curly-haired biker glanced their way, then nudged the shorter man from Washington. The two from Oregon briefly followed their gazes, but quickly dismissed her and Rocky and returned their attention to the bartender wearing the top hat. The Washington men kept their backs to their friends, elbows resting on the bar behind them, not bothering to mask their interest.

The barmaid placed two drinks on the table. Janelle was thankful for the interruption. Giving those two attention would only spell trouble. Janelle handed the waitress her credit card and asked to start a tab. Turning back to Rocky, Janelle snapped her fingers, attempting to draw her friend's focus back from the no-doubt felons.

"As gorgeous as you are, you can get any man you want. Showing those two interest is just asking for trouble."

Rocky picked up her cosmo and took a quick sip. "I wish. Flying off to different locations for shoots doesn't leave me time for relationships. Besides, you know how my last one ended … in disaster. Had it not been for the quick response to my 911 call from the bathroom I had barricaded myself in, I'd likely be dead. Thank goodness he's behind bars for a good long time."

Janelle didn't need to be reminded of the asswipe who had threatened to kill Rocky if she left him. The man had gone for his gun and had shot several times through the locked door of the bathroom, thankfully only nicking Rocky in the thigh with one of the stray bullets before the authorities arrived and arrested him.

"You have a habit of attracting trouble. He wasn't your only abusive relationship. Remember the one who refused to leave your side and went to all of your jobs? It took me threatening to shoot his dumb ass if he didn't take a hike."

Rocky shrugged. "Apparently, I'm not a great judge of character."

Janelle briefly glanced at the bikers again. "Or, you're just attracted to the wrong kind of man. These guys" —her thumb indicated the men behind her— "you'd best run from, not to, girlfriend."

"And what fun would that be?" Rocky winked at her. "Maybe you ought to end your dry spell and give one of those bad boys a shot. For crying out loud, live a little."

Janelle's thoughts bumped right into Vlad. Talk about a bad boy. He made her libido stand up and yell, "Hell yes," but she wasn't about to introduce him to Rocky. Especially since she wasn't sure if Vlad was even human.

"Excuse me?" teased a deep voice from behind her. Rocky's widened gaze told Janelle exactly who now stood directly behind her. "Are these seats taken?"

Wonderful.

"There are two stools over by the bar—" Janelle trailed off at the same time Rocky was pulling out a chair.

The blond took the seat to the left while the dark-haired and olive-skinned biker sat to her right. Janelle's original assessment of him being Native American seemed incorrect, as bright green eyes peered out from thick black lashes.

The blond reached across the table. "I'm Gunner and this here is my right-hand, Smoke."

Janelle shook his hand. "Nice to meet you, Gunner."

"Is it?" Gunner's laugh was as deep and throaty as his voice. "You look as if you'd rather be anywhere but here. We don't bite … unless you want us to, of course."

His broad smile made Janelle think he was quite serious and not jesting at all about the bite. She could easily imagine his pearly whites biting down on a neck or two. His partner in crime, Smoke, said nothing, probably the quieter one. His green gaze strayed to Rocky, making Janelle realize he was the reason the two of them were now sitting at the table, letting Janelle off the hook. Though handsome in his own right, Gunner wasn't her type, which brought Vlad slamming back into her thoughts.

Rocky thankfully rescued Janelle from having to reply to Gunner. "I'm Rocky Barta."

"The model?" Gunner asked, tapping his forefinger on the table before pointing it at her. "Of course. I knew you looked familiar. Are you from around here or just visiting?"

"I'm from Eugene, but I also have a flat in New York City."

"Smoke here—"

Gunner was interrupted from saying anything further when the heavily muscled biker approached. "Hate to break this little party up, but we have to go."

"Jesus, Ryder, can't you see—"

"Fuck this shit," the man called Ryder said, anger evident in his whiskey-colored eyes. "Kane called, said Vlad's at the clubhouse. We need to return immediately. Wrap this up and meet me and Xander out front."

Not waiting for a response, Ryder and the one called Xander headed for the exit. Gunner jumped to his feet, Smoke following suit.

"Sorry, ladies," Gunner grimaced. "Duty calls."

Without another word, both men followed the other two like a fire lit their heels.

Vlad was at the clubhouse.

One mention of the man's name and the bikers seemed to jump into action. Was he that important to their organization? Maybe Janelle had been incorrect in thinking he wasn't a part of the Sons of Sangue.

Maybe he silently headed the gang of bikers. Like a kingpin to the cartel, Vlad Tepes appeared to call the shots. And if he wasn't wholly human … what about these men who seemed to follow his request without question?

Blood.

Sons of Sangue.

Sangue was the Italian word for blood.

Sons of Blood.

Vlad visiting her in the middle of the night, razor-sharp fangs sinking into her throat, floated back into her mind. A vision? Maybe not a dream after all.

Vampire.

Blood vials hanging around the necks of several of the Blood 'n' Raves barmaids and patrons?

Jesus! What the ever-loving-fuck had she just stumbled across?

CHAPTER EIGHT

V LAD STOOD IN THE LARGE MEETING ROOM BEHIND THE seats reserved for the president and vice president of the MC. Members of the Sons of Sangue filed in, each taking their respective chairs circling the oversized table. The vampiric death skull, the same one decorating the back of their motorcycle vests, had been carved into the center. A thick piece of glass protected the design.

Some of the members of the Washington chapter, along with those who hadn't earned their patches, stood along the walls, filling the room to overcapacity. Even the large oak doors couldn't be shut without the place becoming claustrophobic.

It warmed Vlad's heart to see his grandsons' circle grow. These men and their mates were nearly as much a part of his clan as Kane and Kaleb. Should they ever need his help, he'd be there for them at the bat of the eye. He hoped the commitment was mutual. With his brother creating a small legion, he'd need every man at hand to stop the son of a bitch.

Not all of those present were vampires. Some of them were prospects and hangarounds. Though Vlad wouldn't allow them to put themselves at risk against his kind, they might prove useful as lookouts.

Kane picked up the wooden mallet and struck the plate, the din of conversation instantly dying. From the earlier whispers, Vlad gathered most had no clue why the emergency meeting had been called. His grandsons had likely waited for him to take the lead.

While numbers were a good thing, before they delved into the thick of things, the humans would need to leave the room. This was a matter the vampires needed to handle. Humans would only get themselves killed going up against Mircea's personal army.

Christ, Mircea's carelessness alone made Vlad want to end the son of a bitch's life. His temerity was going to expose what Vlad had spent years keeping hidden. Living side-by-side with humans would never work. There would always be a militia of want-to-be heroes aiming to take their heads.

Kane stood by his seat at the head of the table, everyone giving him their attention. Curious gazes briefly strayed to Vlad, no doubt wondering about his appearance when he normally stayed away from club business.

"First, I need all of those not patched to fall out into the main room of the clubhouse. This part of the business is to be conducted by members only." Kane motioned some of those by the exit to take their leave, waiting for the large doors to close behind them before continuing. "Vlad has news we need to hear. This isn't good, so listen up."

Vlad stood behind Kane as he took his seat next to Kaleb. Resting a hand on the shoulder of each of his grandsons, he glanced around the room at the men gathered. Everyone gave him their undivided attention, including those there from the Washington chapter. Besides him, there were three other primordial vampires present: Kane, Kaleb, and Ryder. If need be, Kane had said they could enlist the help of Draven Smith and Brea Gotti, who also carried primordial blood.

Those newly made vampires Mircea was creating all had his brother's blood, making them primordials as well. This little party of vampires sharing the same vengeance could become a shitfest real quick. Vlad needed to contain the problem and shut his brother and his plan down.

"You all know my brother is out there gunning for Kane and Kaleb, and indirectly, all of you. He wants to take me down and will try to do so through my grandsons. Other than his ultimate goal of killing my kin, I'm betting he's also trying to get the authorities to focus on the club for these murders. Get you scrambling so you can't hone in on catching the cagey bastard."

Heads nodded and murmurs of agreement filtered through the room.

"I don't think you need to be told this threat shouldn't be taken lightly." Vlad rubbed a hand down his short-cut beard. "Mircea has been a nuisance for some time and I take the blame for allowing his transgressions. No more. My brother is to be stopped at all costs."

"Agreed," some of the men murmured.

"I stopped by the coroner's office a few days ago. I hypnotically entranced the medical examiner into believing the lethal wounds were not caused by bite wounds, hoping to deflect law enforcement from the real cause."

"Let's hope that works," Kane said. "Last thing we need is locals snooping around. I'll have Cara keep an ear open at the Sheriff's Office."

"Good idea, Kane." Vlad glanced around the table. "If any of you come across him, do not try to take him out on your own. Make sure you have one of the four of us, me, Kane, Kaleb, or Ryder present before you attempt to cross him. He's strong and growing stronger every day."

"How so?" Anton asked.

"He's consuming a lot of blood, which will aid in his power. All his senses will be heightened. He'll know you're coming long before he spots you."

"How the hell will we get the upper hand if he knows we're there?" Alexander chimed in.

Vlad took in a deep breath before letting out a heavy sigh. He wished he had an answer. "Somehow we need to mask our scent. Any of us can scent a vampire in the vicinity. We need something stronger so Mircea can't detect us, or we'll never catch the son of a bitch. I'm open to ideas."

"GQ has some cologne you'll smell a mile away." Grayson chuckled.

"Fuck you, Gypsy." Alexander wadded up a piece of paper from the table and threw it at him, striking him in the forehead, which only made him laugh harder. "India likes it just fine."

"On the serious side." Grigore, home from the first leg of his touring with his pop star mate, Caitlyn, all but growled.

"Years ago, when I hunted, I used something called skunk spray. It covers a human scent so they can't be detected by animals. I'm pretty sure that shit will even deaden a primordial's sense of smell."

"What does it smell like, Wolf?" Grayson asked.

"Shit smells just like skunk."

Alexander's lips turned down. "And you want us to spray ourselves with it?"

Grigore shook his head as a grin blossomed on his face. "You can if you want. But good luck getting that shit off you, Xander. You spray the ground, your boots, anything near you. I doubt even a primordial will scent a vampire over that stench."

"It's certainly worth a try," Vlad said. "Where do you get it?"

"Any hunting store carries it." Grigore shrugged. "I can pick some up if you want to give it a try."

"Pick us up a bottle. If it works, we'll order a whole damn case." Vlad looked around the room. "Any of you want to be the guinea pig?"

"Why not Viper or Hawk?" Bobbie suggested.

Kaleb's gaze widened, and he used his thumb to indicate his brother. "I volunteer Viper."

"You would volunteer me, Hawk. Coward." Kane laughed. "I'll do it. Wolf, get us a bottle of that shit. If it works, as Vlad said, we'll want a case. Let's just hope it does. But remember, we spray around us. I don't want to wind up being the stinkiest sons of bitches on motorcycles."

Grayson shook his head and laughed. "I won't be riding downwind from you, Viper."

"If this shit works, Mircea certainly won't know what hit him," Vlad said. They'd only get one chance. "Because once he figures out what we're doing, he'll know damn well we're coming because of the stench."

"We could always go back to GQ's cologne idea." Grayson laughed, earning a smack on the back of his head by Alexander.

Laughter and chatter filled the room until Kane used the mallet again to gain their attention. "We'll use the prospects and hangarounds to look out for anything unusual."

"They know about us, Kane?" Vlad asked.

He nodded. "The prospects do. The hangarounds haven't proven themselves. I'm not sure they've earned our trust yet, but this could be a way of testing that. If they fail in any way, we'll hypnotize them into forgetting and cut them loose."

"Sounds like a viable plan, Viper." Hawk glanced around the room. "We use the prospects to keep an eye on them. They travel in pairs and groups. No man on his own. If they see something, they are to call us. If a prospect feels a hangaround isn't holding up his end, then we'll be informed."

Grigore shook his head. "Not sure they should be trusted with our secret just yet."

"Why's that, Wolf?" Kane asked.

"I still live by the old Benjamin Franklin adage, 'three can keep a secret, if two of them are dead.' Anyone outside this room, I don't trust. Including prospects. I know we need them, and thus far they have been loyal. After we catch Mircea, I say we patch them over. But the hangarounds? I say they take a hike until this problem is dealt with."

Kane looked at Kaleb. "What do you think, Hawk?"

Kaleb shrugged. "Let's put this shit to a vote."

Vlad continued to watch as his grandsons conducted their business, happy with the vote outcome. The hangarounds were to be cut loose for the time being and out of club business. They could come back once Mircea was caught. Grigore was correct, Vlad didn't need people who hadn't yet proved their trustworthiness knowing their secret. With the prospects having something to gain, obtaining their patches for a job well done, they were more likely to keep their lips closed.

Kane looked to Ryder. "Any news from the Washington chapter, Ryder?"

"Gunner informed me they're on standby should we need them."

"Unless Mircea crosses the border, we got this shit handled," Kane said.

"I agree." Vlad patted Kane and Kaleb's shoulders. "Looks like you have this end covered. If anyone sees my brother and Kane, Kaleb, or Ryder are present, then take the son of a bitch out. No need to wait for my permission. The same goes for the little legion he's created. We need to stomp these minions out and quick."

"You got it, Vlad." Kane stood and addressed the group. "We'll call in the prospects and hangarounds and finish this shit up. Wolf, you get us some of that skunk spray and I'll give it a test."

Grigore nodded. "You got it, P."

Kane walked to the double doors and swung them open. Vlad said his goodbyes as the other young men filed in. He didn't need to be present for the rest of this. He had a brother to hunt down. But first, he needed blood. Maybe he'd use the Blood 'n' Rave and their donors for a little sustenance. And while he was at it, check out the other primordials, Draven Smith and his mate.

JANELLE'S SCENT TICKLED HIS nose the minute he cleared the back door to the club. The question was, what was the bewitching special agent doing in a place that offered blood to vampires?

Music, if that's what the awful noise could be called, blared through speakers. He'd prefer something softer and more soothing than the loud industrial stuff now pounding his eardrums.

How the hell did one converse?

Vlad walked through the small storage room that doubled as an office. He'd need to talk to Draven about getting a donor since he wasn't used to feeding in this establishment. He had his own harem of blood hosts back on his island. Otherwise, he simply hypnotized those he fed from whenever the need arose. Vlad supposed using donors was a safer way of doing things, less chance of getting caught sipping from arteries out in the wild.

He doubted any of the donors inside would recognize him as a vampire since he didn't wear Sons of Sangue colors.

Little did they know, they'd be feeding the eldest of his kind.

Draven Smith leaned against the bar, and the woman whom Vlad presumed to be his mate sat on the other side. The owner nodded in Vlad's direction, not surprised to see him, conceivably having scented Vlad long before he walked through the office door.

Draven righted himself. "Vlad Tepes, to what do we owe the honor?"

"I need one of your donors."

Vlad's gaze went to the smaller woman, no doubt the one Kane called Brea Gotti, who could be no taller than five-foot-two when she stood. Her highlighted brown hair had been shaved short on one side, the tresses on the opposite side falling to just past her chin. She sported a tiny diamond in her left nostril. She might be small in stature, but Vlad could sense the power coming off her in waves. Brea Gotti wasn't one to be fucked with, in part because she also happened to be the descendant of Vlad's long-dead brother, Radu.

Vlad gripped Brea's small hand, bringing it to his nose. "Amazing, my brother's scent still lives in you and in the one they call Ryder. Take care of his heritage. As far as I know, you two are the end of his lineage when all these years I thought none were left."

Brea smiled warmly, her blue eyes, much like those of his brother's, twinkled in the bar lights. "It's a pleasure to meet a great uncle ... far down the line, of course."

Vlad glanced over his great niece's shoulder, spying Janelle Ferrari sitting not far away, next to another beautiful young woman. Though pretty, she had nothing on the special agent. His nostrils flared, scenting her rich blood. His fangs punched through his gums, tingling with his hunger. Christ, he needed to get a hold of himself. His blood ran hot just at the sight of her. Too bad she wasn't on the menu.

He'd need to get this little dine-and-dash done before she spotted him, leaving him to answer a lot of uncomfortable questions. After all, the Blood 'n' Rave wasn't the type of establishment he normally frequented.

Vlad turned back to Draven. "You have someplace I can go while I await a donor? I prefer to do so quietly and away from all of this flashiness."

Draven smiled. "Right. I wouldn't think you'd come here to hang out. What does an old vampire like you do for entertainment?"

Vlad damn near rolled his eyes at the mention of his age. He could kick Draven's ass on a bad day. "I entertain women."

"I bet you do." The barkeep chuckled. "Maybe you ought to try a mate one day."

"You can't be fucking serious." Vlad's eyes rounded. "Why in the hell would I want to tether myself to just one?"

His gaze traveled back to Janelle, who had yet to spot him. Of course, he'd never want a mate or the responsibility that came with a bond. The idea was ludicrous, even if the blood now burning through his veins called him a liar. Taking another female had lost its appeal since he met the special agent.

Christ, when the hell had I allowed that to happen?

He'd lost his first wife centuries ago, and still the anguish stayed with him. The idea he hadn't protected her from the Turks and she had jumped to her death had damn near crippled him with guilt. Vlad couldn't saddle himself with that type of responsibility … or heartache ever again.

It made him weak.

Draven laid a hand on top of his mate's, squeezing it. "I may have thought the very same thing until Brea."

"Keep it that way." Vlad all but growled, restlessness settling in.

Nothing ruffled his feathers, ever … until Janelle. Not only was the woman devastatingly beautiful, but something about her was alluring like the call of a siren. Vlad needed to remember nothing good could come from their union. Any kind of relationship could only end badly.

"Room?"

"My, aren't we in a hurry?" Draven pointed to a curtained doorway. "Take the stairs to the top. There's a room with a door. If you want a sip of whiskey while you wait, the room is stocked with Gentleman Jack per your grandsons' requests."

"Thank you," Vlad said, taking one last glance at Janelle.

Satisfied she still hadn't spied him, he disappeared behind the curtain and took the stairs two at a time. The lights had already been turned on, offering a soft glow to a comfortable room, complete with wine-colored carpeting and matching draperies. Tasteful. A tan Italian leather sofa sat at the back, with oversized cushions. Vlad headed over, taking the bottle of whiskey from the cart with him. If he hung out in Oregon much longer, he might just develop a taste for the amber liquid. It certainly did a fine job of warming him from the inside, much the way sipping blood did.

Vlad sat, crossed one booted foot over his knee, unscrewed the cap to the whiskey and took a long pull from the bottle. His mind conjured up Janelle. Hell, it was bound to. Her scent still wafted up the stairs and roused his libido, hardening him, and he had yet to take a single sip of blood. Christ, what would drinking her blood do to him?

Too bad he was unable to hypnotize her.

He wouldn't have minded finding out what she tasted like.

Hell, fucking her while he sipped from her neck?

The thought alone had his dick throbbing. He needed to finish what he came here to do, which had nothing to do with any horizontal action. Vlad needed sustenance, not a quick lay. Fucking tonight's donor wasn't going to happen, even if his vampire side ached for more. Unfortunately, his heart wasn't tempted to feed his other hunger even if it were offered, which left him pissed off and horny.

Maybe Draven was right. Vlad needed to find a new form of entertainment, like hunting down Mircea. That or he needed to fuck Janelle and rid her from his system. Which, of course, couldn't happen if he was unable to hypnotize her. There was no hiding the vampire in him when sexual desire took over.

Vlad scented a human and her red blood cells entering the stairwell before he heard the footfalls coming up the steps. A pleasingly plump blonde cleared the landing and walked into the room, padding softly across the carpeting. Her fair skin, ruby red lips, and heart-shaped face lent to her beauty. This blonde had womanly curves and a nice set of large tits, though she was petite in height. She normally fit his type, but unfortunately couldn't hold a candle to the woman downstairs who seemed to have captured his attention.

"What's your name, sweetheart?"

"Ivy," she answered, closing the gap.

This one didn't seem bent on conversation. Good. Ivy knelt at his feet between his now spread thighs and pulled her bobbed hair to one side, exposing her neck. Vlad could tell Ivy was no newbie at feeding vampires. No nonsense, no need to chitchat. Exactly the way Vlad wanted it … at least for the day. Feed and get the hell on the road.

He had a brother to catch.

And a sexy-as-sin woman to avoid.

Vlad's eyes heated, further bringing out the vampire. It had been nearly five days since he last fed. Primordials could go a bit longer before the death chill would settle in, though he could use the sustenance. Ivy didn't look as if she'd suffer from losing a bit more blood than normally required. It was about damn time he fed more regularly, as well, if he wanted to build his strength against Mircea. Hard telling how much the fool was consuming.

Running his tongue along the soft side of her neck, he cringed as Ivy's responding soft moan carried to his ears. Vlad's nostrils flared, inhaling the deep, rich bouquet of her blood. His stomach cramped from hunger. He couldn't help wondering again what Janelle's blood might taste like, a thought he damn well shouldn't be entertaining. Vlad didn't need the trouble she'd bring, not when he already had enough of his own.

One of Ivy's hands gripped his leg, while her generous breasts pressed into the V of his thighs. Sex wasn't what he came for.

Nor was Janelle.

Vlad released her and gently pushed her from him, anger flaring hot within him at no longer wanting to feed … at least not from the pretty blonde. He couldn't keep his damn mind focused and off of fucking. Maybe not Ivy, but most definitely someone else in the building.

"Mr. Tepes?" Ivy stood, twisting her hands in front of her.

"I'm sorry, Ivy, but apparently I'm going to go without sustenance tonight, which is not your fault." His fangs had already retreated. "Let me escort you downstairs and buy you a drink."

"If you're sure." Her warm smile normally would have appealed to him. Not today. "I could use a glass of wine if you wouldn't mind."

Vlad couldn't help but wonder why Ivy hadn't been already scooped up and made a mate to someone. Placing an arm around her shoulders, he led her down the stairs, through the curtains, and to the bar.

Brea had left her spot, but Draven remained. "I hope Ivy was to your satisfaction."

Vlad licked his lips, not about to reveal his lack of desire where Ivy was concerned. He couldn't have the barkeep thinking it was somehow the fault of the blonde. "She knows how to please a man."

"Is that so?"

Janelle's cold response washed over him like a bucket of ice water. Of course, she'd pick that moment to approach him. Vlad sucked in a deep breath, dropped his arm from around Ivy, and turned to the woman who had his dick in a knot. His remaining erection lay proof of that.

Holding Janelle's icy stare, he said to Draven, "Get Ivy anything she wishes and put it on my tab."

"Absolutely," came the barkeep's response before Vlad tuned out everything but the woman in front of him. He had to wonder what had happened to her friend. "To what do I owe the pleasure?"

"Or displeasure." Janelle raised a delicate brow, one he wouldn't mind easing with a trace of his finger. Her gaze briefly took in Ivy at his back. "Girlfriend?"

Janelle had handed him the perfect opportunity to keep her at arm's length. But his hardened cock had other ideas. "I don't have a girlfriend. Offering?"

Janelle harrumphed.

"What are you doing here, Special Agent Ferrari? Taken to following me again?"

"I'm off the clock, Vlad. Don't flatter yourself."

"This doesn't appear to be your type of club. I picture you knocking back beers with other law enforcement, not partying with teenagers."

"They're all of age," he heard Draven intervene. Great, they had a fucking audience.

Vlad hardened his jaw, gripped Janelle by the forearm, and said to the barkeep, "I'm occupying your room upstairs again. Make sure no one, and I mean no one, fucking bothers me."

Draven gave him a salute. "You got it, big guy."

"I will not be sloppy seconds." Janelle fought his grip to no avail.

"Then how about fucking firsts?"

Janelle's gasp carried to his ears as he lifted her off the floor, threw her over his shoulder and smacked her ass hard. Parting the curtains, he didn't stop until they reached the top floor, slamming the door behind him.

CHAPTER NINE

*W*HAT. *THE. HELL*? JANELLE SPRAWLED OVER VLAD'S shoulder, one arm securely anchoring her. No doubt her ass sported a large red handprint from the solid swat that stung her flesh. As she pounded his rigid muscles, he effortlessly took the stairs two at a time, carrying her as though she were light as a feather. Her bathroom scale screamed to a different tune, one that involved removing articles of clothing in an attempt to lower the numbers.

What did Vlad do for a living? Lift weights? He certainly didn't seem to be someone who spent hours in the gym.

Lord, she bet he could do his own calendar shoot and make a mint, giving the New York City firefighters a run for their money. Vlad created a new definition for the term fit. By the feel of his ungiving back muscles, Janelle swore he was made of granite.

"Put me down, you big oaf."

"Excuse me?" he grumbled, the sound coming from deep within his large frame. "I'm not a beast."

"You could've fooled me with your Neanderthal toss of me over your shoulders and dashing up the stairs."

Reaching the top, Vlad strode into a large room, ignoring her request to be put down. But before she had time to insist he comply, she found herself sliding very slowly down the front of an uncompromising chest when he simply could have dropped her. The last man she'd dated wore preppy glasses, had a short military-style haircut, and a nice dad-body.

The opposite of … *this*.

Vlad did not have a soft spot anywhere on him, including the impressive erection now trapped between them, searing her abdomen. She bit back her spike of desire, heating her to the core. The continuing sting of her ass and the heat pooling between her thighs pretty much proved she was out of her league with this man.

Janelle used her palms to push away from his rock-hard chest. "What the hell do you think you're doing? You can't just treat me like a belonging. And smacking my ass? I should shoot you for that."

He smiled, mischief twinkling in his gaze. "You liked it."

"I…" She glanced away from those impossibly dark eyes so he wouldn't see the truth. Christ, it had been a turn-on, but she'd die before admitting as much. "I didn't."

His arched brow mocked her. "Liar."

Vlad gripped her by the back of the neck and pulled her in to him, her breasts bumping against his chest. Suddenly, she regretted not wearing a bra. Her taut nipples scraped against the cable knit of her sweater, only intensifying her hunger. Traitorous body. Good thing her sweater hid her physical reaction. The last thing she needed was Vlad knowing she desired him. Hell, desire didn't seem like a fit description for the hot sweaty sex she fantasized about. And if she allowed herself to indulge, Janelle was pretty sure he'd deliver.

Regardless of his denial, the man was an insufferable beast, arrogant to a fault, pretentious, and … and…

Vlad looked down on her, stealing her thoughts and muddling her brain. Her gaze drifted from his eyes to a perfect set of temptingly kissable lips; probably the only thing soft about him. His hand snaked about her bare back, searing her flesh, and pulling her flush against his groin again. His sizable erection nudged her abdomen, causing heat to nearly liquefy her thighs. Jesus, much more and she'd become putty. Damn good thing his arm anchored her or she might've fallen at his feet like the no doubt countless women before her. Vlad didn't seem like a man used to being denied. Normally she had a will made of iron, but something about him had her libido high-fiving her and cheering her on.

Sleeping with Vlad would be a very, very bad thing.

Janelle brought her gaze back to his smoldering one. Heat warmed her like the hot sun to asphalt. Much more and she'd be fried. No doubt detecting her train of thought, thanks to ogling his sinful lips, his gaze dropped to her mouth.

If she allowed him the kiss, Janelle wasn't so sure she'd stop him from going further. Sex had been the last thing on her mind since breaking up with her ex last year. Work had been all-consuming. She lived for her job, hence all the long hours. Rocky had been correct. The truth of the matter was Janelle didn't get out enough. When she wasn't at work, she was at home working.

Janelle could hardly deny the hunger now sluicing through her veins.

She wanted Vlad Tepes.

They were adults and what two consenting grownups did was nobody's business. Well, other than the barkeep downstairs who likely already assumed they were doing it anyway. Vlad gripped her chin more tenderly than she imagined a man of his power was capable of.

He lowered his head, sealing her lips with his. Janelle slid her hands up his chest and tangled her fingers in his thick soft-as-silk hair, more to maintain her upright position than to keep him from pulling away. What started as a gentle meeting of their mouths quickly turned possessive. He slanted his head for a better angle, then breached the seal of her lips.

Janelle moaned, her tongue mating with his in perfect rhythm. Vlad tasted of warm whiskey and vanilla. She knew she should stop him before they went any further. There would be no takebacks once the clothes came off. But Lord, she needed this man naked more at this moment than she cared about her DEA case or catching his criminal brother. Her libido wasn't about to be curbed, not this time.

Vlad kicked the door closed with the toe of his boot, then backed her against the nearest wall. His groin ground against her soft abdomen, telling her he had no intention of stopping at a mere kiss. It was a heady speculation having someone so sinfully hot desiring her. Janelle had always thought of herself as average, especially next to her beautiful friend Rocky. And yet, Vlad made her feel desirable.

The pretty blonde who had been up here with him moments ago slipped back into her thoughts. His comment of fucking firsts should have solidified the fact he hadn't done anything with the other woman, and yet she needed to confirm as much. Her ego needed validation.

Janelle stepped away. Vlad dropped his hold, and seemed intent on avoiding her eyes. A sliver of fear ran through her. Not wholly human. Her suspicion came crashing back, causing her to shiver as he appeared to hide something of himself. Had the lab made a mistake? Everything about this man seemed human, right down to the impressive erection still straining the front of his jeans. Other than his odd ability to scramble electronics and hypnotize a person's way of thinking, he seemed completely mortal. She couldn't help but wonder if the DNA results were nothing more than a horrible lab mix-up.

Her visions, though, the dream she'd had of Vlad sinking fangs into her throat….

Another shiver passed through her, this one oddly arousing.

"I'm sorry," he apologized, mistaking her reason for retreating.

"You and Ivy" —Janelle palmed his cheek, gaining his darkened gaze— "did you two?"

"Have sex? Absolutely not. You have no reason to be jealous."

Her brow creased. Before today, Janelle wasn't typically one to be envious of anything or anyone. "I couldn't care less what the two of you did."

"No?" He smiled, warm and arresting, sending a jolt of lust straight to her womb. "Then what are you asking for?"

She nearly laughed at the double entendre. Never had she asked for a man's cock before, but with Vlad, she was damn tempted. "I refuse to be second."

"We already established that isn't the case." His face sobered. "I can scent your need, *iubi*. Tell me what you desire and it's yours."

Janelle was tired of pretending she didn't want this man. Taking a shaken breath, she whispered, "You."

"Christ," he mumbled, right before he drew her in for another kiss, this one scorching, damn near melting her where she stood.

God help her, she had not once needed anyone the way she did this man. Janelle slid her hand down the smooth cotton of his T-shirt to his jeans, before palming his erection and hearing his growl.

Breaking the kiss, wanting to see his answering desire, she opened her eyes and locked gazes with him. An odd blackness seemed to fill his eyes, taking over the sclera until no white could be seen. Janelle sucked in a shallow breath at the unnatural change. Vlad quickly averted his face, but it was too late. She had already noticed the supernatural transformation.

Vlad gave her his back, but Janelle wasn't about to allow him to retreat, not now. She had already seen the worst of humans. Whatever this was Janelle was pretty sure she could handle it. Part of her already knew the truth, her erotic dream months back telling her as much.

Was this the same man she had researched, the long-dead ruler who had impaled his victims?

She shook her head. *It couldn't be.*

"Vlad?"

"Go." His response was curt. "Leave before we do something you'll live to regret."

His voice seemed somehow thicker, as though two razor-sharp fangs truly did fill his mouth. Janelle needed to see them firsthand. If her dreams hadn't frightened her, neither would the vampire standing inches away. The thought of him sinking his fangs deep into her throat didn't sicken her as it should. No, it only intensified her desire.

Janelle laid a gentle hand on his rigid spine, causing him to increase the separation. But instead of allowing him space, she wrapped a hand about his biceps and forced him to face her. His brow protruded unnaturally above his deep-set obsidian gaze, the abnormality supernatural and inhuman, but taking nothing from his allure. His cheekbones rose high on his face, hollowing out his cheeks. When he drew back his lips and hissed, the vision in her dreams came to life. Two very long canines stood out in stark contrast to the deep red of his lips.

Gooseflesh popped out along her forearms.

Janelle raised a hand to her throat, where she could feel her blood pounding in her pulse.

His gaze followed her action. "Relax, *iubi*. I have no intention of feeding from you."

"Because you already fed from the blonde?"

He shook his head. "It was my intention to, but no. After one scent of your sweet blood downstairs, I lost my appetite for hers."

"Then you'll feed from me?"

Truth be told, she wasn't even affronted by the idea of Vlad drinking her blood. Hell, if he so much as touched her with those razor-sharp fangs... A shudder ran through her. Vlad the man was heady enough to deal with. But Vlad the vampire? He was down-right intoxicating.

"Would you drain me?"

"Never, *iubi*," he whispered, his hand palming her cheek.

"Why do you call me *iubi*?"

"Would you prefer I call you love, baby, or sweetheart? It's all the same in Romanian."

Janelle smiled. "If any other guy called me baby, I'd probably deck him. Oddly, it seems sexier coming from you."

His black gaze narrowed and he dropped his hand from her cheek. "You still find me sexy, even as a monster?"

"I don't see a monster."

"Then what do you see?"

Janelle licked her dry lips. "A vampire that could choose to be lethal."

"I would never harm you, *iubi*. Although you should probably run far away from me."

"Why?"

"Because if you don't, I may not drain you of your blood, but I will fuck you. I can scent your desire and it's driving me to the breaking point. You want this." He gripped her hand and placed it back over his erection.

Janelle drew her lower lip between her teeth. "God help me, I do."

Before she had a chance to say more, he turned her so her ass now cupped his erection. Vlad fisted her hair and pulled back on her head, exposing her neck. Janelle's pulse thundered through her, her senses waiting for his canines to pierce her tender flesh.

Vlad leaned forward, his nose just centimeters from her carotid artery, and licked a path from her bare shoulder to her ear. "The time to stop me is now, *iubi*. Say the word and walk away. Otherwise, I will fuck you like no other and rid you of every memory of anyone who came before me."

Talk about ego, but damn she believed every word. Her mouth dried. Janelle didn't think she could work up the words to stop him, even had she wanted him to. But she didn't. If he slid his hands into her panties, he'd find her wanting... So. Damn. Much. Instead of vocalizing her need, she pushed back against his erection, earning her another growl.

Vlad reached around her, slipped the button from her jeans, then pushed the tight denim from her hips, her thong following. Sliding his hand up her bare torso and under the cable-knit sweater, he cupped one of her breasts, finding the nipple pebbled.

"Jesus," he blasphemed, his fingers tugging on the pert tip.

Janelle leaned into his touch, her breasts achy and tight. Her bare ass pressed against the roughness of his jeans. If she slid her center along the material, she could easily climax. Janelle moaned, damn near ready to beg. His fangs grazed the tender flesh of her neck.

Would his bite hurt?

Vlad, sensing her readiness, released her breast and placed one hand in the middle of her back and anchored her over the arm of the sofa. She fisted the pillow, tucked into the corner; her breath came in short pants. The hand securing her slid down her back to her ass, just before the rasp of his zipper sounded, followed by the hot tip of his erection pressed against her. The heat of his cock brushing against her wetness drove her mad, spiking her hunger. Desperately, she ached to feel him slide inside. The anticipation alone nearly had her climaxing.

Janelle bit back the impending orgasm, wanting to feel him inside her before she gave way. Vlad positioned his cock while he continued to hold onto her hair, arching her back and leaving her neck exposed. She moaned and pushed against him.

"Christ, you're fucking hot."

Vlad pushed slowly into her, withdrawing slightly before fully seating himself. His name tumbled from her lips. He was thick and hot, deliciously filling her. Rocking back into him,

Janelle encouraged him to take her fast and hard. Vlad tightened his grip on her hair, thrusting energetically enough to move the couch beneath her.

"Vlad." She panted his name, a hairbreadth away from orgasm. "Christ, bite me already."

Vlad growled, then sank his fangs deep into her neck. White-hot lights flashed behind her closed lids, stealing her breath. Janelle convulsed around his thickness as he held her tight against him. His lips were suctioned to the tender flesh of her neck as he drew her life's fluid, sucking the red cells from her artery. Janelle cried out as she climaxed a second time.

Never had she thought one could have an out-of-body experience without death, but damn if she didn't feel as if she were floating, looking down upon their joined bodies. Vlad withdrew his fangs with a soft pop, before licking the twin holes and appeasing the ache left from his fangs.

He thrust one final time before he tensed, his hold on her tightening. His curse echoed through the room before he released his grip. Janelle collapsed to cushions beneath her, bare ass still in the air.

"I'm wrecked."

Vlad's chuckle and the rasp of his zipper was her only answer.

CHAPTER TEN

V LAD SHOULD'VE BEEN TROUBLED BY THE FACT HE HAD JUST fucked and fed from a woman he couldn't hypnotize into forgetting. Hell, she was law enforcement and could effectively walk out of this room, expose the truth about vampires and bring him to his knees.

Once the euphoria wore off, he'd no doubt realize how much he had screwed up and potentially placed his family and their friends in danger. But at the moment, he couldn't seem to wipe the stupid grin off his face. Special Agent Ferrari was still bent over the sofa, with her bare ass in the air.

"I'm wrecked," resonated through his thoughts, making him want to strut like a fucking peacock, stroking his ego and then some. Not that he wasn't already confident when it came to women, but this one … this one had been somewhat of a challenge. And damn if he didn't want to wrap those long lean legs about his waist and do it all over.

Now was not the time to be patting himself on the back, though. Mircea needed to be found and dealt with. Fucking a human and worrying about the consequences was wasting his precious time. The longer Mircea was allowed to walk the earth, the larger his brother's army grew. This situation, if it wasn't dealt with, could become catastrophic.

And now? He had another issue he needed to get a handle on. Janelle's knowledge of vampires couldn't be erased. For whatever reason, hypnosis didn't work on her and scrambling her thoughts only left her confused about the events, not forgetting them entirely. Vlad had fucked Janelle and used her for sustenance.

Talk about disastrous.

This woman intoxicated him. Vlad was beginning to wonder if she hadn't somehow bewitched him. Everything about her called to his baser needs. The last time he had desired a woman the way he did Janelle, she had leaped to her death rather than be captured by the Turks, devastating him and leaving him hollow. The idea he might feel something for this female scared the bejesus right out of him.

"Janelle?"

"Hmmm…," was her muffled reply.

"Everything okay?"

He heard her answering chuckle before she lifted herself from the sofa and stood. Christ, she was beautiful, bedraggled and all. Janelle gripped her jeans and sexy-as-hell black lace thong from about her ankles and pulled them up, shimmying them over her hips before righting her sweater. Under which she wore no bra. The thought alone had him hard as concrete and ready for round two.

Talk about being wrecked. If he wasn't careful, this woman could easily destroy him. Janelle pushed her long brown tresses from her face and smiled, looking well-fucked and sexier than ever. Vlad bit back his rising need.

They needed to go.

He had a brother to catch.

And now that Janelle knew about him and his kind, he wasn't going to let her out of his sight until he figured a way out of this horrible mess he had gotten himself into. Flipping the tables, Vlad was about to become her fucking shadow. Janelle wouldn't be given a choice, not with the vampires' entire existence at stake. Humans had proven time and time again untrustworthy. Why should he expect her to be any different?

Janelle took in a deep breath before letting it out slowly. "*That* was incredible."

One of his brows arched. "I'm glad you think so, *iubi*. I wouldn't mind another go-around, but I'm afraid we must head out. My brother needs to be stopped and we've wasted enough precious time."

"Will you call if you find him?"

"Call? I'm afraid, *iubi*, you and I are now stuck like glue. Where I go, you go."

Her mouth rounded, bringing to mind something else she could use her sassy mouth for. His phone buzzed in his pocket, stopping her from challenging him. Kane's name appeared on the screen. He swiped his thumb across the surface and took it to his ear as he held up one finger for her to give him a moment.

"Talk to me."

"I just got a call from one of our prospects. Lefty and his partner Chad were in Eugene and came across one of Mircea's parasites."

"Lefty? Is he one of yours?"

"Prospect. He's not yet a vampire but he's trustworthy."

Vlad scratched the back of his ear, his guilt rising with Janelle's knowledge of their existence.

"Look, we need to act quickly. Your brother's army is going to grow out of control if we don't stop him. We don't have time to be fucking around."

"I agree."

Vlad's shame grew. Kane was correct. Time was of the essence. He should have been out there looking for his brother instead of fucking Janelle, causing yet another obstacle. He jammed a hand through his hair, shoving the strays from his face.

"Keep them on the tail of this *nenorocitule* and send me the whereabouts. I'm heading out. I'll tear the son of a bitch's head clean from his shoulders before he has a chance to cause more trouble."

"Jesus," Janelle whispered.

"Where are you? Wolf, Rocker, Hawk, and I are already on our way to Eugene."

"Florence, at the Blood 'n' Rave." He glanced at Janelle who looked at him in concern. He had to give her credit, any normal woman would have freaked the fuck out. "You're closer than I am, but I'm not going to use normal modes of transportation. I'll be there before you boys arrive. Text me the whereabouts."

"You alone? I thought I heard a female voice."

"No, but I don't have time to explain. You find the freak of nature before I do and don't take his head until I get there. I want to see if he'll roll on Mircea. We need to know where my brother is operating from as of yesterday."

Vlad didn't wait for a response. He ended the call and pocketed his phone. "I'm taking you home."

"My car is outside. It's not necessary—"

"I'll have Draven deal with our vehicles. They'll only slow us down."

Her gaze pinched. "I don't understand."

"You will when we get outside."

Vlad grabbed her hand and led her down the stairs and through the curtains. Draven continued to man the bar, but there weren't any Sons present.

"You have someone who can take our vehicles back to the penthouse?"

Draven nodded.

Vlad tossed his keys onto the bar then grabbed the pen and paper from the wooden counter and jotted down the address. He held out his hand to Janelle, who laid her keys in his palm without question.

Draven picked up the pad and looked at the address. "Done. And her?"

"She goes with me."

His gaze darkened. "She's not one of us."

"You don't think I fucking know that?" Vlad all but growled, irritated by the fact this barkeep would question him. "I'll take care of her. You take care of the fucking cars."

Draven sneered but didn't question him. "You got it."

Vlad pulled Janelle through the office door and out the back of the club. It was pitch black, the night sky covered by clouds threatening a storm. His vampire vision could see perfectly in the dark and into the forest beyond the back of the establishment.

"Get on my back."

Janelle halted, pulling on his grip. "Excuse me? You seriously can't think to piggyback me to wherever you are taking me."

"I can and I will. Stop wasting time and crawl on, unless you'd prefer I cradle you like a child."

"Wouldn't taking your Aston be faster?"

"You're about to find out." Janelle's gaze questioned him, obviously skeptical. But instead of wasting more valuable time, she thankfully did as she was told. "Hang tight."

Gripping her legs at his waist and praying her grip at his neck was strong, Vlad took off for the forest and headed in the direction of her apartment. Janelle needed a change of outfits. He sure in the hell wasn't letting her traipse around a band of vampires dressed as she was, not to mention the impracticality of her fuck-me heels. If he was going to keep an eye on her twenty-four-seven, then he needed her suitably dressed, not to mention wearing a bra. Janelle had a set of great tits, but he didn't need everyone else knowing that.

Those he planned to keep for himself, at least until he figured a way out of his predicament.

JANELLE WALKED, MORE LIKE stumbled, into her apartment and headed for her master bedroom, not caring if Vlad chose to follow. Motion sickness had her equilibrium off-kilter and her stomach rolling. Bouncing off the hallway walls, she eventually made it to the doorway. Her large king-sized bed had been left unmade, tempting her to lie down until the wooziness passed. Too bad Vlad hadn't given her more time, like eight hours for a good night's rest. She couldn't have been dizzier if she had stood in place and spun for several minutes.

What the hell had just happened?

It was as if she had stepped into a nightmare of paranormal activity. Vampires? Until an hour ago, Janelle had been 100% a realist, believed in things as they were. Things that went bump in the night didn't exist to her … until now.

Vlad Tepes had not only proven the lab's result that he wasn't human, but he had superhuman abilities, like being able to run through the forest at the speed of light, her motion sickness proving as much. Next time, she'd insist on taking her sturdy SUV and following the posted speed limit. Lord, she hadn't even begun to process all that had happened in the past hour. Janelle had not only had sex with a very seductive freak of nature, but she had also allowed him to feed from her.

And she had liked it.

Lord, she was going to need to see a psychiatrist when this was all over. No one would likely believe her anyway.

Walking to the mirror centered above the dresser, she glanced at her bedraggled self. Sticks and brush stuck out at odd angles from her tangled hair, gathered from their break-neck run through the forest. Surely, she'd never get a comb through it. The twin holes at her neck drew her gaze down. Angling her head for a better look, she noted they were nearly gone, as though he hadn't sunk his fangs into her artery like she was his version of a Bloody Mary.

Bile churned in her stomach. Janelle was about to lose every drop of alcohol she had consumed. She was never allowing Rocky to pick the nightclub again. If her instincts were correct, the bartender was also a vampire.

Did the Blood 'n' Rave patrons even have a clue?

Judging by the little vials she had noted strung around their necks, Janelle was betting they did. She planned to ask Vlad about the waitresses, seeing as how Ivy had also worn one.

Was she the only one in the dark about these nightcrawlers?

And if Vlad was a vampire, how the hell did he walk about in the daylight?

"What's taking so long, *iudi*? We need to move. I can't lose this son of a bitch Kane had called about. We need to eliminate this piece of work before he hurts more humans."

Eliminate?

Janelle startled at Vlad's approaching steps, his footfalls muffled by her area rug. She turned so quickly it caused her stomach to climb up her throat. Without a thought or care if the blasted vampire watched, she ran to the en suite and emptied what little she had consumed. Tears ran down her cheeks and snot gathered in her nostrils. She was but a hair-breadth away from losing her shit, praying this was all just another damn dream.

She didn't have to look to know he stood behind her. Instead of accusing her of wasting his precious time, he knelt on his haunches and gathered her hair gently in his fist as she puked again.

Great. Just great.

Hot sexy vampire had now seen her at her absolute worst.

"Humans can't always handle that high rate of speed." His deep tone soothed her. "I should've taken more care. I'm sorry."

When she emptied the last of her stomach, Janelle sat back against the adjacent wall. Vlad stood, grabbed a wash-cloth from the shelf, and wetted it before handing it to her. She grabbed the offered cloth and scrubbed her mouth, then her nose, before tossing it into the nearby sink.

"A warning would have been nice. I don't suppose we travel by car from here."

He chuckled. "Sorry, *iubi*. We left those back in Florence. I promise to go a bit slower from here. Kane and Kaleb may very well beat us there by now."

Janelle dragged her hands down her hot face. If Vlad arrived too late to *eliminate* whoever needed a fast ticket to hell, she'd be to blame.

"Who are you looking for?"

"One of my brother's bastard creations."

"A vampire?" His nod was her answer. Her hand covered her neck where he bit her. "Am I going to become one?"

Vlad knelt beside her again, caressing her cheek with his knuckle. "No, *iubi*. You won't become a vampire. I merely drank from you."

"Then how does one become…"

"You have to drink from our blood. Even a droplet would do so."

Janelle thought back to the night she had visited him at his penthouse. "Your hand, when you cut yourself, is that why you took such care getting rid of the blood?"

"That and the DNA. If someone were to come across it, they might discover our chromosomes are much different from those of humans."

The lab had discovered the new species thanks to her. Janelle's face heated, but she wasn't ready to let Vlad in on her blunder. Had he let her in on his secret to begin with, she wouldn't have been so foolhardy as to hand it over to the crime lab. Janelle could only imagine the studies they were likely doing right now on the simple hair follicle, looking for answers.

Instead of confessing, she rose to her feet, feeling much firmer than moments ago. "We should probably go."

Vlad stood, then led her from the room. "I'll call Kane and see if they arrived." He pulled out his cell, tapped the screen a few times then put it to his ear. The other end obviously picked up when Vlad said, "What's the scoop?"

His jaw hardened as he began to pace the room. "Lefty and Chad there?" There was a pause. "Good. What's the address? We're five minutes away."

He hung up the phone then turned back to her. "Sorry, Janelle. But I'll need you to crawl on my back again. You think you can handle it?"

She sucked in a deep breath. "Better than staying here."

Vlad chuckled. Following her quick change of clothes, he led her to the door where she hopped onto his back. "Close your eyes. It will help."

Janelle did as she was told, feeling the wind rush through her already tangled hair. The clock on her wall at home had indicated she had about five hours before she needed to be at her desk. Something told her she was going to be using one of those rarely taken personal days from work. Seeing her boss, Robby Melchor, with what felt like the king of all hangovers wasn't at all appealing. Besides, she needed time to herself to sort out this mess she had gotten herself into.

Gripping Vlad more tightly about the neck, she squeezed her eyelids closed, calling forth a mental image. Her visions had returned, this one more frightening than any from her past.

A man with short dark wavy hair and eyes very similar to Vlad's stood in a darkened doorway. Garbage and stench littered the alley, so much so, Janelle could damn near smell it.

Kane, the man she had seen at the Sons of Sangue's clubhouse months ago, and several others stood around a headless corpse, blood leaking onto the cobblestones beneath their feet.

One of them broke off from the group, as though looking for something, someone. Maybe the perpetrator. He passed several darkened doorways in his search, now several yards from the crime scene. A gleam from the security light glinted off the long piece of steel the wavy-haired man withdrew from his back and lopped off the other man's head.

Janelle's eyes opened and she let out a terrifying scream.

CHAPTER ELEVEN

V LAD STOPPED A COUPLE OF CITY BLOCKS SHY OF HIS DES- tination. Janelle's scream had caused him far more concern than finding Mircea's creation. Let his grandsons take care of the miscreant. Releasing his hold on her legs, Janelle slid down his back. Feet planted on the ground and white-faced, she bent over, placed her hands on her knees and gasped for air.

Something had frightened Janelle; he could sense her fear as if it had come alive and crawled inside of him. Vlad was pretty sure with what she did for a living she had already seen a lot of ugly in the world. He couldn't imagine what could incite such terror.

Pulling her to the rear of a nearby tavern, he backed her against the brick wall, bracing his palms against her shoulders. "Talk to me."

An errant tear slid down her cheek. "He took his head clean off."

Uneasiness washed over him. "A vision. What exactly did you see?"

"Oh my… For fuck's sake." Janelle wet her lips. "I haven't had a vision in months."

"Focus, *iubi*. Who did the head belong to?"

125

"I don't know." She shook her head. "I've never seen him before."

"Can you describe the assailant?"

"He wore a long charcoal trench coat over black slacks and an off-white colored sweater. His eyes," she said, looking up at him. "They were icy blue in color, but the shape of them reminded me of yours."

"Mircea," he whispered on a curse.

"His hair, though black like yours, was slightly graying, worn short, wavier."

It had to be the son of a bitch. "Can you describe the man whose head he took?"

"He wore a Sons of Sangue vest. Long dark blond hair now stained red from the blood. Jesus! So much blood. His back was to me. I have no idea who he was. I saw the man wielding the sword. The steel blade sliced clean through his neck. Blood flew everywhere."

Vlad needed to know the identity, though her description didn't sound like either of his grandsons. He released his hold and pulled the cell from his pocket, quickly dialing Kane's number. It went straight to voicemail. Vlad then dialed Kaleb's, but got the same result. He tipped his nose to the sky, faintly detecting the spill of vampire blood. They had to be close.

He shoved the cell back into his pocket and gripped her hand. "We'll take the rest of the way on foot. We aren't far. Are you going to be okay?"

Janelle nodded. Holding her hand, they took off on a jog, following the scent of fresh blood and other vampires in the vicinity. He couldn't chance leaving her behind should Mircea still be in the area. He was going to kill the *nenorocitule.*

Janelle kept up with his pace, her tennis shoes clopping against the pavement behind him. The closer they came to the address Kane had given him, the stronger the stench of spilled blood. He could also smell each of his grandsons' unique scents, telling him they were still alive. Mircea was either no longer in the vicinity or had managed to somehow mask his scent.

Kane met him at the front of the alley where they came to a stop. He lifted his chin in the direction of Janelle. "What's she doing here?"

"My business."

Kane's jaw hardened; his fangs prominent against his red lips. "If she knows about us, it's club business."

"Then it's a fucking good thing I'm not in your club." Vlad glanced over Kane's shoulders. "Who?"

"I'll expect you to take care of her, Vlad. She can't know about this."

"You're one to talk."

"I made Cara my mate. Are you prepared to do the same with this female?"

Vlad's brittle laugh was the only answer he was about to give his grandson. No one questioned him or his motives. Ever. Not even his great-grandsons.

"Who did Mircea take out?"

Kane's angry gaze softened to one of sorrow. "Peter Vasile. He went by Rocker. Christ! He was a good man, a friend of Wolf's. He didn't fucking deserve this." A muscle ticked in Kane's jaw as he glanced back at the carnage about twenty feet away. "How did you know?"

"Janelle." Vlad glanced briefly at her. "She had a vision. She saw my brother cut off Rocker's head."

Kane rubbed his whisker-stubbled jaw as he apparently took in the fact the woman with Vlad was gifted with visions. Instead of commenting on it, his grandson took a deep breath, then let it out slowly. "We never scented the motherfucker. How the hell did he get so close?"

Vlad glanced around at the garbage overflowing from bins. The stench of it was everywhere. "My guess is Mircea rubbed himself with trash so you couldn't distinguish him from your surroundings. What about the vampire Mircea created?"

"Dead. We got to him before…"

Vlad's gaze swept the area. "My guess is he's still in the area. This smells like a setup. He wanted you to find his lackey. While you were concentrating on taking him down, Mircea snuck in and took one of yours."

Kane hung his head, no doubt feeling the weight of that responsibility. Vlad placed a hand on his grandson's shoulder. "This isn't your fault, Kane. You couldn't have known."

"I should have. Damn it." Kane jammed a hand through his hair. "I left Rocker unprotected. I told him to keep watch while we took care of the newly turned vampire."

"Not your fault, Viper," Kaleb said, clapping his brother on the shoulder as he and Grigore came to stand with the group. "I'm going to kill your rat-bastard brother."

"By all means, Kaleb. You have my blessing."

The bodies of the dead, arms and legs askew in spilled blood, lay nearly a block apart. The first was at the opening opposite of where Vlad and his kin stood. Peter's body lay mere feet away.

"Mircea is our main focus," Grigore assured Vlad. "I'm going to get that skunk spray. Mircea will be shitting himself looking for the creature causing the stench. Next time, we'll be ready."

"We should pan out, scan the whole area for Mircea." Kaleb glanced down the street. "Maybe even head out and scan the forest beyond."

"He's no longer here," Janelle said, gaining their attention.

Vlad turned and gripped her by the forearms. "Another vision?"

Janelle worried her lower lip, her gaze unfocused as she wobbled on her feet.

"I see the same man, standing…" She gasped. "He's in my apartment."

"SON OF A BITCH."

Vlad wasn't about to explain his actions. There wasn't time. Mircea had crossed the line. *Nenorocitule!* His psycho brother knew where Janelle lived. Cold fear snaked down his spine and grabbed him by the balls. Like it or not, Janelle

Ferrari had touched his cold, dead heart. He glanced at the woman leaving him vulnerable to worry and pain, something he hadn't experienced since his first wife had taken her life. She had entrusted him with her care only for him to fail her. He wasn't about to allow history to repeat with Janelle. Damn it, but he'd not allow his brother to get his hands on Janelle, even if he had to keep her under his protection twenty-four-seven.

Vlad gripped her biceps. "You need to go with my great-grandsons. They'll see that you're kept safe."

Janelle's widened gaze went from the dead bodies lying in the alley behind them to Kane. Her mouth dropped. "Seriously? Great-grandsons? How old are you?"

"Old" Vlad grimaced. "I'll explain later, *iubi*. You need to go with them."

"No fucking way," Kane interrupted, shaking his head. "I'm going with you, Vlad. You're not facing this bastard on your own."

"Not to mention someone needs to clean up this mess behind us." Kaleb used his thumb to indicate the alleyway. "Though I don't give a rat's ass about the other guy, we can't leave them for the authorities to find. Besides, Rocker needs a proper ashing. I want to kill the motherfucker for Rocker alone. Sorry, Grandpa, but your brother is a piece of shit."

"I won't argue." Vlad took in a deep breath. His brother had already caused too much pain and they had him to blame for it. He should have allowed Kane to kill him when he had the chance. "I'm sorry for your friend. Jesus! This shouldn't have happened."

"Viper can go with Vlad. I got this." Grigore's deep timbre cut in, his tone full of emotion, his eyes glassy. "We'll catch up with this fuck, Vlad. We don't pick our families or who we're related to. You can't take the blame. You're right, though, this shouldn't have happened. Rocker didn't deserve this, man. He was one of the good ones."

"Agreed, Wolf." Kane cleared his throat and placed a hand on Grigore's shoulder. "We'll all be there for the ashing, send him off right."

Grigore nodded, his Adam's apple bobbing in his throat. "I'll have Xander bring the box truck around and help take care of the mess. We'll meet back at the clubhouse. Hawk, you take Ms. Special Agent here back to safety."

"Wonderful. I get babysitting duty," Kaleb grumbled.

"I'm entrusting you with her care, Kaleb." Vlad pointed a finger at him. "Something happens to her and you'll be answering to me."

"I wouldn't dream of allowing harm to come to her, Grandpa." His sarcasm didn't go unnoticed. Vlad would deal with his lack of respect later. He knew his grandson was disappointed at being left out of the chase but keeping an eye on Janelle was more important to him than catching his bastard brother.

Kaleb placed a hand on Janelle's shoulder and led her in the direction of the motorcycles. "Let's go, sweetheart. We're about to become close friends. Where I go, you go."

Vlad growled though he knew Kaleb wouldn't dare touch her. But allowing her to ride behind Kaleb on two wheels with little protection? Almost made him send Kane off to find Mircea without him. Jesus, she had gotten beneath his skin.

Kaleb noted Vlad's discomfort, handing Janelle a helmet. "She'll be fine. Relax, Grandpa, I've been riding one of these much longer than you've been using your cage with four wheels."

Janelle looked at the black skull cap in her hands, then turned her glare on Vlad. Even when trying to protect her, he had somehow earned her scorn. *Women*. He'd never understand them.

She tried to hand Kaleb back the helmet. "I'm going with you, Vlad. I'm not a two-year-old and I don't need a babysitter."

Anger heated his blood. Why the hell was everyone so bent on arguing with him? He didn't have time for this shit. "Like hell."

"I work with hardened criminals daily. I don't think your brother—"

His humorless chuckle cut her off. "He's a vampire, *iubi*, even worse, a primordial. You're out of your league. We'll talk when I get back to the clubhouse."

Vlad, not waiting for further argument, took off in the direction of Janelle's apartment with Kane fast on his heels. They had wasted too much time. He could only hope Mircea had dallied overlong. City buildings blurred as they traveled faster than the human eye could detect. The wind whistled through his ears and tangled his hair.

Within minutes, they stood in front of her locked apartment door, everything appearing as it should. Vlad lifted his nose, detecting the slight odor that Mircea had indeed been there along with the much stronger stench of garbage. Vlad had been correct. His brother had used the trash from the alleyway to keep from being easily detected.

Gripping the doorknob, he found it to be locked. He squeezed the handle, hearing the metal crunch beneath his grip as the inner workings were rendered useless. The door pushed open, giving him a view of the ransacked room. Vlad strode through the apartment, not finding Mircea. He had managed to give them the slip again. By the looks of the broken latch on the window, he knew how his brother had managed to enter the apartment. Looking three floors down to the empty street below, people bustled by but Mircea was nowhere to be found. Even his scent was starting to fade. The third-floor apartment surely was no problem for Mircea. He likely leapt to the asphalted street below.

"*Nenorocitule*," Vlad growled.

"He certainly is a motherfucker, but he can't hide forever," Kane agreed.

Vlad's booted feet echoed about the vaulted ceilings as he entered the living area. The picture window to the back of the room overlooked the city of Eugene. Lights lit the sky, making the stars impossible to see. The city was alive with activity. Mircea would easily blend in.

Vlad scanned the streets, coming up empty, but he couldn't shake off the notion of being watched. Mircea was out there. He could feel it in his bones. Kane approached from behind and came to a stop beside him. Vlad's frustration nearly crippled him. Mircea continued to win as long as his brother drew breath.

"I'm coming for you, Mircea," Vlad roared. "You son of a bitch!"

The faint sound of laughter drifted back across the breeze. Mircea had been close enough to hear. Vlad slammed his hands against the plated glass, rattling the metal frame, though not hard enough to shatter it.

He'd have the door and window latch fixed, but Janelle would no longer be staying here, not until his brother was caught. He couldn't allow Mircea the chance to get his hands on her. Jesus! Just the thought of what Mircea might do to her had him wanting to annihilate the bastard. No more mercy.

"You want me to give chase?" Kane asked.

Vlad's blood ran hot. "Don't waste your time. It's what he's counting on. We won't find him. Let's have a look around, then I'll speak with the apartment manager about getting the door and window fixed before heading back to the club-house."

Vlad did a sweep of the living area, finding nothing out of the ordinary other than Janelle's things strewn about. Mircea was sending Vlad a message and he heard it loud and clear. He canvassed the other rooms quickly, finding nothing but the same mess. He was just about to head out when Kane called to him. Vlad jogged to the kitchen where his grandson stood with the refrigerator door ajar.

"Your brother left your girlfriend a message."

"She's not—" It was all Vlad got out when he saw the bloody message left behind. Apparently, before leaving Rocker behind, Mircea had torn a hole in his chest and pulled out the man's heart, which now lay in a bloody pool on the glass shelf.

Tacked to the congealing blood was a note: Vlad will never take your heart, but I will.

"He's one sick bastard," Kane mumbled.

"He's fucking dead!" Anger like he'd never felt before coursed through Vlad. He wanted to hurt something ... or better yet, someone. Mircea had drawn a big ass target on his back. Vlad didn't plan on missing this time.

"Where do you think he went?"

"The coward will hide among the forest. That area is much larger to get lost in."

"Then we need to play the son of a bitch's game. Let's try out the spray Wolf was talking about."

Vlad's brows raised. "You're going to spray Wolf with that shit?"

"Fuck, no. He'd never allow it. I'll let a prospect do the honor." His grandson laughed. "We'll follow in behind."

CHAPTER TWELVE

J ANELLE STEPPED OVER THE BIKE SEAT AND TOOK OFF HER
helmet. Angry didn't begin to describe the emotion running through her. Sure, Vlad was trying to keep her safe. But,
damn it, she was not a child and had dealt with hardened
criminals daily. Being shuffled back to the clubhouse like a
two-year-old who didn't know her way around a crime scene
was beyond infuriating.

Shoving the helmet at Kaleb, she turned without a word
and headed for the clubhouse. It wasn't his fault his great-
grandfather had placed him on babysitting duty, nor had he
asked for it. She wasn't exactly being fair to the man, but her
anger had overruled her actions. A glance back at the handsome vampire proved he followed and had her wondering
again just how old Vlad was.

Not waiting for Kaleb, or an invite into the clubhouse, she
stepped up onto the small cement porch. The door swung
open. A pretty, short-bobbed brunette holding a toddler
greeted her with a warm smile. The toddler looked too much
like the wavy-haired vampire behind her not to be his.

"Hi," the woman said, stepping back to allow Janelle to
enter. "I'm Suzi. The grumpy one giving you a ride, that's my
mate. You must be Vlad's—"

"I'm not Vlad's anything," Janelle grumbled before turning her frown into a smile. "I'm Special Agent Ferrari. But you can call me Janelle."

"Nice to meet the woman who seems to be giving Grandpa a hard time." Suzi laughed, placing her toddler on the floor. He ran off to his daddy, who scooped him into his arms and kissed the boy's brow. "Grandpa needs someone like you."

Janelle stopped, her breath having caught in her throat. "We're not ... I mean we aren't—"

"Too bad." Suzi's answering smile was stunning. It was easy to see what Kaleb saw in his ... *mate*. What was that? Some kind of term for vampire wife? "I'd quite enjoy watching someone give him a run for his money."

"Just how old is Vlad?"

Suzi's questioning gaze went to Kaleb's. "She knows, piccolo diavolo. Apparently, Vlad's got loose lips these days."

Janelle drew her brows together. "I'm not following."

"You know about us ... vampires. Normally, should someone discover our true nature, we hypnotize them into forgetting." Kaleb placed the boy back on his feet and he ran off to the living area where he pulled out a box of toys. "Much safer that way for our kind."

"Vlad tried to hypnotize me. It didn't work."

"Oh my," Suzi giggled. "Now isn't that a conundrum? I wonder why that is."

Janelle shrugged. "I have no idea. Maybe because I have visions."

"Visions? Like a psychic?"

"I guess, though I've never labeled myself as one. I see past and future events at times, things that have or have yet to happen. I've used them to help solve cases for the DEA. Once I met Vlad, they stopped … until today."

"I see." Suzi folded her hands in front of her. "I bet that could prove to be quite useful in your line of work."

"It can at times." And then there were times like today when her visions could be downright chilling.

Kaleb walked over to the bar and grabbed a bottle of whiskey. "Would you like a drink?"

"Please." Janelle joined him at the bar. "After tonight, I could certainly use it."

"Suzi?" Kaleb asked.

She walked over to him and wrapped her arms about his waist, kissing him briefly on the lips. "None for me."

Kaleb poured two glasses, offering one to Janelle. She took the glass and downed it in one gulp, causing him to chuckle. He poured her another. "I suppose tonight would be quite frightening for you, or at the very least unnerving."

Janelle gripped her glass between her palms, resting her forearms on the bar. She wanted answers, even if they didn't come from Vlad. Kaleb seemed a bit more forthcoming. "Is this an everyday occurrence for a vampire?"

"Maybe not an everyday, but we do lead a colorful life." He took a sip from his glass. "I would say not much different from your life of chasing criminals."

"The DEA usually deals in investigating and preparing prosecution of drug-related criminals, drug gangs, drug trafficking. That sort of stuff. But when murderous crimes crossover into our territory, yes, I do then deal with violent offenders."

"Like the cartel," Kaleb added.

"Yes, like the cartel, not to mention some motorcycle clubs."

Kaleb threw back the rest of his whiskey. "We don't deal in drugs."

"I didn't mean your club, but our office has investigated some of your rival MCs, like The Devils."

"You had quite the bust a while back."

"Yes, thanks to one of your members, Rogue, for going undercover."

"Glad he could help," Kaleb said. "It was quite the ordeal since we had no knowledge he was working with the DEA."

"I'm sure it was." Janelle took a sip of her whiskey, not wanting to hash up old cases, especially since she had not been a part of that one. "Back to just how old Vlad is…"

Suzi laughed, leaning into Kaleb's side as he draped a tattooed arm across her shoulders. "He's lived five centuries."

"He's over 500-years-old?" She gasped. "I may need a paper bag."

Kaleb's brow creased. "What the hell for?"

"I think I'm going to hyperventilate."

He chuckled. "Because you just had sex with a 500-year-old man?"

"I … that is…"

His humor increased. "We could scent the fact you had sex the minute you arrived back at the alley."

"I … what?" He had to be joking.

"Maybe Grandpa should've told you." Suzi grimaced. "Vampires can scent things like desire, sexual activity, other vampires."

Well if that wasn't a palm-to-head moment. "You mean this whole time Vlad could smell if I desired him?"

Suzi nodded before poking Kaleb in the side for his continued laughter. Wonderful. So now they all knew what she and Vlad had been doing before they arrived at the alleyway.

The toddler picked that moment to run across the wooden floor. "Daddy," he yelled, reaching for his father's arms and thankfully saving Janelle from further embarrassment.

Lord, just open a hole in the floor and swallow me.

Her face heated, likely turning a deep shade of red. Kaleb picked up his son and tossed him in the air, earning him a round of giggles.

"What's his name?"

"Stefan," Suzi told her.

"Vampires can reproduce?" Janelle quickly snapped her mouth closed. She supposed she should come with a filter. "I'm sorry. I didn't mean to pry. He's adorable."

"We aren't the undead like in the movies. We're very much alive." Suzi smiled. "But thank you. Stefan can be a handful, like any other toddler."

"Is he a vampire too?"

"Not yet. He'll grow into his genes. Feel free to ask whatever you want, Janelle. I was curious at one time too. Vampires can only reproduce with vampires."

"Oh." Well, that certainly answered the question of why Vlad hadn't concerned himself with a condom. "You said you were curious … weren't you always a vampire?"

"No. Women aren't born into the life. Only men are born true bloods like Stefan. And not all men who are vampires are true bloods, some are simply turned like women. Once a vampire chooses his mate, he shares his blood with her and they're mated for life."

Suzi was a bundle of knowledge. Janelle couldn't help but wonder what Vlad might think of her learning so much about his secret. 500-years-old? Janelle wasn't sure what to think of that.

"So there are no women who became vampires without the aid of a man?" Janelle took another sip of the whiskey. At this point, she might need the whole damn bottle. "Definitely a chauvinistic society … I meant no offense."

"None taken," Kaleb said with a crooked grin. "The only time I'm aware of a female vampire who had turned a man was Brea Gotti. Her mate, Draven, took some of her blood and he was surprisingly turned. Turns out she's a descendant of Vlad's long-dead brother Radu. We figure her genetics made her able to do things a normal female couldn't."

"So you aren't dead and sleep in coffins?"

"And we aren't put off by crosses, holy water, or garlic either. Though we do tend to sunburn faster than a normal human, we don't burn up when we're out in the daylight. I have a king-sized bed I share with Suzi. We're quite normal." He tilted his head, his gaze going to her throat. Janelle raised her hand and self-consciously covered the area Vlad had bitten. "Vlad drank from you?"

Janelle worried her lower lip. "I'm not going to turn into a vampire, right?"

"As I said, you would've had to ingest some of his blood for that to happen." Kaleb paused, his gaze hardening. "You didn't, right?"

A shiver ran through her at the thought of drinking someone's blood. "Absolutely not."

"Good."

"Why?"

Kaleb's grin returned. "Because then you would have been mated to Grandfather for life and that would make you my grandmother."

Suddenly, Janelle wasn't feeling well at all. What parallel universe had she just stepped into? No wonder they chose hypnosis. She might've been better off not knowing about these vampires, no matter how sexy Vlad was.

Scratching her nape, she asked to use the bathroom. Janelle shut the restroom door behind her and stared at her reflection. The tiny twin holes, just beneath her ear, had vanished.

Just the thought of Vlad biting her and drawing her blood kicked up the heat in the restroom. She heard Kaleb say, "For the love of all that's holy, quit thinking about the old man. We can scent your desire all the way—," followed by a thud, likely Suzi elbowing him again, followed by a groan.

Janelle gripped the sink and bowed her head. There would be no secrets with this group, not when it came to her lust for a 500-year-old vampire.

VLAD FOLLOWED KANE INTO the Sons of Sangue clubhouse, anger simmering beneath the surface. While they had come close to catching Mircea, his brother always seemed to be two steps ahead. It was as if he had anticipated their next gambit; it was a game at which Vlad was currently losing. And he fucking hated to lose. By the time they caught a whiff of his scent, it would dissipate quickly.

The chase had been for nothing. They hadn't spotted any of Mircea's minions either. Christ only knew how many he had already created and were currently running rampant in Eugene, not to mention all of Oregon.

One of Kaleb's brows rose as he stood by the bar, several of the Sons also in attendance. "Any luck?"

A muscle ticked in Kane's jaw, his gaze blazing with fury. "Mircea knew we were coming. He hid in the forest among the vegetation where there was no way to mask our scent. The son of a bitch might as well have been toying with us."

Vlad shrugged, his palms turning to the ceiling. "Going in I suggested covering Kane in deer feces."

"Listen to you." Kane rolled his eyes and shook his head. "I didn't hear you offering."

"What the hell do you think I had you along for?"

Guffaws traveled through the crew along with a few off-color comments. Vlad's attention shifted to the living area where the women congregated. His gaze stopped on the stunning brunette who had occupied far too much of his focus. Janelle sat cross-legged on the wood-planked floor next to a box of toys. Stefan pulled out a fire engine; his face animated as he proceeded to tell her a story. Though Janelle kept her fascination riveted on the boy, her scent gave away her reaction to his proximity even if she refused to acknowledge him.

Janelle was likely still pissed he hadn't permitted her to go on the vampire-hunt, but she was out of her league on this one. He couldn't allow her anywhere near Mircea for fear of what his brother might do, should he manage to get his hands on her. Christ, the cold dead heart in her refrigerator said as much.

"I have that covered," Grigore said, gathering back Vlad's attention. He opened a bag, withdrew a spray bottle and set it on the wooden counter. The word Skunk Scent was printed in bold black letters across the white label. "With this, he won't stand a chance of knowing we're in the area."

Kaleb's nose turned up. "The scent alone will send him running."

"Surely, the motherfucker isn't scared of a little white-striped polecat," Grigore argued.

Alexander picked up the bottle and read the ingredients. "One-hundred percent skunk urine. This shit stinks bad enough without having opened the seal."

"Damn, Wolf." Kane plugged his nose. "Take that shit outside. You'll stink up the whole fucking clubhouse. You may not care about sleeping with the scent of skunk hanging in the air, but I'm sure Caitlyn would."

"She left this morning, headed back to her place in Crescent City so she can begin working on her next release. I'll be heading back in a few days, but I don't suppose she'd be too welcoming if I smell like this shit."

"You need to sell her place in California," Ryder said. "There's some prime real estate along the coast for sale, not far from us. You living in California ain't right, bro. That's Devil territory."

"Yeah, well, Crescent City is closer to where her recording studio is. When we come back here, staying at the clubhouse is convenient and free."

"Fucking tight ass." Alexander cuffed him on the shoulder. "With her money, you guys could afford a mansion along the coast. I sure in the hell wouldn't stay here with the prospects."

Grigore chuckled. "Fucking prospects know it's me she's taking to bed. Besides, most of the prospects stay elsewhere when I'm in town. Only Lefty's staying here now and he's spending a good share of his time with Chad. He ain't interested in what my old lady has. We'll be looking to buy a second place in Oregon soon enough."

Silence descended among the men as they realized Peter "Rocker" Vasile wouldn't be returning to his room at the clubhouse.

"Jesus." Grigore cleared his throat and scrubbed his face with his palms. "You know I'm going to kill the son of a bitch, Vlad, brother or no. For Rocker, man. He didn't deserve what he got."

Vlad laid a hand on Grigore's shoulder. "Duly noted, son. One of us will surely get the job done."

"Aye, aye," Kaleb said raising a glass of whiskey. The men followed suit, toasting to the fallen Son. "We'll send him off with a proper ashing, Grigore."

"Thanks, Hawk," he said, blinking the moisture from his gaze.

Suzi walked over, her hand covering her nose and lightening the mood. "Could you guys please take that stuff outside. It's stinking the place up."

A grin split Kaleb's five o'clock shadow. "I know what cures that."

Suzi groaned. "You think sex is a cure-all."

"Isn't it?" Grigore shared in the humor before grabbing the bottle from Alexander and placing it back into the baggie. "I'll set it out on the porch, Miss Suzi."

She rose on her tiptoes and kissed his whiskered cheek. "You're one of the good ones, Wolf."

A blush traveled up his neck and reddened his cheeks. Rather than call more attention to his soft heart, Grigore walked over to the door and placed the bag on the stoop before returning. "It'll do its job as long as he stays to the woods. We'll need to come up with something else should he be hiding out in Eugene."

"We chased his scent into the surrounding forest." Vlad rubbed his short-cut, bearded jaw between his thumb and forefinger. "I don't think he's going into town unless it's to feed. Mircea knows we're looking for him, so he'll want to stay off our radar. What better way than to hide amongst the critters?"

"Lefty and a couple of the other prospects stayed back in Eugene to keep an eye out for more of Mircea's vampires," Kane told the group. "Should they come across any more, they'll call us."

"What about Chad?" Kaleb asked. "He shouldn't have knowledge of what's going on, he's not one of us."

"I took care of that before we left. He's been hypnotized."

"Thanks, Xander," Kane said. "Should Lefty become a Son," Kane said, "we'll deal with Chad and what he's allowed to know then, that is unless Lefty chooses him as a mate. Otherwise, we handle him the way Xander did, same as any other human."

The door to the clubhouse opened and Grayson strode in, followed by Tamera and Lucian. She placed the boy on the floor and he toddled over to Stefan and the box of toys. Janelle was no longer on the floor, but sitting on the sofa next to India and Cara. Tamera joined the women. Just before Vlad looked away, he caught Janelle's side-glance. She might be trying damn hard to ignore him, but she wasn't getting the job done. Vlad kept the smile from inching up his face, not wanting to have to answer for its origin.

The scent of skunk suddenly filled the air, sending some into a coughing fit while others gagged. Jesus, that shit was strong. Seconds later, Grayson laughed as he turned and headed for the door with Grigore fast on his heels. Thankfully, most of the smell followed the big guy out the door. Suzi and Tamera jumped to their feet, opening windows and the door trying to air out the lingering scent of skunk.

"Fuck, that stinks." Kaleb pinched his nose. "If Wolf doesn't beat Gypsy's ass for that, I just might. No way Mircea will scent a vampire over that shit."

Alexander smirked. "Wolf will handle Gypsy, no doubt in that."

Ryder chuckled. "Better him than one of us. Well, at least now we can test Wolf's theory. If we don't scent him coming back into the clubhouse other than the smell of the skunk, we can call it a win."

The sound of Grayson's laughter continued as Grigore's growl drifted through the opened windows. As fast as Grayson was, it might take Grigore a bit to catch up. Vlad couldn't help the chuckle that bubbled up through him. Apparently, Grayson was the prankster of the bunch. No one seemed a bit surprised by his antics.

Seconds later Grigore and Grayson entered the clubhouse, both stinking to high heaven. Vlad wrinkled his nose. This would be one time their vampire sense of smell was a bad thing, a very bad thing. The women quickly cleared the house with the toddlers in arms.

Kaleb plugged his nose. "Jesus! You two stink."

Grigore laughed, trying to rub up against the VP. "Well, at least we proved it worked."

"Don't count me in on using that shit," Alexander said. "It's all I can do not to dry heave just standing next to you two idiots."

Grigore grabbed hold of Alexander and wrapped him in a bear hug that he couldn't get out of. "Just showing you some love."

He finally dropped his hold and Alexander smacked him behind his head, only to cause a round of guffaws.

"Anyone know how to get rid of the smell?"

"You should have thought of that before you started spraying my ass, Gypsy." Grigore shook his head and laughed. "Lemon-scented dish soap, lemon juice, and some peroxide should do the trick. I accidentally got sprayed years back when I used to hunt before coming out here."

One of Grayson's brows rose. "Do we have lemon-scented dish soap here?"

Kane rolled his eyes. "You guys stink to high heaven. I volunteer to go to the store to get the supplies. Next time, spray the forest vegetation when we track Mircea, not one of us."

"I volunteer to douse the son of a bitch in it when we catch him," Kaleb added.

"You boys won't get the chance to get to him if I do first." Vlad ran both hands through his hair and let out a deep breath. "While you're fucking around with this stinky ass shit, I'm going to be out there looking for him."

"He'll scent you coming." Kane raised a brow. "You won't catch him without cover."

"Then I'll send one of you fools in ahead of me. Keep that shit away from me. It's burning my damn nostrils." Vlad started backing for the door. He needed to get the hell out of there before that stench was all he could smell for days. "I'm taking Janelle back to my place for now. Kane, send someone over to her place to clean up. I don't want her looking in that refrigerator."

"What the hell is in the fridge?" Kaleb asked.

Kane's eyes grew misty and he cleared his throat. "Rocker's heart, bro."

"Jesus," Grigore growled. "I'm going to kill the motherfucker."

"Get in line, Wolf," Vlad said, before walking out the door, drawing in copious amounts of fresh air and looking for Janelle.

CHAPTER THIRTEEN

J ANELLE STUMBLED OVER TO THE SOFA AND SAT HEAVILY onto it, framing her face between her palms and leaning forward. Vlad noted he'd need to stick to normal modes of transportation in the future as she didn't seem to handle a high rate of speed very well.

"You aren't going to get sick, are you?"

She groaned, not bothering to look at him. "No, but what would you care?"

"Because I'd rather you didn't puke on the floor."

She sat up, her gaze snapping to his. "Seriously? You, who snacks on humans, are afraid of a little bile?"

Vlad grumbled under his breath. A little gratitude for keeping her safe wouldn't hurt. "It's the sensitivity to the smell. I can scent things better than a human and the smell of bile is almost as unpleasant as the damn skunk urine."

"Which brings up the fact you can smell when I desire you."

He raised a brow. "And?"

"You could have warned me." His chuckle followed. "Not funny, Vlad."

She leaned forward again and groaned. It was obvious the poor woman had trouble with motion sickness. He couldn't help but wonder if planes weren't her thing either.

"Does this happen often?"

"You mean not feeling well after traveling the speed of light?" Her reply was muffled by her hands as she leaned into them. "I don't normally go running faster than the eye can track. I swear my eyes are twitching in their sockets."

"If you're going to get sick—"

"Oh, for crying out loud." Janelle stood so quickly, she wavered on her feet before plopping back onto the sofa. "I'll walk myself home right after I get my bearings so I don't soil your damn penthouse suite."

He cleared his throat, pretty sure this wasn't going to sit well with her either. "You can't go back to your apartment."

"Why?" Janelle attempted to level her gaze at him, her eyes indeed moving rapidly. No wonder she was feeling ill. "I'm capable of cleaning up whatever your brother did to my place. I don't need your help. I just need a second to get this damn room to quit spinning."

Vlad walked over to the large picture window overlooking the Eugene skyline. Red tinged the horizon as dawn loomed. Janelle would no doubt be expected to be in her office soon. She didn't have the luxury of not having a time clock to punch. He'd need to talk to her about that as well. It might benefit them both if he were to keep a close eye on her, should she take a leave of absence. He supposed that would be met with the same animosity of not going home.

"You have a job to go to," he said matter-of-factly.

"You just figured that out?"

Vlad didn't miss the sarcasm in her tone. He wasn't used to being disrespected; why he allowed it from her he wasn't sure. One thing was for sure, though, she'd be staying with him. And if she refused to take a temporary leave from her job, he'd shadow her regardless of her employer or her thoughts on the matter.

"Maybe you should call in."

Janelle leaned back in her chair, looking a bit less peaked. Her gaze traveled to the large clock on the wall. "I'll be fine. I'm not due in for about an hour and a half. I have plenty of time to get home, shower—"

"*Iubi*, you aren't going home."

She stood, wobbled a brief second then caught her bearings. She propped her fists on her hips. "You can't order me around like I'm one of your grandsons. So unless I'm being held against my will, I'll be leaving. No need to drive me, I can call for an Uber."

"Kane is sending someone over to clean up your place."

"What?" If looks could kill a vampire, he'd be dead. "Why on earth would you send a stranger into my home?"

"It was ransacked by my brother."

Janelle took a deep breath as though she were dealing with an unruly child. Christ, he was only trying to protect her. "I'm capable of cleaning the mess. Besides, how will they get in? Not to mention how I'm supposed to know if anything is missing."

"I broke the knob on the door to get in. I'll have it fixed," he quickly added. "As far as missing possessions, I doubt you have anything of use to my brother."

"Why would he break in?"

"To scare you."

She opened her mouth to reply, then shut it as if she thought better of it. Janelle seemed to be mulling over Mircea's reasoning, then said, "I won't be intimidated. I'll report the break-in, send the lab over."

"You can't do that."

"Why the hell not? You're seriously starting to piss me off, Vlad."

Vlad scrubbed his face. Why couldn't he have been obsessed with someone a bit less frustrating? "*Iubi.*"

"Stop calling me that. I'm not your damn love or your baby."

"There's a human heart in your refrigerator."

Janelle's legs gave out and she fell back onto the sofa. "Jesus. Your brother's a psychopath."

"He's worse."

"What could be worse than a person with who lacks morals and kills without conscience?"

"An immortal vampire who has zero regard for humans." Vlad walked over to the sofa and knelt in front of her, taking her hands in his. "He's promised to take your heart."

She licked her lips. Good, he was finally seeing an inkling of fear in her eyes. A shiver passed through her. "Whose heart is in my refrigerator?"

"The vampire you had a vision of, the one where Mircea took his head. He used his heart to send you a message."

"I need to send the crime lab—"

"You can't. The DNA would be all wrong. We can't let the authorities to get their hands on it. There would be too many questions." Vlad let go of her hands and placed a palm against her cheek. "We take care of our own. That's why you can't go home and it's also why you need to take a leave of absence. I can't keep an eye on you twenty-four-seven if you're doing your job."

"What?" Janelle batted away his hand. "You can't order me around. I have a job to do and I won't be intimidated. If I don't go to work, I won't have a job to go back to."

Vlad should have known she'd be stubborn about this. "Then I'll trail you at work."

She chuckled. "You can't be serious. What would I tell my coworkers? My boss?"

"You let me handle what we tell them." He needed to use another strategy to get her to see reason. "With me by your side, you stand a much better chance at catching Mircea. Without me, you have a zero percent chance."

Her gaze darkened, undoubtedly offended. "You seriously doubt my skills as a special agent then."

"Not at all, Janelle." Vlad stood, paced the floor to the window and looked out again, giving Janelle his back. "I know my brother's skills as a vampire. He can get places you can't without being seen. He can scent your arrival long before you get there. He's stronger than you and your coworkers. And the worst of it, he's stronger than most vampires, which says a lot. You can't go tracking a 500-hundred-year-old vampire and expect to live."

"If he's that damn strong, then how do you expect to stop him?"

Vlad turned, wiping all emotion from his face. "Because I'm more powerful. I made him."

JANELLE STARED AT VLAD. WHAT kind of hell had she stumbled into? 500-year-old vampires. Fangs. Heartless killers. Not to mention these demons had been on earth longer than she'd been alive.

How had they stayed in the shadows without detection all these years?

Vlad had mentioned the dissimilarities in their DNA and how they needed to keep it out of the hands of the authorities, more specifically out of the hands of the crime lab. Heat traveled through her body, shame for what she had already done by giving the lab Vlad's hair, his DNA.

Not wholly human.

Janelle needed to confess, make known her faux pas, though she shuddered at the thought of telling him. Vlad would be furious and rightly so. Maybe she'd sneak into the lab, find his hair and DNA results, and destroy it all. Unfortunately, doing so would not erase the technician's memory. The cameras protecting the lab would also prove her wrongdoing and solidify a criminal case against her, marking her as a felon, gain her jail time, and make sure she'd never work in law enforcement again.

It might be reasonable to think she'd at least be safe from his psychotic brother in a six-by-eight-foot cell, but Vlad had already said no prison system could hold him, which meant Mircea could get to her as well.

"He promised to take your heart."

Janelle was pretty sure that wasn't an idiom and Mircea meant his avowal literally. As much as she hated to admit it, she needed Vlad. Not once had she had to rely on another for her safety. Janelle prided herself on being a top-notch special agent. She may have had partners who'd watched her back while in the field, but never had she felt so defenseless.

Moisture filled her eyes, though she refused to succumb to tears. Janelle had worked years for the DEA; being hardcore was second nature. Breaking down over a vampire wanting her dead wasn't going to happen any more than if Mircea was part of a Mexican cartel.

Pull up your big girl panties, Buttercup.

Janelle had always known of the possibility her life might one day end on the job. It was a fact every special agent knew, kept in the back of their mind, and worn like armor. To forget could cost them or their partner's life.

But how could she possibly defend herself against an immortal?

The answer was quite simple. Her gaze rose to the vampire standing just feet away. He looked sexy as hell all decked out in his jeans and T-shirt and unquestionably deadly. He held his shoulders back, his spine straight, his hands folded in front of him while looking at her with real concern. This vampire who had better things to do than babysit a DEA special agent had taken it upon himself to see she stayed out of the hands of his scary-as-fuck brother, the one from her latest visions.

Vlad Tepes, a real-life badass vampire, was prepared to kill for her. Janelle more than liked this vampire and that thought alone scared her more than his brother's threat to take her heart. She had no business falling for a vampire, let alone one old enough to be her great grandfather many times over. Talk about him robbing the cradle, not that he had any 500-hundred-year-old prospects. Did he?

"Are you okay, *iubi*?"

Love. Surely, it was a term of endearment and nothing more. With his looks and the fact he had probably been around the block many times already, she doubted this sinfully hot vampire would fall for someone as ordinary as her.

"I'll be fine." And as much as it killed her to say so, she added, "With your help. You've convinced me I can't do this on my own."

Vlad took the few steps separating them and knelt before her again. "I won't let anything happen to you."

Janelle believed him, that this deadly immortal would kill for her. Vlad didn't strike her as someone who was in the habit of making false promises.

"We need to come up with a plan. I can't just take a leave from my job. My boss wouldn't allow it on such short notice without me being damn near on my deathbed. Otherwise, I wouldn't have a job to go back to when this nightmare ends. And you shadowing me on the job? I need his permission for that."

"Then we'll get it."

"How?"

"How easily you forget my powers of persuasion. I'll hypnotize him into doing my bidding, then no one will question my being with you. I'll no longer need to use my," he paused, giving her a wink, "parlor tricks."

Janelle couldn't argue with his plan as it did make sense. Vlad would have access to anything she did and everywhere she went. He'd be by her side protecting her from his noxious brother.

"I need to go to the office soon."

"I'll go with you. You'll introduce me to your boss and I'll make sure he allows me access to you and your cases."

"What will we tell him?"

"That I'm a special agent undercover with the ATF. The case you were handling dealing with the drug smugglers who got their throats ripped out by a rival cartel is also on our radar for smuggling guns. It will look like we're working the same case and I need you and your office's cooperation."

"Why undercover?"

Vlad smiled and stood back up and began pacing. "If I tell him that I need you to go undercover with me, we'll no longer have to worry about your nine-to-five office. We'll periodically report back with false statements to placate him until we annihilate my brother. Then you'll be able to return to your job when our supposed case falls apart and I'm called back by my superiors."

Captain Robbie Melchor was far too astute to accept their story at face value. He'd want to get affirmation from Vlad's supervisor.

"What if he wants to talk to your boss? Captain Melchor is a control freak. He'll want to cover his bases should something go down while we're undercover. He won't take your word. He'll want verification so he's not to blame."

"I'll give him Kane's number. He can act as my superior. With my prior hypnosis, he'll believe whatever Kane says."

Janelle didn't like this one bit. What if hypnosis didn't work on Robbie the way it didn't on her. This plan was far from foolproof. Vlad might be able to walk away when this was over, but she'd be jobless and Robbie would make sure she wouldn't be able to get another position in law enforcement.

She let out a sigh, leveling him with her gaze. "This better work, Sir Bites A Lot, or I'm out of a job, and I'll be holding you responsible."

He chuckled, his eyes twinkling in merriment. It was a stunning sight since the big guy didn't seem amused often. "'Sir Bites A Lot?' Sounds like a name for a cartoon character and not a frightening immortal."

Janelle smiled. "What would you've preferred?"

"A carnal vampire with impure thoughts when it comes to my sidekick."

"A bit too long for a nickname. So I'm your sidekick?" she asked, liking the sound a bit too much.

"You are for now." He placed a finger next to his lips. "How about smoking hot vampire?"

She raised a brow. "Egotistical much?"

"I don't hear you complaining, not to mention the fact I can scent your desire when I'm near proves as much."

He had a point, causing her to groan and her face to heat. "If we're going to be spending a lot more time together, then we need to set some ground rules."

"Which are?"

"No biting."

Vlad laughed again. "Fine. No biting as long as we can have—"

"No sex."

"Well, that certainly does suck." He grumbled. "So much for what I was going to add."

"If we're to keep our eyes and ears open, we need to focus. Finding your brother is our top priority, not getting into each other's pants."

"But you'd like that." She rolled her eyes, causing him to laugh again. "We can't afford distractions."

"Well, if I'm Sir Bites A Lot, then you're Ms. I'm No Fun."

Janelle couldn't help but chuckle. She was seeing a whole new side to this man, one she happened to like. "I need to borrow your shower before we head to the office. I can wear what I have on, but we'll need to stop by to my place later to get some clean clothes."

Vlad rocked back on his heels, looking sheepish as if there was something he wanted to add.

"What is it?"

"I don't suppose I could watch."

Her breath caught in her throat. Surely, he hadn't meant what she thought after the rules they had just discussed. "Excuse me?"

"You shower … in the shower. I could do some wicked mind tricks that are quite orgasmic and it wouldn't be breaking your stupid rules. Or I could just wash your back."

Janelle groaned, placing her palm against her face. She was definitely in over her head. Spending too much time with this one was a temptation she might not be able to resist. Giving Vlad her back, she headed for the shower and wondered about those newly mentioned parlor tricks of his.

CHAPTER FOURTEEN

J ANELLE LEFT THE DEA'S VISITOR OFFICE WITH VLAD CLOSE
behind. She didn't have to look to know he was there.
She felt him in every pore of her body. Working alongside him
and keeping her desire in check was going to be a challenge.
Not that anyone normal would know. But the fact he could
scent when her libido kicked up in his presence took embar-
rassing to an entirely new level. She chomped on the gum
she had just stuck into her mouth, hoping to keep her
thoughts off the sinfully hot man who trailed her.

Focus, damn it. You have a job to do.

The first step in their hatched plan had gone off just as he
said it would. Vlad Tepes, aka ATF Special Agent Val Tepp,
had managed to print an obviously fake ID and pass it off as
the real thing by his powers of hypnosis. He had enlisted his
grandsons to secure a more legit-looking one should they
need it in the future through some of the Sons of Sangue's
more shady connections. Janelle didn't bother asking about
those unknown associates. She figured the less she knew,
the better off she'd be if this all blew up in her face.

Vlad wore a pair of blue jeans, worn in all the right places
with that lived-in look, cupping his ass quite nicely. Not that
she noticed, of course. They had just left the secondhand

165

shop about an hour ago where she had picked out a few out-fits that might pass off as something a cartel soldier might wear. Soft flannel stretched over his broad shoulders, worn over a vintage Journey concert T-shirt. A pair of scuffed black military-style boots helped complete the look, left unlaced at the top. A bandana loosely circled his neck should he need to disguise the bottom half of his face, the same way many of the cartel hitmen and street gangbangers did.

Using one of her rubber hair ties, she had banded his black hair in a messy ponytail at the nape instead of his nor-mal loose style. His mane no longer softened the harsh an-gles of his face or the square of his jaw, making him look scary as fuck. In short, his appearance now fit his undercover story.

The visitor's pass gave him clearance to accompany her through the DEA building with no more than a few cursory glances. Vlad no longer had to use his hypnosis or parlor tricks as no one would question his being here if he stayed by her side.

"Have a seat, Val." Janelle smiled, loving being able to order him around. They had a part to play. He did as she instructed, though the straight line of his lips, shadowed by his beard growth, told her he wasn't used to taking directives. "I'll call Captain Melchor and see if he has time for us."

"I'm not spending any more time than necessary in this box you call an office." He growled. "Make it happen."

"You're here as my guest." Janelle smiled, holding back on the humor. "Play the role."

"I'm playing the role of an undercover operative, a hitman for the cartel." He didn't so much as smile. His take-no-shit attitude was hot as hell. "I don't take orders from anyone except the kingpin, not even you."

She swallowed, failing at keeping her desire in check. "You play well."

His nostrils flared, one side of his lips turning up. "If you don't get that libido in check, Special Agent Ferrari, I'll show you exactly how well I play before we go visit that boss of yours."

"Seriously?" Janelle shook her head. "I'm trying to focus. I can't control everything, especially how your presence affects me. We made a deal. No sex."

"Good to know you can't control yourself around me." Janelle groaned and he chuckled. "You made that deal. I never said I agreed."

Vlad stood to his full six-foot-six height and swaggered around the desk as if he knew she thought he was the sexiest man on the planet. He had her pegged. Janelle blew out a steady stream of air and held out her palm to stop him.

She was in trouble.

His grin told her he knew exactly what her thoughts were. "We could lock the door—"

Her palm connected with his solid chest.

"Vlad," she warned, feeling the heat of the contact clear up her arm, warming her from the inside. "We need to get out there looking for your brother. We can't do that if we're distracted. Mircea is going to count on that. Why do you think he threatened me? It's not because I'm a threat to him. He somehow believes he can get to you through me."

"What's one quick—"

"Vlad!"

He chuckled again. "You're right. I don't need the added distraction. Let's go see your boss."

"COME IN AND SHUT THE door," Janelle's boss said, following her knock.

Captain Robbie Melchor stood and held out his hand. Vlad couldn't help but give the man's hand an extra firm squeeze as he shook it. The captain tried to hide the fact the greeting had pained him by rubbing his hands together. Vlad stood a good half a foot taller and had him by several pounds. He'd give the man credit, his face hadn't shown the slightest intimidation. Maybe his bravado was due to the fact there were dozens of special agents who would come to his beck and call should this meeting go south, though little good it would do.

"Janelle told me when she requested this meeting that you're working undercover for the ATF, that one of our cases may impede the success of yours, the Flores case to be specific. You're undercover attempting to infiltrate the cartel. You have my utmost respect."

Vlad shrugged. Although Janelle's superior rubbed him the wrong way, he kept his thoughts to himself. There would be no mutual return of respect. Janelle may care about her boss's opinions, but Vlad did not. He'd bet if he looked close enough, he'd find a few dings in the captain's armor, not to mention some dirty deals along the way.

The little bastard no doubt thought because of his rank he was above reproach. If Melchor hadn't sucked dick to get his present position, then his superiors had worn blinders at the time of his promotion. Vlad would no doubt be doing the world a favor if he decided to drain the arrogant fuck. He had no use for men who used their power to get what they wanted, of which Melchor was no doubt guilty.

Janelle had been wise in her request to be the one to speak since Vlad wasn't one to mince words. One disrespectful comment from the arrogant bastard and Melchor would be picking himself up off the floor.

Clearing her throat, Janelle took a seat across from the captain's stark white Formica and steel desk. A large monitor and keyboard sat to right on the desktop. Vlad couldn't see the screen from his vantage point. "It's been requested that we back off the Flores case as it may impact all the work Val's already put into this. Not to mention put his life in jeopardy should he be outed."

The captain took his own seat, a look of indifference on his face. "You know I can't do that on his word alone. I'm going to need someone to verify his story."

Vlad remained standing, clasping his hands behind his back to keep from reaching out and grabbing the man by the throat. "I have a supervisor. He's the only one who knows about my mission. Blow the undercover work I've done so far and I'll come back and seriously fuck you up. I'm not playing games out there. I'm risking my life."

Janelle shot a dark glance at Vlad. She obviously wasn't happy with him speaking out. Vlad had handled Melchor's type before. Allowing a woman to speak for him would send the wrong kind of message. He needed to make sure her boss knew the consequences of crossing him.

Captain Melchor blanched. "I assure you, it's not my intention to impede an ongoing investigation. Validating your story is covering all my bases. I have people to answer to as well. If need be, you have my permission to use Special Agent Ferrari."

Vlad bit back his actual retort. The fact this poor excuse of a human was willing to throw his special agent into the cartel's den rankled his ire. "I plan to. Don't count on her reporting back unless necessary. I can't afford the risk and I report back only to my superior. You want to know any details, call him."

"How did you meet Special Agent Ferrari?"

Vlad held up a hand, stopping her from interrupting him. He was sure to catch hell once they left Melchor's office. At least Vlad was no longer scenting desire on her like an aphrodisiac. Christ, it took all his willpower not to toss her on her desk a few moments ago and fuck her from his senses.

Her anger was much easier to handle.

"She was sticking her nose into the Flores case, trying to pin the murders on the La Paz cartel. I tried my best to shake her, to keep her from their radar, but it was becoming increasingly difficult. I don't have to tell you what happens when the cartel feels you're getting all up in their business. I felt it best, for the sake of the case and Janelle's wellbeing, to let her in on my undercover work, maybe bring her in as my old lady."

Captain Melchor looked at Janelle. "And you want to be a part of this? You've never done anything undercover. You sure you can handle this?"

Janelle nodded. "I'm sure."

"I do hope so, Special Agent Ferrari. The cartel doesn't fuck around," the captain said. "Who is your superior, Val, and how do I get a hold of him?"

Vlad smiled. The man was too easy to manipulate. Hell, he hadn't even had to use hypnosis to get him to do his bidding. Withdrawing a worn piece of paper from his pocket, he slid it across the table with a phone number jotted in black ink across it.

"This number is used for the operation only. We can't chance calling the ATF office directly. If you do, they will deny knowing me and the operation."

"Your superior's name?"

Before leaving her office, Janelle had found a higher up's name from the ATF they could use for their ruse. They needed a real person should her boss look up the validity of his superior. Vlad had called Kane and let him in on their plan before entering Captain Melchor's office.

Vlad said, "Acting Director Kenneth Turk. He'll be expecting your call."

CHAPTER FIFTEEN

"SHOWTIME." THE BURNER PHONE KANE HAD ACQUIRED earlier vibrated on the counter with an incoming call. He picked it up and looked at the number on the screen. It had to be Melchor.

"You got this?" Kaleb looked at him in concern. "Your history with this asswipe could blow this if you lose your shit."

"As long as he doesn't compromise us finding Vlad's brother, then I'm good. He steps out of line, I'll tear out his throat."

Kaleb chuckled. "That's my brother."

Hitting the answer on the screen, Kane placed it on speaker. "Turk here."

"Acting Director Kenneth Turk?"

Kane's hate ran deep for Robbie Melchor due to the man's past with his mate, Cara. She and Robbie had briefly dated long before Kane and Cara had gotten together. Apparently, the man didn't know the definition of the word "no." Cara hadn't told any of her co-workers about Robbie having raped her because she felt they wouldn't have likely taken her word over the decorated officer's. Cara had packed up her belongings, quit the police department, and moved to Lane County where she became a detective.

Kane couldn't have been more thrilled with the outcome, though. Had it not been for her arrival in Pleasant, he might have still been quietly admiring her from afar.

Thanking Melchor for his fuck up? Wasn't going to happen.

"Who the fuck is asking?"

Robbie cleared his throat. Kane pictured him using a forefinger to loosen his collar. No doubt still a yellow belly. Typical pencil pusher with credentials, not having the actual balls to do the fieldwork.

"I'm Captain Robbie Melchor with the DEA office here in Oregon. Special Agent Val Tepp one of yours?"

"He gave me a heads up you'd be calling. He's working on a case for us. Call me again and I'll deny it. Blow his cover and I'll come find you."

The smirk on his twin's face told Kane his brother was humored by his reply.

"Thank you, Acting Director Turk. I appreciate your time." Kane could hear Janelle speaking in the background, telling him that she and Vlad were currently in Robbie's office. "One of my special agents, Janelle Ferrari, will be working with your man."

"See that she doesn't fuck this up. I agreed to bring her on because she was sniffing around where it might get her hurt or jeopardize the case we're building. Special Agent Val told me he could use her undercover as his old lady. You need to touch base, go through me and use this number. Otherwise, forget she exists until we make our case. Got me?"

"I don't plan to jeopardize your case. I'd be happy to share what we have on the Flores case."

"Have your special agent give it to me. I'm not here to make friends." Kane ended the connection and placed the cell on the bar. "Damn, that felt good, though it might have been more fun seeing his face."

Kaleb guffawed. "Not once did he argue or question you, just threw Janelle to the wolves, so to speak. He likely doesn't care about her wellbeing, only his damn reputation. What a fucking pansy."

Kane grinned. "You won't get an argument from me."

"MAKE SURE YOU KILL THE son of a bitch this time," Vlad growled into the phone.

"I would've last time but as I recall someone stopped me." He heard the smile in Kane's tone, telling him Kane jested. Vlad supposed he deserved it. "I'll take some of my men with us. We'll canvas the area. We'll find him. His hours are numbered. I'm not giving Mircea days. This ends now."

"Call me when you find him."

"I'll call you when he's dead."

Vlad ended the call and pocketed his cell.

Like a caged animal, he paced the floor of his penthouse. He wasn't used to holing up in one place overlong, not even on his island. The itch to get back on the road crawled across his skin like a thousand ants. He needed to find his brother and get the hell out of Oregon. Ever since his captivity centuries ago he hated being confined, even to a luxury pent-house, which is why his island had become his sanctuary with twenty-plus acres in which to roam. Human interaction could be kept at a minimum and only out of necessity.

He had developed a certain dislike for people.

They provided the nutrition he needed for survival, a way to sate his sexual desires, and little else.

The decline of civilization had become quite obvious over the years. Vlad supposed he could blame the lack of parent-ing. Politeness had all but disappeared. Work ethics had gone out the window. And people conversed by way of elec-tronics or skipped conversation altogether and spent their time watching television.

Hell, kids were killing kids these days.

He shook his head and gritted his teeth. In his time, he had ruled with an iron fist, and if the crime called for it, a wooden stake. Vlad was feared as well as revered for the way he held court. There were penances to be paid. Anything less and his enemies would have considered him weak.

The world had grown soft.

Vlad couldn't get back to his self-isolation soon enough. How much worse could humanity get? He wasn't sure he wanted an answer. One thing was for sure, though, he wasn't about to allow his brother to contribute to the darkness a mo-ment longer. Mircea needed to be stopped before the cat, or in this case, the vampire was out of the bag.

Janelle shifted in her seat, quietly watching him stew. She had been the one bright star in his otherwise bleak existence;

the one human he had actually enjoyed. Even in the face of evil, she didn't cower. Hell, no. She wanted to be out there on the front lines, helping him bring down his brother.

As if she had read his thoughts, she said, "I hate that we are sitting here doing nothing. Strength comes in numbers. How do they plan to find him anyway?"

The whiskey tone of her voice stirred him in places he was having a hell of a time ignoring. Visions of her on her knees flooded his brain and stirred his cock, making his pants a bit uncomfortable. Tracking Mircea was but a mere blip in his present muddled brain, proving Janelle was a distraction he shouldn't be entertaining. His weakness where Janelle was concerned rankled his ire and very well should have.

"If you're referring to my ass of a brother, I don't know," he snarled, giving his back to her, hoping she hadn't detected her effect on him.

Christ, she was quickly becoming his Achilles' heel, proof in that he stood here babysitting her rather than combing the woods. "He's near. I can feel it in my blood, but damn if I can get a read on his whereabouts. It's like the son of a bitch anticipates my moves and it's driving me to the brink of madness. I can't help but wonder if my brother somehow mastered the art of blending in with his surroundings. Being able to sneak up on the Sons in the alley speaks of some sort of trickery."

"You won't catch your brother in here pacing the floor."

Still miffed, Vlad whirled on his heel, heat pooling in his gaze and no doubt blackening his eyes. "You think I don't know that?"

Flames of fury licked up his spine. Lord, she didn't deserve his rage. Self-loathing washed over him from his uncalled for outburst. Vlad was the one at fault, not Janelle. She had done nothing more than offer her help. It was his damn sentimentality months ago that had Vlad unwilling to end Mircea's life and thus imprison him. His brother had enlisted his servant Nina and escaped his island, making Vlad the biggest of fools.

Kane was right. This must end.

But instead of being out there tracking the bastard down with his grandsons, he stood there with his dick in his hand. Had Janelle not held her libido in check and he scented the slightest essence of her desire, there would be no stopping the beast from emerging. Drinking from her had been a colossal mistake. One taste of her sweet blood and she was his heroin and he the junkie.

Lord, he was the one who needed to check his libido.

Biting back the emergence of his fangs, he once again gave her his back and peered across the horizon. Nightfall had descended. Downtown high-rises were illuminated, lighting the skyline and leaving the forest edging the city dark and impassable for humans. Not that the blackness would hinder his or his kin's sight but it would render Janelle nearly blind.

He wasn't about to take her along for the hunt and put her in jeopardy, not with Mircea's threat to take her heart. Kane and Kaleb were quite capable of sniffing out his trail. If they didn't kill him on sight, then Vlad would once they gave him the coordinates.

Vlad braced his large hands against the cool glass. "We won't catch Mircea in the city," he said more to himself, before giving Janelle his attention.

"What makes you think so?"

"Because the forest offers him better cover. Nearly fifty percent of Oregon is covered by woods. Besides, I'm betting Mircea dislikes people as much as I do. If I were him, it's what I'd do."

"Sometimes hiding in plain sight is the better choice. He could be taking advantage of the background and blending in with the crowds."

Anything was possible, Vlad thought. Mircea could assume he'd easily blend in with the city's residents. Hopefully, Vlad hadn't allowed his arrogance to count out other possibilities.

"What do your visions tell you?"

Janelle smiled. "They don't work that way, Vlad. I wish they did, then I could catch a lot more criminals, not to mention tell you exactly where your brother is. Unfortunately, I have no idea when one will show up."

He could tell by her restlessness she wasn't one to sit idle, not when there was a job to do. Vlad liked that about her, but unfortunately the special agent was out of her league on this one.

"We shouldn't be sitting here," Janelle continued. "We need eyes out there looking for him. The more people the better the odds are of catching him."

And he damn well would have been out there now, had it not been for his need to protect. No one could scare up Mircea like Vlad, not even his grandsons. Helplessness settled over him, further souring his mood. But allowing Janelle to tag along wasn't an option. Mircea would show her no mercy, if for no other reason than to watch Vlad suffer.

Vlad supposed his killing of Mircea's stepdaughter and secret crush, Rosalee, and Mircea's later imprisonment had caused some of his anger issues. The killing of his brother's mate Nina was no doubt another sore spot, even if Vlad hadn't been the one to do so—he had handed down the order. Hopefully, Kane, Kaleb, and the Sons would successfully capture and kill Mircea, ending his brother's revenge on his own family.

"Vlad," Janelle broke into his thoughts again. "If he's such a danger and needs to be stopped, I don't understand why we're wasting our time. More people could die."

He resisted the urge to roll his eyes at her naivety. Hell, she could die should they join the chase. If he told her his reasoning, the determined beauty would demand they go on the hunt regardless of being put at a risk.

"Damn it, *iubi*. Stop questioning my motives."

Fire flared in Janelle's crystal blue eyes.

Good. He had pissed her off.

She stood, striding over to him, only to stop mere inches from touching him. Her forefinger met his chest. Heat blossomed through him at lightning speed, causing his fangs to punch through his gums and his cock to instantly harden. No way he'd hide the effect she had on him now.

He wasn't one to ignore his hungers. Being the oldest of his kind, Vlad was in the habit of taking what he desired and not having to apologize for it. Hypnosis had served him well over the years ... that is until Janelle. And right now, she was what he desired most, to hell with Mircea and everyone else. The world could fucking wait.

"Don't you dare order me around. Stop being so damn stubborn and let me help."

Vlad glared down at her. "You can't."

"Why the hell not?" Christ, even her anger was a turn-on.

"Because Mircea would kill you upon sight and that's not acceptable."

"He won't know I'm there. I'll stay out of sight."

"He'll be able to scent you long before you ever get close to him."

Janelle jabbed him again. "Why not let me decide—"

Vlad gripped the hair at her nape, effectively shutting her up. Yanking her against him, her breasts bumped into his chest, her nipples already pebbled. *Well, if that wasn't a mistake...* Her desire scented the room and surrounded him like a cape, further hardening his dick. Vlad had meant to silence her. Now he coveted a kiss. Who the hell was he kidding? Nothing short of fucking her again would be enough.

"You're walking a fine line, princess. "

"I'm not a princess." Her lips thinned; her gaze heated. "I can handle anything thrown my way. Ask anyone I've worked with. I've gone up against some pretty chilling criminals and not backed down. You don't frighten me, Vlad Tepes."

"You should be frightened. This is not what's best for you."

"It's dangerous. I get it. No situation is guaranteed safe, and yet I'm good at my job because I don't worry about what's best for me."

Vlad chuckled at her misunderstanding. He was no longer referring to his brother and imminent death. "I'm what's not best for you, *iubi*. But treating you like a princess? Definitely not what I had in mind."

She licked her lips "There is one thing we think alike on."

"This won't end well." He tilted her chin with a slight tug of her hair. Vlad didn't want her to mistake where this was going. "When Mircea is dead, I'll go back home. This isn't some romantic flick. There is no forever—not for me."

One side of her lips tilted up. "Did I ask? Check your ego, Vlad. I'm married to my job. I don't need candlelight dinners. Although, wine might be good…"

"*Iubi*…"

Vlad released his grip and cradled her skull. Sliding his other hand down to the base of her spine, he anchored her against the hardest part of him. Damn if it didn't want to be appeased. His gaze dropped to her lips. Vlad should've given someone else babysitting duty because she sure in the hell wasn't safe with him. Standing this close, scenting her desire, not to mention the sweet bouquet of her blood racing through her veins, and he had already lost the battle.

Sealing his lips over hers, he kissed her fiercely, telling her of his intentions. This was no sweet kiss. There was no stopping him. Not since the loss of his wife so many years ago had he felt such all-consuming desire. This woman not only had him by the balls, but by the heart. If he wasn't careful, Vlad was in danger of falling hard and losing his soul to this woman. He had told Janelle he didn't do forever. But he'd be damned if he knew how the hell to walk away.

Janelle fisted the soft cotton of his shirt, stepping up and leaning into the kiss, opening for him. Vlad wasted little time sliding his tongue past her lush full lips and into the soft cavern of her mouth. His fangs nicked the soft pad of her tongue. The metallic tang of her blood flooded his mouth and called forth his vampire DNA.

Every part of him needed appeasing.

Needed to feel her from the inside.

Thirsted for the sanguine fluid sluicing through her veins.

Reaching down, he placed a forearm behind her knees and picked her up as easily as if she were a doll, cradling her against his chest. Heading for the California king-sized bed, Vlad toed open the partially closed door with his booted foot. His long strides reached the bed in short time where he laid her upon the cotton comforter.

She was the angel to his devil.

Lying on the bed, her hair haloing her head, he could easily picture wings spread out beneath her. Christ, that alone should have him running. Instead, it left him wanting to crawl into the bed, encompass her and never let her go. She alone could save him from the darkness that consumed his life. The four-letter word mocked him, the one word he swore to never use again when it came to a woman, not when the confession brought with it weakness.

The desire he saw in her electric-blue eyes, scented on her, damn near crippled him. He wasn't worthy of the adoration. It was reason enough to send her away. Instead, his heart pained at the idea of never seeing her again. He knew what it felt like to be wrapped in her heat, to partake from her artery. And right now, he wanted nothing more.

Love.

He was a fucking fool.

"Please tell me this isn't what you want, *iubi*. Christ, tell me no."

"Yes."

Vlad groaned. The battle was lost. "Why the hell can't you listen?"

Janelle sat, gripped the front of his T-shirt, and pulled him to the bed. He came to rest between her spread legs, his cock cradled in the V of her thighs. Her heat further warmed his hardness. Palming her cheeks again, he kissed her slowly, one full of possession, one full of promise. And if she could read what he was feeling … she'd know it was one filled with love.

Janelle kissed him back, moaning against his mouth. She mattered. Not Mircea. Not his grandsons. Not the world beyond the penthouse. Breaking the kiss, he slid a hand down her abdomen, into the waistband of her pants and beneath the thin scrap of lace she wore beneath, finding her already wet.

Vlad slicked his fingers along the silky center … and the cell phone rang. Damn it, he should ignore it but knew better. His grandsons were out there doing his bidding, what he should have done long ago.

Nenorocitule!

Vlad withdrew his hand from Janelle's jeans, earning him a groan of frustration. He rolled from her and withdrew the cell from his pants pocket. He saw Kane's name and let out a curse. Sliding his finger across the lock, he then answered the phone.

"This better be good."

"Grumpy much?" Kane clipped. "We found Mircea."

CHAPTER SIXTEEN

JANELLE STEPPED INTO THE SONS OF SANGUE CLUBHOUSE where the vampires gathered, the scene looking like something straight out of a horror flick. These men weren't actors with realistic stage makeup, though. They were scary-ass motherfuckers with fangs. The members had morphed into their vampire egos and looked ready for the hunt.

A shiver passed down her spine as she realized the lethal world she had stumbled into. These vampires were out for blood. Janelle fought the urge to tuck beneath Vlad's arm. Funny, he had also taken on his vampire manifestation and yet she felt safe by his side.

"Where is he?" Vlad's anger-filled tone seized everyone's attention and the room grew silent.

Malice and hatred toward his brother, Mircea, was clearly written in his black gaze. Janelle had seen Vlad's anger firsthand, but this fury was far more deadly. Not a single vampire in this room seemed to challenge his authority. No, they clearly looked upon him as though he were the governing power. Even his great-grandsons who led this group appeared ready to do his bidding.

"A small abandoned cabin several miles from here, near the summit of South Sister, about sixty-five miles east. Probably the home of a long-dead mountain man or hunter," Kane provided. "Wolf called in the sighting. He and Gypsy picked up Mircea's scent. Apparently, your brother finally let down his guard. Gypsy was able to get close enough to the cabin to spot Mircea."

"Mircea nose them out?" Vlad's gaze overflowed with excitement, no doubt for the coming chase. He rubbed his hands together.

"The skunk spray apparently kept them from detection. I told Wolf to hold his distance. We didn't want them getting too close and chance driving Mircea from his hideout due to the stench."

"And he's still there?"

Kane nodded.

"Best fucking news I've had all day." Vlad glanced at the thickly muscled vampire to his left. "Ryder, you take Janelle back to your place. See that she's kept safe."

"Xander's been appointed babysitting duty." Ryder growled his displeasure at the idea, showing his razor-sharp fangs. "I'll take her there, but I'm not missing out on the hunt. Gabby, Adri, and India are already under Xander's care. What's one more? Once I have Janelle secured, I'll head up the mountain and meet you all there. Someone needs to send the coordinates to my cell. You may need my primordial strength if some of Mircea's turned vampires are in the vicinity."

"You have a point, Ryder. The women will be safe enough since they aren't Mircea's target," Bobby Bourassa added. "I'll ride with you."

"Thanks, Preacher. Make sure Xander understands Janelle is targeted though," Kane said. "Don't take Mircea's threat lightly. Xander needs to keep a close eye on her until we rip Mircea's fucking head off."

"He's my brother, Kane. My mistake. If we're all there when we catch up to him, then I get the honors of ending the son of a bitch."

Kaleb patted Vlad on the shoulder. "Understood, Grandpa."

A muscle ticked in Vlad's cheek, obviously not fond of the term. He bared his teeth at his unfazed grandson. "Vlad."

Janelle didn't blame him. Vlad certainly didn't look grand-fatherly. Hell, he didn't look a day older than the rest of the vampires who were obviously younger.

"Let's get the show on the road." Kaleb ignored Vlad's set-down. Janelle would have chuckled had the situation been other than it was. She'd bet Kaleb was the more obstinate of the twins. "Janelle, you'll be safe with Ryder and Preacher."

Lord, she wanted to argue, wanted to stay by Vlad's side and make sure he stayed safe. But she'd be an unneeded distraction to him, one that might cost him dearly. Besides, the idea she could help was laughable at best, even if she was a damn good marksman. The criminals she chased on a daily basis had nothing on these lethal vampires.

Ryder handed her a helmet. "Let's go, sweetheart."

Vlad narrowed his gaze. "You tell Xander anything hap-pens to her, he answers to me."

"She'll be safe enough," Ryder assured him. "No one even knows I live there. The house is in Gabby's name."

Janelle took the helmet, but instead of putting it on, she gripped Vlad's forearm. "Can we talk? In private?"

His dark gaze dropped to hers. "This can't wait, *iubi*?"

"No."

Vlad sucked in a deep breath then released it, no doubt impatient with the delay. Time was wasting and if the men dallied overlong his brother could give them the slip once again. But a few minutes couldn't hurt, could it? What Janelle needed to say wouldn't take long. Besides, she might not get another chance.

He firmly gripped her by the hand and led them through the building and out the door, slamming it behind him. His anger was palpable, but it didn't change her need to confess. He could be angry with her all he wanted, but she'd have her say.

"What is so hell-fire important that this couldn't wait? My brother is a cagey bastard and the last thing I want is him slipping through my fingers while I stand out here having a chit chat."

Janelle ignored his insolence.

"What if you don't return?" she whispered, hoping to keep her admission from prying vampires' ears.

Vlad harrumphed in response.

"There's always a chance—"

"Get on with it so I can get up that damn mountain."

The idea something might happen to Vlad didn't sit well with her. If she had a vision, she might be able to prevent a possible catastrophe. "Let me go with you."

His answering chuckle spoke volumes. "Non-negotiable. You'll not only put yourself at risk but me as well."

"You?"

His gaze softened. "Christ, *iubi*. You have to know…"

She drew her lower lip between her teeth, hoping he felt more for her than a casual friend with benefits. "No, I don't."

He pulled the hand he held to his lips and placed a kiss to the back. "Go with Ryder and when I get back we'll talk."

Janelle didn't want him going on this ruthless mission without knowing how she felt. The idea he might not make it back strangled her heart. It was foolish to care, or worse yet to fall for the man. Dear Lord, he wasn't even mortal. She had no idea how a relationship with a vampire could even work. And yet her heart had picked the eldest of them all to take a nose-dive for anyway.

There was no way this was going to end well.

Her heart would be left in tatters.

Foolish didn't begin to describe her mistake in having fallen in love with him. It wasn't like he'd return the sentiment. After all, he had already told her he didn't do forever. The words had stung at the time but she had hidden behind her excuse of being married to her job. He was a vampire, for chrissake. Of course, there could be no future for them. Janelle would wither away and die while Vlad lived on to see another century. And then another, and another.

Gripping his shirt, Janelle pulled him down for a brief kiss. "Come back, okay?"

His eyes twinkled with his grin, revealing two large white fangs. Instead of inducing fear, though, the thought of him sinking them deep into the artery at the side of her neck sent a shiver of pleasure down her spine.

"It's certainly my intention, *iubi*."

"What I'm trying to say is" —she cleared her throat— "I, um, care." Fear of rejection kept her from admitting the full truth. It hadn't taken much for her to fall in love with him, stupid as it was.

Vlad gripped her nape, pulled her in for another kiss, this one far deeper and full of promise. The door opened behind them and Vlad released her. She heard the approaching footsteps as Vlad stepped back.

His gaze continued to hold hers hostage. "Ryder, take Janelle to your place. Make sure Xander knows what he has."

"You got it, big guy." Janelle glanced at the man to whom she was being released. His head tilted toward the row of motorcycles. "Let's go, Janelle."

Without another word, she turned and followed the two bikers over to the row of Harley Davidsons. Ryder stepped over the seat of his motorcycle and sat down, strapping a skull cap to his head. Janelle put on the one he had given her, clipped it beneath her chin, then stepped onto the back peg and seated herself behind him.

Ryder took one of her hands and wrapped his waist with it. "Hold on, sweetheart. We aren't going to be following the speed limits. We'll be at my place shortly. And don't worry, I'll take care of the big guy. Even if he doesn't need my help."

Janelle wrapped both arms about his middle. "I'm holding you to that."

Ryder's chuckle was his response as he started the engine, kicked up the stand, and circled the parking lot. The other biker she heard them call Preacher followed them out of the lot. One last glance back told her Vlad watched until they turned out of sight. Whether he wanted to admit as much, she knew he cared for her on some level. Janelle felt it in the desperation of his kiss and had read it in the depths of his black eyes.

She leaned forward and shouted into Ryder's ear. "Make sure he comes back."

Ryder turned his head slightly so his words could be heard. "Sweetheart, that man doesn't need my help, even if I implied as much. Whether he comes back to you? It's really none of my business. But if that kiss was any indication, I'm pretty sure he'll be looking you up when this is over. So you mind Xander and stay put."

Janelle wasn't about to cause Vlad more distress. She'd listen for now, but if she had another vision and it told her he was in any kind of trouble, all bets were off. She'd find a way up that damn mountain.

THE PHONE VIBRATED ON THE stand just before the jangle split the silence of the cabin. Mircea strode over to the table by the window, picked up the cell, swiped the front of the screen, then took it to his ear.

"Tell me you've spotted my fucking brother."

"No, but you have company."

"How many?"

"Two vampires. I was doing a sweep of the woods. Fucking skunk smell had me staying away from the south side of the cabin as I sure in the hell didn't want to be sprayed. I was downwind taking a wide arc around that area when I caught movement. It was too damn big to be a polecat."

"They see you?"

"No. And they didn't detect me either since I was quite a distance downwind from them. After I spotted them, I hightailed it out of there and called you."

"It was only a matter of time before a couple of those sons of bitches found me. They likely already called in the rest of their crew with my brother on the receiving end of the call as well. I want these two taken care of before the cavalry arrives. Are you alone?"

"For now. But there are three others within range, not too far off the path. I had them doing a wider sweep of the forest."

"Call them and get them up here. You boys take care of business and get the hell on the road before any of the other Sons arrive. Don't be hasty … they'll arrive damn quickly. Keep your guard up. If you get caught unaware by any of these boys, they'll take your head."

"What about you?"

"I'll be long gone before the party starts."

"You know, you and I could take these two out ourselves."

Mircea chuckled mercilessly. "What the hell do you think I created you for? I'm not about to take a chance that they might get the upper hand. You wait for the three other vampires I created that are near, then take out our unwanted company. Your numbers will give you the advantage. Wait for the rest of the Sons to arrive and you don't stand a chance."

"And if your brother shows up?"

"Take his fucking head." Mircea ended the call.

Stepping up to the window, he pulled aside the threadbare curtains and peered out. The scent of skunk was definitely stronger from the south side of the cabin. If his little snitch was correct, he had spotted two of the Sons directly in the scent's path. Mircea would bet his left nut the Sons were using the stench to cover being detected. He had stupidly thought there was an actual skunk out there in the forest, costing him precious time.

The point went to the Sons but the game was far from over.

There were far better ways to blend in with one's surroundings. Thankfully, his brother hadn't tapped into that particular ability yet. It had been by sheer luck that Mircea had discovered the usable talent. When he finally caught up to Vlad, he wouldn't scent Mircea's approach and he'd take his damn head before his brother ever spotted him.

The little cat and mouse game was getting old. It was damn time he rid the earth of his egotistical brother and take over as the eldest of all vampires. He'd make sure even the Sons followed his lead, or he'd kill every damn one of them.

Movement in the trees caught his attention. Mircea dropped the curtain back into place. "Not going to be your day, boys."

He smiled, pocketed the cell, and headed for the other side of the cabin. The woods were particularly dense on the north side. Luck was for once on his side. Within a few hours, Mircea would be miles away and the Sons of Sangue would have two fewer members. Vlad would no doubt amp up his search, angling for Mircea's head.

"Not damn likely, bro."

Mircea still had one or two aces up his sleeve and he planned to play one of them post-haste. No way in hell his brother would chance putting Special Agent Ferrari in jeopardy by dragging her up the mountain chasing a fool's mission. Mircea planned to find out just where she was being held, and when he did, he'd take her in more ways than one.

Vlad Tepes was about to pay for his sins in spades.

CHAPTER SEVENTEEN

V LAAD STEPPED THROUGH A CLEARING NEAR THE CABIN. The place appeared to be abandoned for several decades. The logs no longer fit nicely together, bearing holes in most of the chinking as though a good strong wind might blow the place down. The windows and trim looked in need of serious repair, most panes either broken or missing, leaving tattered curtains fluttering in through the openings. The tin roof bore years of rust and pine needles. Moss grew on the north side of the building, leaving what was once brown a dark green. The smell of must and dirt was strong. Vlad bet, other than his brother, this cabin hadn't seen occupants in over a century.

Mircea seemed to sniff out these old discarded cabins. It wasn't his first time holing up in the backwoods. And unless Vlad cut his brother's life short, it probably wouldn't be his last. The *nenorocitule* was like a rat playing hidey-hole.

Four dead vampire bodies lay side-by-side on the needle encrusted ground, their heads no longer attached. Vlad glanced at the pair of Sons who had arrived at the scene before him. Both Grigore and Grayson were damn near coated in the blood of their victims, the rest soaking the foliage at their feet. Neither looked the worse for wear from having faced off against four of Mircea's primordial minions.

Vlad turned his nose up, sniffing the air. Fury raced through him at his brother having given them the slip again.

"The fucking coward sent his newly turned vamps to fend you off while he vanished. The general leaving his soldiers to certain death." He shook his head and growled his displeasure beneath his breath. "His scent is stamped all over the area. Christ, we just missed his sorry ass again."

"The son of a bitch probably fled while Gypsy and I were here parrying with his fucking gnats." Grigore brushed his blood-stained hands against the legs of his jeans, though little good it did. "I'm afraid I failed you."

"You did no such thing, Wolf," Vlad snarled. He couldn't very well fault Kane and Kaleb's men. Hell, they were out here doing him a favor. "Mircea knew exactly what he was doing. Had you not been spotted by Mircea, we might have gotten the upper hand. Not only did the scent of the skunk help you get this close without detection, but it also kept you from smelling my brother's creations before they were upon you. He likely had them combing the woods. Given the shitty situation, I'd say you guys did a damn fine job."

"They may have had your brother's primordial blood running through their veins," Grayson said, "but they were easy enough to beat, most likely because they were newly turned."

"Five minions down." Kane wrung his hands together. "How many more to go?"

"Six down," Vlad added. "Don't forget the one I took out early on. You can bet if we don't catch up to Mircea, there will be more."

"Takes 'em a week to turn."

"It does, Gypsy, which means we need to find the son of a bitch before he gets started on more. Fuck!" Kaleb groused. "We were so close to ending this."

Vlad patted his grandson on the shoulder. "You're no more disappointed than I. He's got to run out of luck sooner or later. And we'll be there."

"One thing is for sure," Kane chuckled, "we have the motherfucker scared and on the run. Otherwise, he would've stayed to help out his vampires. Instead, he led them to slaughter. Great job, Wolf and Gypsy. I just wish we would've gotten here sooner to help."

Grayson grabbed the band from his arm and pulled his blood-encrusted hair away from his face and into a messy knot. "Think nothing of it. Other than being in need of a good shower, I don't think I got more than a few scratches. It was way more fun this way."

"I don't doubt that for a minute." Vlad noted the approaching vampires long before he spotted Kane's other men coming up the mountain from the south side. His sense of smell picked them up long before Ryder and Bobby stepped into view with the scent of the skunk urine now dissipated. "What are you two doing here? Where's Janelle?"

"Safe with Alexander. The women were glad for the company."

Vlad gave them a nod of approval. "Thank you, Ryder. I owe you."

The other vampire smiled before his gaze dropped to the corpses at their feet. "You don't owe me a thing, Vlad, but damned if I'm not pissed over missing the festivities."

Bobby hissed, his fangs jutting below his upper lip, which was partially hidden by his long, full beard. "I always seem to miss the fun."

Grayson winked at the hulking vampire. "Then I'll give you the honors of disposing of these sons of bitches, Preacher."

"The hell you say. You and Wolf made the mess. You get to clean it up." He brushed the overlong bangs from his eyes and looked at Vlad. "Any idea where your brother took off to this time?"

"No fucking clue." Vlad's fangs still hung well past his lips, telling of the rage still coursing through him. "One of these fucking days, Mircea's time will be up and I'll be there."

"And I hope I'm there to watch the show." Grigore's hand indicated the four bodies. "What do you want done with these?"

"Torch them," Vlad said. "We can't risk a hiker accidentally coming across them and alerting the authorities. They'd no doubt want to run tests in hopes of discovering their identities. Throw them in the cabin and burn it to the ground."

Grayson grabbed two of the headless corpses. Grigore handled the other two, dragging them toward the back door of the cabin. Bobby gripped the hair of the heads, carrying two in each of his big paws and followed his brethren. It wasn't long before the entire cabin was engulfed by flames.

VLAD: SONS OF SANGUE | 201

Vlad turned to Kane. "You and the rest of the Sons stay here, make sure this doesn't get out of hand. I don't need a forest fire to contend with. Use water from the creek just beyond the clearing if you need to."

His brow furrowed. "Where are you off to?"

"To find my damn brother."

"You aren't fucking going alone." Kane's black gaze flared. "The boys can be on fire watch. But Kaleb and I? We're going with you. You may be able to take your brother, but hard telling how many of his cretins will be called in for his protection."

"We took out six of them."

"Exactly, Vlad. How many more are there?"

Kane had a point. Vlad had no doubt he could take on his brother one-on-one and win. But add in a handful of newly turned vampires and Mircea might just get the upper hand. Allowing his grandsons to tag along would ensure he had a fair fight. Vlad needed to keep his wits about him and not act on the anger raging inside of him, burning as hot as the cabin.

"You and Kaleb may accompany me," Vlad agreed. "We'll head north and see if we can catch his scent and find the path he took. The rest of you head back to the clubhouse once the threat of the fire spreading is gone. We'll meet up with you there later. We'll either find the son of a bitch and end this now or we'll need to come up with a new plan. This has gone on far too long."

"I'M FINE, ROCKY."

Janelle stood on the veranda of Ryder and Gabriela's coastal home, overlooking the Pacific while talking on her cell. A glass panel rail wrapped the deck so the million-dollar view from inside the house remained unobstructed. Small waves crashed off the rocks below, but did little to soothe her.

"I just wanted you to know I might not be around for a few days."

"Is everything okay?" Rocky asked. "I worry about you."

She chuckled. The truth of it, Janelle should be worrying about her friend and not the other way around. Rocky had a habit of attracting trouble. And yet here Janelle stood...

"I'm fine. Just doing some undercover stuff for work, shit I can't talk about."

Janelle hated lying to her bestie. But telling Rocky they were chasing down a crazy-as-a-loon vampire wasn't an option. The world Janelle had stepped into wasn't hers to reveal, even if she were to be believed that paranormal creatures existed.

Xander, the model-handsome vampire who was put in charge of her keeping, and his pregnant mate, India, were anything but bloodthirsty monsters. In fact, they were pretty tolerant of her being foisted on them, making sure she had everything she needed, including a little space so she could make her phone call in private.

From what Janelle had learned, this beautiful estate belonged to Gabriela Trevino Caballero. She had yet to become the mate of Ryder, the biker who had given Janelle the ride. Apparently, Gabby wasn't ready to be turned into a blood-drinker. Christ, Janelle couldn't blame her. The thought of becoming one made her blood run colder than the chilled breeze coming off the ocean.

Adriana, Gabby's friend from Mexico, had no clue vampires were a thing even though she lived in their guest house. When Gabby's father, the kingpin of the La Paz cartel, had been killed by the Sons of Sangue, Gabby brought her friend along when she had moved up the coast to be with Ryder. Since humans weren't allowed to know about their existence, Adri had been kept in the dark. Gabby, on the other hand, had been an exception since she had been technically mated to one of the Sons.

According to Gabby, Adriana's ex-fiancé had taken over as kingpin and Adri was no longer safe to live in Mexico. When Gabby found out that Janelle also knew about the Sons' secret, she'd become an open book, answering Janelle's questions. Once Adriana returned to the party fresh from the shower, though, all talk about vampires ceased.

Maybe, Janelle needn't worry so much about Rocky after all. Her life seemed tame compared to this world. In the future, though, she'd steer Rocky away from the Blood 'n' Rave. Her bestie would need to find a different biker to satisfy her bad boy obsession, not one from the Sons of Sangue.

"Does that mean we can't go clubbing?"

"Yeah, about that—I was thinking you should stay away from those bikers we met the other night."

Rocky sighed. "As much as I'd like to pursue Smoke, I was thinking of heading back to New York for a bit anyway."

Janelle gripped the steel railing housing the glass panels, her hair picking up in the light breeze. A seagull dipped, picked up a small fish in its beak, then flew farther down the shore. She envied Rocky's carefree life where she could so easily fly away. Normally, Janelle would try to convince her to stick around longer, hating when she couldn't see her bestie for long periods. When Rocky moved back to New York, it was typically six months or better before she came home. This time, Janelle knew it to be for the best.

"Any reason you're leaving?"

"My agent called. There are a few jobs she thinks might be perfect for me, not to mention the swimsuit cover shoot coming up next month in Saint Thomas. It's easier being closer to my agent when jobs come up. I thought maybe I'd head for my apartment in the city."

Janelle smiled. "You mean your shoebox?"

"An awfully expensive shoebox." Rocky laughed, but Janelle detected a note of sadness in her tone. "Granted, my apartment here is three times the size, but it's not in New York City either. I was hoping we could get together before I leave."

"When are you heading out?"

"In three days."

Janelle looked out across the endless horizon. "I don't think I can make that happen, Rocky. I'm sorry. It's just this case—"

"I get it. We'll catch up later next week by phone."

"You know I hate that."

Rocky chuckled again, this time the sound much lighter. "We both have jobs. Love you, bestie."

"Love you too. Safe travels."

"You stay safe yourself," Rocky said and the line went dead.

Rocky never was one to say "Goodbye." And she had always hung up before Janelle could say the words. Janelle supposed her best friend was correct. Goodbye carried a final connotation. Rocky tended to take shoots to tropical locations during the winter months, flying back to the West Coast in the spring. Who could blame her? Oregon was heading into the coldest part of the year. Janelle shivered just thinking about the coming snow and pulled her sweater tighter around her, warding off the chill.

Rocky would also be far away from Smoke and the rest of the bikers she seemed drawn to and that was a good thing. Hopefully, before Rocky made her way back, she'd have a new obsession, one far less dangerous. A last look across the blue horizon, Janelle turned, slid open one side of the sliding glass wall and walked back into the house.

"Could you leave it open?" India asked from her seated position near the doors. She rested one hand on her extended belly. "The ocean calms me."

"Absolutely." Janelle couldn't help being curious. "When are you due?"

"Any day." The dark beauty smiled. Her chocolate-colored skin was flawless. India could certainly walk runways with Rocky, she was that beautiful. "Not soon enough. Xander tells me I'm too anxious because once the little guy arrives, we won't get a moment's peace."

"I suppose that's true." Janelle laughed. "But I'm sure you're anxious to be a mother."

Her smile widened. The warmth of it flooded her dark gaze. "I can't wait to cuddle him. I feel like I've already been waiting for a lifetime."

"She had a miscarriage first time around," Alexander provided. "The first trimester of this pregnancy she was a complete wreck."

"So…" Janelle glanced around the room and noted Adriana's absence along with Gabby's. The last thing she needed was her big mouth spilling the beans to Adri. "Vampires can have miscarriages?"

Alexander sat on the arm of the chair where India reclined and wrapped his arm around her shoulders. "Not that I'm aware. Our DNA allows us to heal at a rapid rate, so I would assume the same would go for our unborn son. Her miscarriage was with an old flame."

India grunted, smacking him with the back of her hand and making Janelle wonder about the story. "Not even close. He was a psycho. This baby is born out of love."

"Of course. Anyone can see the love you two share. I'm curious, though, he's born a vampire?"

"Technically, he's a true blood. He won't develop into his vampire genes until around the age of sixteen or later." Alexander looked down and rubbed India's belly before continuing. "I developed mine much later. There's no time limit when that happens. But the children grow up much like human babies. They survive on breast milk and when they get a bit older, they eat normal food. At some point, that will no longer satisfy their needs and they'll develop their bloodthirst."

"I suppose born into it they would know no other way, making it seem" —Janelle shuddered, unable to hide her reaction to the idea of drinking blood— "somehow normal."

India adjusted her position, seemingly uncomfortable. It had to be hard to get comfy while a baby lay on your bladder and other organs. Her protruding belly moved, causing India to giggle before her mouth rounded.

Alexander looked at his mate with concern. "You okay, *gattina*?"

India breathed slowly through her pursed lips, then ran her tongue along them. "Just a sharp pain. I'm sure it was nothing."

Alexander looked more than a little worried as he stood and knelt before her chair, resting his hands on her bent knees. "Do you need me to get you anything? Blood—"

"Oh, please, I'm fine…" She sucked in air again. "This can't be happening. Not now."

"What is it? The baby?"

"I think he's coming." India cried out in obvious pain, her hand resting at the top of her belly. She glanced at Alexander and started breathing deeply. "We got this, right?"

A smile lit his handsome face. "We sure do, *gattina*."

Janelle watched as everything began to unfold, wondering why no one was calling for a squad or heading for a vehicle to take her to the hospital. They did have something other than a motorcycle, right? India was in no shape to get on the back of one. Wait, she did see a car in the drive when she had arrived with Ryder and Preacher.

"Who should I call? What hospital is near here?" Janelle asked.

Alexander turned his head, giving her his brief attention. "We don't need a doctor. I've delivered babies before. We can't chance they'll run tests on our DNA. Do me a favor and get me some towels and hot water."

"What? You can't think to—"

"Towels?" His curt reply put her in action, looking for the nearest bathroom.

"I don't know where they are. I'll get Gabby." Janelle was about to look for her when Gabby and Adriana came running into the living room from the outside deck, out of breath. Adriana's complexion had drained of color as if she had seen a ghost.

Alexander looked up as India's pains seemed to momentarily subside. "What's up?"

"Adri thought she saw Mateo," Gabby said. "There was a huge yacht just offshore and she was positive it was the one belonging to her ex."

"You want me to have a look?" Alexander stood. "Someone needs to stay with India, but I'll go check it out."

Gabby's mouth dropped as she looked to India. "You're in labor?"

"I was having pains, but they're gone for now." She gripped Alexander's hand. "Go. See what's going on. I'll be fine."

Alexander held her gaze a moment longer, then headed out to the deck followed by Janelle. "You should stay indoors. Vlad will have my ass if anything happens to you."

"It's Adri's ex, so that's the immediate concern. Not Vlad's brother."

Looking offshore, there was a mega yacht moored several hundred feet away. It wasn't close enough to be troubling at present, but it was there just the same.

"Should I call someone? Maybe alert the DEA if you know for sure it's cartel-related?"

"Until I see the bastard, I'm not sure he's of concern." Alexander ran a hand through his hair. "Gabby and Adriana were careful not to publicize where Adri was living. They didn't want Mateo finding her. So unless the bastard steps on the grounds, I can't be sure he knows she's even here, nor do I want to alert him of her whereabouts. Let's get back inside and lock up, just in case."

Janelle followed Alexander back into the living room. He turned and closed the glass wall of doors and slipped the lock. "Gabby, make sure all the doors and windows are secured, just in case the bastard comes this way. Unless we know he's aware of Adriana's whereabouts, we can't be sure he's here for her."

Adriana nodded. "I agree. I might be overreacting."

Alexander laid a hand on her shoulder. "You need to tell us when you suspect anything. I don't want to be caught unaware, Adri. It's better to know than be left in the dark."

India cried out again, both hands on her stomach as she bore down. Alexander looked at Gabby. "Towels? Hot water?"

She ran off to do his bidding while Adriana paled again. Alexander knelt at India's feet and spread her thighs. "My baby boy is on his way."

CHAPTER EIGHTEEN

GABBY RETURNED QUICKLY, HANDING ALEXANDER THE RE-quested items, and none too soon. India cried out again, bending forward and bearing down. Sweat beaded her brow and upper lip. Alexander looked up at his wife in adoration. There was no doubt this man loved his mate heart and soul as he soothed her with whispered words of encouragement.

The birthing process seemed to progress at a rapid pace, more so than humanly possible, probably due to their vampire genetics. Good thing they hadn't been en route to the nearest hospital. Surely, they wouldn't have made it out of the driveway.

"I see the head, *gattina*. One more push."

Janelle stared in awe. Gone was all thought of Adriana's ex possibly being in the vicinity as they witnessed the small miracle of a baby being brought into the world. It amazed Janelle how much these paranormal creatures were still human.

India did as instructed and moments later the tiny infant slid into Alexander's capable hands. Gabby handed him a pair of scissors that had been sterilized with a good dose of whiskey to cut the umbilical cord. Janelle assumed the cord would easily heal itself since the baby had his parents' DNA, nor did Alexander bother with clamping it off.

It wasn't long before the infant was wrapped in a small blanket and placed into India's arms. Tears gathered in India's dark eyes as she looked upon her wailing baby boy. She cooed and whispered to the child, soothing him with her voice. The calmed infant nuzzled against her chest, closed his eyes, and made a sucking motion with his lips.

Gabby and Adriana took the soiled cloths from Alexander and helped him quickly clean up the mess. Janelle, however, couldn't take her eyes off the child. He was perfect, right down to his ten little fingers and toes and rounded head. He seemed human in every way. It was a ridiculous notion that the baby might come out sporting fangs, even if Janelle fought the urge to look.

Alexander stood and circled the chair. Placing a hand on India's shoulder, he stared in wonder at the tiny baby.

Suddenly, Janelle felt as if she was intruding on their private moment. "I'm going out to the deck to give you two some privacy."

Glancing at her, Alexander said, "We've secured the house and I'm pretty sure Gabby turned on the alarms. It'd be best if you stayed inside."

"Then I'll join Gabby and Adri in the kitchen."

Janelle just missed getting hit by the swinging door as the women came running through, skidding to a halt. Gabby damn near screamed the word, "Smoke."

Alexander's nose tipped up. "Jesus."

He left India's side and ran toward the kitchen and pushed open the door. The acrid smoke rolled through the opened doorway, stopping him from entering. Turning, he headed for the other side of the house. Thick black smoke already billowed down the long hallway, blackening the white walls.

Janelle's eyes burned as the rapidly spreading fire trapped them in the living area, giving them only two ways to exit. Janelle guessed it to be Adriana's ex, Mateo, and his men, orchestrating their moves. Should they leave the house from either direction, surely they'd be ambushed.

"Christ! I fucked up!" Alexander moved from the hall to the glass wall looking out onto the deck, staying just out of sight.

Janelle knew the rocky oceanfront couldn't be seen without standing on the edge of the deck and looking down. There was no way to see who waited at the bottom of the steps.

She needed to think quick before the entire house went up with them in it. Janelle turned to Gabby. "Is there another way out, other than the obvious?"

"Yes." A smile appeared on her face, one Janelle was surprised she could muster with her multi-million dollar home burning down around them. "There's an underground pathway that goes to the guesthouse where Adriana stays."

"Seriously?" Alexander helped India to her feet, not bothering to question the logistics of a tunnel or the need for one. "Show us."

"Follow me." Gabby turned and headed for the basement stairway.

214 | PATRICIA A. RASEY

The strong scent of gasoline mixed with the stench of smoke made seeing and breathing more difficult by the second. They quickly took the stairs down. Being the last through, Janelle closed the door behind them.

"Why in the world is there an underground tunnel to the guesthouse?" Janelle wondered aloud.

"Well, thank the good Lord there is one," India said, cuddling her baby close to her breasts.

They made their way to the back wall of the basement. Gabby reached behind a stack of books on a shelf, pulled a lever, and the built-in bookcase slid quietly open. The cement underground tunnel automatically illuminated. Once they were all safely tucked inside, Gabby pulled another lever on the wall and the case slid shut behind them.

She turned and led the troop through the tunnel. "Rumor was the man who built this house had it put in so he could visit his mistress while his wife slept. Apparently, he was dicking the nanny. It was never discovered until he died of a heart attack in the nanny's bed. The woman was so distraught she confessed everything to the wife. The previous owner had the entire place renovated, but left the tunnel. He related the tale to Adriana and me when I was house hunting."

"Well, thank fuck for his insight," Alexander growled.

Reaching the end of the corridor, Gabby pressed another button that swung open the door at the end. The five of them and the baby quickly passed through and traveled up the steps.

Alexander stopped at the entrance to the guesthouse. "Stay here until I see the coast is clear. These fucks likely already scouted this place and found no one to be here, but I don't want to take the chance they're watching the place."

He slipped through the door, letting it close softly behind him. Adriana's hands trembled as she tried to maintain a semblance of calm. Her face paled whiter than a sheet.

Tears streamed down her face as she worried her lower lip. "I should try to talk to Mateo since I'm the reason they're here."

"What? No!" Gabby swung around to meet Adriana's gaze. "You can't be serious?"

"My God, Gabby! They're burning down your house. Don't you see? Mateo will stop at nothing to get me back. He'll kill all of you if he has to. I should've stayed in Mexico. I'm so sorry."

"No!" Anger flared in Gabby's eyes. "You have nothing to be sorry for. This is the bastard's fault, not yours. You're safe as long as you're with us. Alexander is capable of getting us out of here."

"He's one man against an army. It's hard telling how many men Mateo brought with him." Adriana gripped Gabby's hands. "Let me go to him—"

Alexander opened the door, blood dripping from his hands and forearms. His shirt was splattered in crimson. "Let's go."

Adriana dropped Gabby's hand and covered her mouth at the sight of so much blood. Her eyes widened in shock, rendering her immobile.

Gabby gripped her shoulder, shaking her and getting Adriana's attention. "Let's go, Adri. Look at me, not Xander."

Adriana slowly nodded.

Following Alexander into the guesthouse and out the back door, the five of them stole through the woods. Alexander brought up the rear, keeping an eye on their surroundings. Thankfully, they had managed to clear the guesthouse undetected. Janelle counted three dead cartel soldiers lying face down in the dirt near the exit. Their death they deserved, but she shuddered nonetheless. What seemed like an hour later, they came to a clearing in the forest where a roadway parted the trees.

"I'll call Wolf. He can come to get us. We need to stay out of sight until he gets here with the box truck." Alexander stepped over to India, placing a bloodied hand on the crown of his son's head. "Are you both okay?"

"We're fine. I had faith in you." She smiled, despite the discord her baby had been born into. "I think I have the perfect name for him."

Alexander leaned down and placed a brief kiss on the baby's forehead. "What is it, *gattina*?"

"Chase," India said. "Since he was born amidst the cartel setting us up."

One side of his lips curved up. "More like chaos."

India laid her free palm against Alexander's cheek. "You can use Chaos as his biker name should he stay in the life. But I think I like Chase better."

"Oh, he'll stay in the life." Alexander chuckled. "I have no doubt. As for Chase, it's perfect."

MATEO TOOK HOLD OF THE stainless-steel ladder and climbed aboard his anchored mega yacht from the tender they had used to go ashore. His anger simmered beneath the surface as they set to pull the anchor with three fewer of his men. Christ, their murder had been brutal even for his standards. He wasn't sure what the son of a bitch used to tear out their throats. Or how he had managed to get to all three without one of them firing off a single round, alerting the rest that there had been a problem. It was as if the phantom killer wasn't human but some kind of fucking ghost.

Hell, Mateo hadn't had the time to check to see if the occupants, more specifically Adriana, had made it out alive before sirens sounded in the near distance. He'd bet they had all survived judging by his fallen soldiers, though he had no clue as to how they had managed the feat. Mateo and his men had covered all possible escape routes and yet the five occupants had fled without further detection.

His men had barely enough time to round up the corpses and throw them into the tender. Leaving the bodies behind wasn't an option as it might have given the authorities enough evidence to suspect the cartel. Enough accelerant had been used to warrant an arson investigation, proving it was no accidental fire.

The last of the bodies had been hoisted up and loaded into the stern of his yacht. Mateo wasn't happy having to bring them along. Blood and filth now marred his deck. He detested disorder and foul matter, ensuring a trip to the marina for a good scrubbing once they returned.

Motioning for the captain of the boat to start the engines, Mateo planned to be far offshore before the fire department arrived. They'd be too busy trying to extinguish the flames to note a yacht out to sea. His men raised the anchor and the engine came to life.

Within short order, they were headed away from shore … without Adriana.

Fury over leaving without his absent fiancée licked up his spine, just as the flames had climbed the walls of Gabriela's estate. The bitch was at fault. She had convinced Adriana to leave Mexico and him behind; Mateo had no doubt. He'd see Gabriela paid for her slight. But first, he needed Adriana by his side. Either willingly or kicking and screaming the entire way, he didn't care.

Heads would roll for this fuck up.

Mateo wasn't known for being forgiving.

The plan had been to get in, burn the fucking house down, and drive the occupants out via the front or back of the estate where he and his men waited. Once they had Adriana in hand, they were to eliminate the others. Since his informants had reported that Adriana had been staying in the guesthouse, the now-dead soldiers had been ordered to watch the exit. He had hoped to catch her coming out of the residence once the smell of acrid smoke reached her.

The fact all the home's occupants had been in the guest-house had not been anticipated. Mateo's gaze traveled to one of his men, now overlooking the horizon. Joseph had overseen scoping out the houses before the crew had arrived. It had been his job to report back how many were in residence and where they congregated. No one had been seen leaving the main house in favor of the guesthouse, telling Mateo that Joseph's report had been false.

Mateo gritted his teeth, seething because of his man's fuck up. Joseph was the reason Adriana was not currently at his side. To let it go unpunished showed weakness.

Taking the steps to the bridge, Mateo found his captain behind the panel of instruments. Mateo strode forward, stopped in front of the bank of windows and took in the vast ocean. They were alone; no other boat could be seen for miles. Whitecaps topped the waves but the boat barely swayed as it easily cut through the water. Within moments, they'd be far enough out from the west coast that the boat would no longer be visible to the naked eye. His mega yacht could travel at speeds of seventy knots, about eighty miles per hour, covering a lot of water in short order.

Mateo clasped his hands behind his back. "Once we get far enough offshore, and the coast is no longer visible, stop the boat but don't cut the engine."

The captain nodded his affirmation. "Would you like me to have the men drop anchor?"

"No." Mateo smiled. Delivering due diligence pleased him. "Let the boat coast for a bit. I'll let you know when we can head back down the coast."

Mateo felt the yacht pick up speed as he turned and headed back down the stairs to the stern where several of his men now lounged, Modelos in hand. Christ, he had a notion to throw the whole lot of them overboard. The three corpses lay to the opposite side of the boat, waiting to be tossed over for shark chum.

The men talked and laughed among themselves as if they hadn't just fucked up their boss's plan to get his fiancée back, further agitating Mateo. He ignored the men, stood at the back and watched the coast disappear. A smile pulled up the corners of his lips as he felt the boat slow. Soon, they coasted on the waves of the Pacific.

Mateo turned and looked at Joseph. "Toss them overboard."

"Seriously?" The man didn't bother rising from his seat. "We could take them home, give them to their families for a proper burial."

Mateo closed the gap, grabbed the man by his collar, and yanked him to his feet. "I gave you an order."

Joseph's gaze widened, obviously realizing his faux pas. "I was just—"

Mateo's backhand jerked Joseph's head to the side. Blood splattered from his nose. "Toss the *hijos de puta* overboard."

"Sir." He nodded, grabbing the feet of one of the corpses, struggling to do as he was told.

One of the others quickly jumped to his feet to assist but Mateo held out a hand. The son of a bitch would wrestle the bodies on his own. It was Joseph's fuck up, so it was his to fix. The fool grumbled beneath his breath as he tussled with the heavy weight of each corpse but eventually managed to throw the last body over the rail with a final splash.

Blood marred the once pristine surface of the deck.

"Clean up the fucking mess." One of his men quickly jumped to his feet. Mateo caught him by the forearm and whispered into his ear. "When I go to the inside to the bar to get a tequila, toss Joseph over. Tell the captain to head south until I give him further instructions. The rest of you may then join me once the deed is done"

The man only nodded, keeping his opinion wisely to himself.

Mateo turned and headed through the sliding glass doors. He heard the scuffle behind him, and the final cry as Joseph was tossed overboard. A smile lit his face as he reached for the bottle of Patrón and poured himself a shot.

CHAPTER NINETEEN

THE CLUBHOUSE BUZZED WITH ACTIVITY AND CONVERSA-tion as Vlad and his twin grandsons entered. Irritation and outrage sluiced through him at not finding Mircea yet again. The *nenorocitule* had become a specter, one that was bent on agitating him to no end. He wasn't about to sit idle long, not when he needed to get back out there and hunt the rat bastard down. Mircea's luck couldn't hold out forever. Hell, Vlad would still be in pursuit had the news of Gabriela's house burning down, the exact one he had dispatched Janelle to, not been relayed to Kane.

Thankfully, the reassurance that no one had been hurt came swiftly on the heels of the report. He'd personally kill the son of a bitch who put Janelle in danger right after he took care of his brother. This man, Mateo, wouldn't have to worry about the Sons of Sangue, not when he had just landed himself as runner-up on Vlad's hit list.

Her whiskey-warm voice soothed over him, bringing his interest to the small living area and sofas. Janelle held a baby in the crook of her arm, cooing to the tiny tot as though she didn't have a care in the world and hadn't just survived a fucking conflagration.

She looked up at his approach and smiled. "Isn't he precious?"

Vlad's gaze briefly left hers, long enough to take in the infant with a dark crown of hair. "Yes," was his curt reply before he leaned down, scooped up the infant and handed him to the woman to her right. "I need to speak with you."

Janelle's gaze widened, telling Vlad he was about to get a verbal whiplash. He didn't give two fucks, not with his anger smoldering deep inside. Christ, he could have lost her. "Outside."

She did as asked and followed him to the adjoining parking lot. Vlad didn't bother leaving parting words for his grandsons. He'd see them again soon enough. Leading her to his Aston Martin, he opened the door and indicated that she should get in. Janelle grabbed the door and pushed it closed. Crossing her arms over her chest, she stood defiant.

The rise of her eyebrow told him her opinion on his high-handedness. "What the hell is wrong with you?"

He scratched his nape and grimaced. "Me?"

"I'm not yours to order around."

"Look—"

"No." Janelle slapped a palm against his immovable chest. He felt the hit much harder to the softer muscle in his chest, his heart. It hadn't been his intention to infuriate her, and yet he had. "You want to tell me what this is about?"

"I needed to see you were okay."

"So you see." She put her arms out to the side. "I'm going back inside."

He gripped her forearm. "Give me a moment."

Her jaw clenched; her gaze narrowed at him. "You have exactly one minute."

Vlad ran a hand down his bearded jaw. Sucking in a deep breath, he attempted to calm his amped-up emotions. Man-handling a headstrong woman would get him nowhere. And the truth of it was, he wouldn't have her any other way.

Her narrowed gaze told him he'd need to grovel. Had it been any other woman, Vlad would've walked away. He didn't beg for mercy from anyone and especially not a woman.

"Look" —he raised his hand and brushed a spot of soot from her cheek with his knuckle— "I was worried when I heard about the fire."

"I'm fine."

"I'll have Xander's ass for this," he growled more to him-self rather than to be heard. "He was to protect you."

"He did a great job of that. I'm alive with not one hair harmed."

"He should have anticipated the coming threat."

"Really?" She chuckled bitterly. "He was a bit busy with the birth of his son, you ass. The way I see it, you should be thanking him. Had it not been for him killing the bastards guarding the guesthouse where we made our escape, we'd be on our way to Mexico, or worse yet … dead."

Janelle wasn't helping the fire burning inside him. Her words stoked it back to life. "Fine," he snapped. "He saved you. I'll be sure to thank him for that."

"Vlad…" she warned.

"Get in the car."

"Excuse me?"

"Please … get in the car. I'll be right back." He raised a hand to stop the objection her opened mouth promised. "I will only thank him. You're right. I owe him that."

Thankfully, she did as asked before he headed back into the clubhouse. All eyes turned on him as he strode in, boots clomping heavily against the wood flooring. Vlad supposed he had been a bit of an ass upon arrival. Alexander now sat beside his mate and their baby.

Vlad cleared his throat. "I was rude. Please accept my thank you for taking good care of Janelle. And—congratulations on the baby. You did a fantastic job protecting the women, considering the situation."

A grin quirked up one side of Alexander's lips. The bastard was enjoying his kowtowing. "You're quite welcome. Mateo will pay for his actions."

"I'm sure, just as my brother will once I catch up to the cagey bastard." Vlad turned to Kane and Kaleb. "I'll be in touch."

"Call us when you're ready to resume the hunt," said Kaleb.

Vlad nodded then left the clubhouse, thankful to find Janelle had done as requested, though she now sat in the driver's seat of his Aston. Wisely, he opened the passenger seat and sat down, securing the belt.

"May I ask why you're driving?"

She giggled. "I've been dying to drive your car. Where to?"

Vlad smiled his humor. "My penthouse. I believe we have unfinished business."

The rising scent of her desire tickled his nose. "Glad you hadn't forgotten."

The car slid into reverse. She backed up before circling the parking lot and pulling out onto the paved road. Hitting the gas, the Aston Martin lurched forward.

He glanced over at her, his cock hardening and making the belt crossing his lap uncomfortable. "Forgot? Not a chance."

Janelle's smile held a promise that left him hot for an entirely different reason. "Too bad I'm driving or I'd make the trip a bit more enjoyable."

"Christ," he mumbled. "The pedal to the floor, you little minx."

VLAD'S FINGERS FUMBLED ON the lock of the secured door to his rented penthouse. It was as if he were a bumbling schoolboy all over again and not a seasoned vampire who had bedded numerous women over the past few centuries. Shoving the door open, he entered with Janelle. The unlocked panel banged off the interior wall and rattled the cheap art hanging beside it.

Gripping Janelle by the shoulders, he pushed her against the entry, his mouth slanting over hers.

Janelle fisted his shirt and pulled him forward, sliding her tongue over the seal of his lips. Her boldness spiked his hunger. Releasing his grip, Vlad slipped his fingers into her silky hair and cupped her skull, then opened to her and deepened the kiss. His erection bumped against the softness of her abdomen as he leaned into her, anchoring her against the cool steel door.

Fuck, he wanted her clothes gone so he could feel every smooth inch of her. Reaching for the hem of her sweater, he broke the kiss long enough to push the white knit up and over her head, tossing it to the marble entryway. He covered her mouth again, shoving his tongue past her lips, eliciting a moan. Vlad had waited far too long to take it easy.

He wanted a fast, hard fuck.

Pulling down the cups of her smoke-colored lace bra, he palmed her breasts. Her nipples pebbled against his large, callused hands, telling him she was just as eager, nearly snapping his carefully tethered control. Never had he felt so frenzied with longing … not until Janelle. Vlad broke the kiss again before dipping his head to lave one of the pink, pert nipples with the flat of his tongue. Scraping the tender flesh with his fangs, he fought the urge to sink them gum-deep.

Christ, he craved another taste of her honeyed blood.

Drinking from her before had been reckless and irresponsible. Vlad knew the rules, knew the reasons why humans were kept in the dark. Hell, he had made the rules. And yet, she had broken his iron will. Vlad had caved and tasted the aphrodisiac, making him thirst for more. Only a fucking miracle would keep him from doing so again.

Thankfully, no other room opened onto the penthouse floor because he had no intention of stopping long enough to close the door she leaned against. No, he intended on fucking her right where they stood. He had waited long enough.

Vlad's thick fingers seemed nearly worthless as he attempted to undo the small button on her jeans. No woman had ever affected him to the point of inadequacy. Vlad prided himself on his dexterity and ability to please women. His talents were legendary if one listened to the tales of those he had fucked in the past. But Janelle was different. Not since his late wife had he felt the emotional attachment that came with making love. That damn useless organ in his chest felt near to bursting.

Unacceptable.

Janelle wasn't his to have. He was a vampire, for chrissake. Love had no business entering into whatever this was between them. Too fucking late. When she left, she'd rip his heart out of his chest, though he'd die before ever telling her as much. Janelle had a place in this world. He couldn't ask her to leave that to enter his.

She brushed his hands aside and slipped the button free from the hole, then drew down the zipper with a soft rasp. Vlad pushed the denim past her hips, taking the gray lacy panties with it. Janelle toed off her flats before stepping out of the cotton and lace. Her bra followed, leaving her gloriously naked. Fuck, she was more stunning than anything he had seen in all his centuries. She had soft curves in some places and muscles honed from training in others. The perfect combination. Her long lean legs were perfect for wrapping his waist. She seemed fitted for his larger frame, not some waif he feared he'd break.

"Is everything okay, big guy?" Janelle chuckled. "Or do I need to get dressed? It's a bit chilly—"

"Hell, no." His deep voice echoed about the white sterile room. The cleaning staff was quite efficient. "I was taking in the view. I'm in awe of your beauty."

Janelle looked to her toes.

Using the pad of his thumb, he brought her gaze up. "Christ, you take my fucking breath away."

Her ocean-blue eyes twinkled. "I'm pretty sure I've not heard those words from anyone to describe me before."

"Then they were fucking idiots."

Vlad clasped the base of her skull and brought his mouth back to hers. Renewed hunger blazed inside him like molten lava streaming through his veins. Her naked form melded against his still-clothed one and it was one hell of a turn-on. He swore because of her he could live his life without ever desiring or fucking another. Unfortunately, he might just have to, because he'd never allow Janelle to sacrifice her career and live a life damned with him.

Reaching down, he gripped her leg behind the knee and wrapped his waist with it. His cock lay trapped between them, pulsing against her wet center. Vlad ground against her, desiring to feel her gripping him. The patience to remove even a single article of clothing escaped him. He wanted to fuck her like the beast he was.

Reaching between them, he flipped the button of his pants and pulled down the zipper. Wearing no underwear, he easily freed his erection. The pert-pink tongue that darted out to wet her lips as she looked down upon him in hunger undid him. Vlad caught her about the hips, picked her up, and wrapped his waist with both of her long legs. Anchoring her to the door, he parted her folds and slicked his erection. Resting the tip at her center, he held her gaze just before sliding into her and seating himself to the hilt.

He didn't want to move, not when she fisted his cock like a glove. Nothing had ever felt so close to nirvana. Had someone ended his life at this moment, he'd die a happy, though not entirely satisfied man. Ecstasy was but a few thrusts away and he wasn't about to deny himself. If he had only a short time with Janelle, he planned to enjoy every fucking second of being inside her.

Her red lips parted, sucking in oxygen as he began to move. He couldn't remain still a moment longer, not with his climax gripping his balls like a vise. Every muscle tightened as he increased his pace, thrust for thrust, sending her back sliding up the steel door behind her. She was his every fucking fantasy come to life. Vlad wouldn't last long, not when her inner walls clutched him, damn near milking him. His climax built, heating his balls and throbbing at the base of his cock. Vlad wanted to hold out. He gritted his teeth, tilted his head to the ceiling, and cried out in anguish. Janelle Ferrari had broken him. There would never be another woman for him. Not now, not in a hundred more centuries.

Vlad dipped his head, slanted his mouth over hers, and sealed his fate to centuries of loneliness, pining away for the one woman he could never have. His immortality and existence had finally come full circle and damned him. Jesus, he'd wish for death knowing she was out of his league.

His muscles stiffened with his oncoming climax. Vlad hastened his thrusts, reaching for the edging apex. Breaking the kiss, he looked into her passion-filled gaze and lost his feeble tether. His orgasm began to pulse through him, sending him spiraling over the precipice.

Janelle cried out, reaching her own peak. She tilted her head to the ceiling, exposing her slender neck to him. Dear Lord, it was the most beautiful and tempting thing in the world; the one he'd deny himself. Vlad wasn't about to leave her with regrets, like him having tapped her artery yet again. She might not think it now, but down the road, she'd look back upon their union in revulsion. After all, he was a fucking vampire. This stunning woman would never know that she had captured the beast's heart, and he'd do his damnedest to keep it that way.

CHAPTER TWENTY

JANELLE ROLLED OVER, TUCKING INTO VLAD'S SIDE AS HE LAY on his back, glossy-black hair fanning across his pillow. He stretched one muscular arm around her back and pulled her in tight. Sex-snuggling wasn't something she normally did and she'd bet it wasn't Vlad's MO either. And yet, he didn't look even remotely ready to kick her out. After the hot-as-hell sex against the door, Vlad had closed it, then carried her to his large bed where he had finally removed his clothing, making love to her twice more before she had fallen into an easy slumber.

Something in his demeanor had changed from the entry-way. Once they entered the suite's bedroom and he had laid her upon the duvet, he no longer seemed impulsive or hurried. If she hadn't known better, she'd swear emotions had gotten as tangled up as the sheets. Vlad treated her as if she were precious, maybe even loved.

Crazy.

With all the women Vlad had no doubt slept with in his past, it was insane to think she would be the one to win the king of vampires. He probably had his own harem waiting for him when the mission to find and kill his brother ended.

She trailed her fingers lazily over the light dusting of hair on his chest. Her emotions were the ones getting tied up and no doubt messing with her. In all probability, any affection Vlad had for her would end once he tired of the sex.

Besides, the man was centuries old. Janelle wasn't cut out for his world, even if the idea of blood-drinking no longer repulsed her. Her stupid heart, though, had to get on the same page as her brain. It had gone and fallen in love with him, impossible complications and all. Janelle would be a fool, though, to ever admit as much. When this battle he fought ended, he'd go back to his home, leaving her and her world behind. Vlad didn't strike her as the forever kind, even if Janelle thought it might be remotely possible to continue seeing each other.

"Something has you fidgeting?"

She smiled against his chest. "It's all good."

"Good?" He chuckled, the deep sound rumbling against her ear. "Do I need to be offended? Or maybe I need to show you again just how *great* it is."

"That's not what I meant." Janelle tugged on his chest hair and looked up at his dark gaze. "It was much better than good. I meant lying here with you, it feels good."

He tightened his hold, his lips curving. "I wish I didn't have places to be or I'd suggest not leaving this bed for days."

"Your brother?" A nod was her answer. "You want to talk about him?"

Vlad shifted beneath her. "There's nothing to talk about. I find him, I'll kill him. No mercy this time."

Janelle placed her palm against his whiskered cheek. "You're tormented. I can tell something is eating at you, Vlad. You don't want to end his life, do you?"

Vlad's gaze darkened, unable to hide his affliction. "It doesn't matter, *iubi*. I'll do what I should have done months ago."

"Talk to me, Vlad." He tried to look away, but she brought back his gaze. "Talk to me."

His chest shuddered from his indrawn breath. "Christ, *iubi*, it kills me inside to know I have to take his life, but I've given Mircea one too many chances. He's proven that he's not redeemable."

"Have you told anyone else how you feel?"

Vlad shook his head, the movement rustling the pillowcase beneath his head. "I have to be strong… No, I *am* strong enough to see this through. Me" —he tapped his chest— "not anyone else."

"Why?"

"Because I have to be the one. He's my brother. I can't lay that on anyone else's doorstep. What if I'd wind up resenting them? No, this is on me and I'll do what needs to be done."

She licked her lips. "Then you'll come back here?"

He nodded. And her heart ached for him and what he had to do. No one should have to kill their sibling, even if their deeds were worthy of the sentence.

"When do you need to leave?"

"Probably hours ago." His arm tightened around her. "As soon as I get someone over here to watch you."

Janelle pushed off his chest, holding the sheet to her naked breasts. "You aren't responsible for me. Besides, your brother doesn't have the slightest idea where to find me even if his threat could be taken seriously."

"Oh, he's serious, *iubi*. Don't doubt that." He traced her lower lip with his thumb. "I won't allow him to hurt you."

"I know you won't. You'll get to him first. I have faith in you." Janelle took in a deep breath before hedging over the elephant in the room. "Once you catch him, then what?"

His brow furrowed. "Life goes on."

It pained her that he was so willing to move on without her. "You've said before that outsiders can't know about you or the other vampires. You can't hypnotize me into forgetting, Vlad. What about leaving me behind?"

"Will you tell our secret?"

"Of course not."

"And I believe you. To do so might mean my death and I know you would protect me as I would you." He looked away. "My life, *iubi*… It's complicated."

Janelle gripped his short-bearded chin and forced his gaze back. If he was going to tell her he was leaving, then he'd damn well look at her when he did so. "So, what? You'll just walk away?"

"There can't be an us. Surely, you know that."

Moisture filled her eyes, but she held back the sting of his words. Janelle wasn't one to beg, no matter how much it would hurt when he left. "You'll say a final goodbye?"

"I'm not an ogre." Vlad swore a string of curse words before gripping her shoulders. "Christ, Janelle, I care. You have to know that."

"Then tell me how you feel, Vlad. Or am I just another fling?"

He stood from the bed, giving her his muscular backside before stepping into his jeans. There was anger in his movements as he pulled them over his hips. Janelle had pushed him too hard. Her chest ached at his sudden retreat.

Pulling the phone from his pocket, Vlad looked at the display then slid his thumb over the screen. Dialing a number, he then placed the phone next to his ear. "Where are you?" he asked.

Really? He was going to ignore her now that she had demanded an answer? Obviously, she cared more about him than he was fond of her. Janelle slid to the side of the bed and padded through the bedroom and into the living room where she had left her clothes. Vlad's mumblings carried to her ears, telling her he was still on the phone as she dressed. If she just left…

"Where are you going?" Vlad stood shirtless, jeans hanging deliciously low on his hips, just beyond the bedroom door staring at her, phone gripped in his hand at his side.

It angered Janelle how much she still cared and desired him, but she could no longer take their verbal dance. "It's time, Vlad. You're needed, I get that. But so am I. I'm a damn good special agent and it's time I get back to my job."

Before she could grab the handle, Vlad stood between her and the door—faster than humanly possible. Even though she knew he had special abilities, it still startled her. Vlad could keep her from leaving, but instead of being forceful he ran a knuckle down her cheek.

"I have to go, *iubi*. I missed Kane's call, which is why I called him back. They found my brother's vampires' hideout. The Sons are waiting on me."

"Is your brother there?"

He shook his head. "Kane feels as though he'll show. They have captured one of his minions who's agreed to lure Mircea there in exchange for his life. My brother's curiosity will dictate his actions. He'll show up."

Janelle wet her lips but remained silent.

"You'll wait?"

Even though it pained her, she said, "I need to go home, Vlad."

"And I need you to be safe."

"I'll be fine. Go find your brother."

"Promise me you'll stay put." When she didn't agree, he said, "Kane has already sent Ryder on his way over to watch over you. He'll likely be here before I'm even out of the building."

Janelle all but groaned over her weakness to refuse Vlad. She needed to stay, a glutton for punishment that she was, to see this through. Blowing out a shaky breath, she said, "Fine. I'll stay put."

"We'll talk when I get back."

Vlad turned, opened the door to the penthouse, and left. Janelle quickly bolted the door, though she doubted it would hold one of his kind. Suddenly hungry, she headed for the kitchen, hoping for something other than bags of blood to be stocked in the refrigerator. Otherwise, Vlad would be paying for room service from the lobby's restaurant.

Janelle was surprised to find an array of meats and cheeses, causing her stomach to growl. She pulled out the tray, along with a plastic jug of milk. Funny, she was actually thankful for the bit of time to herself. Since the beginning of this nightmare, Vlad hadn't given her a moment of peace, scared of what his brother might do if he caught up to her. Used to living on her own, Janelle was accustomed to the solitude.

Grabbing a glass from the open shelf, she then turned to the island where the milk sat. The glass slipped from her hand to the marble floor, sending shards of glass skittering across the marble tiles. Janelle gripped the stone countertop as the room she stood in began to fade and a vision took over.

Mircea stood in front of her, all scary-as-fuck fangs and crazed-black gaze, a vampire nearly as big and muscular as Vlad. Before she could run, he grabbed her biceps and turned her, banding a forearm across her chest. Janelle fought against him to no avail. Though she had been trained and had taken men his size, he easily rendered her immobile. Gripping her chin, he tilted her head so she had no choice but to look into the mirror-like gaze of a psychotic vampire.

Taking his free wrist to his lips, he sank in his long, white fangs and tore the flesh. Blood spurted from the opened vein before running down his arm to the worn-wooden flooring at their feet. Pulling down her chin and forcing her mouth open, Mircea took the open-wounded wrist to her lips. Metallic-flavored blood flowed past her lips and onto her tongue, making her nearly gag. Fire began to course through her veins. Dear, Lord, she felt as if she might internally combust.

What's happening?

Janelle blinked and the vision faded, leaving her standing alone in the middle of the shards of glass.

"What the hell?" she whispered to no one.

The ding of the elevator brought her focus back to the now, and her gaze swung to the entrance. No doubt Ryder had arrived for babysitting duty. She'd bet he wasn't too happy about drawing the short straw on this job. Janelle carefully stepped around the broken glass and headed for the entry when it imploded. The door sailed through the air aiming right for her. Janelle put her hands out to ward off the impact. Her thought right before she got run over by fifty-plus pounds of steel? *This is going to hurt.* And then her world went black.

A DIM BULB SWUNG FROM a thin, ratted cord, casting a soft glow about the dank and smelly cabin where she was being held. Janelle woke mere moments ago due to the stench, barely able to open her eyes without the room spinning and nausea setting in. Her head hurt like a son of a bitch, which spoke of a concussion, and the light wasn't helping. Keeping

her eyes closed helped, albeit a little. The last thing she remembered before everything went black was being hit by the
steel door.

Movement in the cabin and shuffling of feet had her lifting
her heavy eyelids again. The man from her recent visions
stood across the room, smiling. Vlad was correct, his brother
was a nutcase.

As luck would have it, Vlad hadn't been able to locate the
psycho, but she had. He stood mere feet away in what she
thought was as an old abandoned hunting cabin, probably so
far up in the woods no one would ever find them. She'd have
to rely on her wits if she were to walk out alive. Mircea, no
doubt, wasn't about to let that happen and probably planned
on using her to lure Vlad. Mircea wouldn't kidnap her just to
kill her. Nope, she was bait.

"You're awake."

His voice was deep, much like Vlad's. Janelle could see
a family resemblance, though Mircea looked more like a
snake oil salesman. A bit smarmy. His hair was short and
curled around his ears, but of the same rich color as his
brother's, shot through with a bit of gray.

Janelle nodded in response.

"Good."

He turned and opened one of the small windows, letting a
small amount of fresh air into the cabin, little good that it did.
Half the panes were either broken or missing, so it hadn't
made much of a difference. Night had fallen; the skies black

beyond the window. She shifted in the moth-eaten chair, unsure how long she had been out.

By now Vlad was surely aware she had gone missing, Ryder no doubt arriving shortly after Mircea had taken her and found the broken entry with Janelle gone. At least Vlad would know she hadn't left on her own and was possibly already out there looking for her.

"What…" Janelle croaked before wetting her lips and trying again. "What are you planning on doing with me?"

"My brother needs to pay for his years of arrogance."

"What's that have to do with" —she tried to clear her dry throat— "me?"

Mircea turned from the window and looked at her. Speaking of arrogance… He shrugged. "I want to make him suffer."

"Why?"

The muscles in his cheeks tautened. "Because he imprisoned me."

"You're free now." Janelle noted she wasn't tied to the chair, though it made little difference. He'd easily catch her, so she'd have to outwit him if she stood a chance of escaping. "Why can't you two just kiss and make up?"

Mircea moved so fast she hadn't seen the slap coming. Her head jerked to the side. "The fool took what was mine and now I will take what's his."

Janelle wiped the blood now leaking from her split lip with the back of her hand, then chuckled, minus the humor. "The joke's on you. He doesn't care what happens to me. Why do you think I was alone?"

Mircea bent down close enough that his horrid breath fanned the fine hairs on her face. Janelle suppressed the urge to be the first to withdraw. "Mind backing up and giving me a little space?"

"Aren't you a sassy one? I'm surprised my brother has taken a shining to you. His normal MO is meek little things that easily jump into his bed." He stood back and rubbed his clean-shaven chin. "Maybe that's it. You're a challenge to him."

"Why not let me go? I'll find Vlad and bring him to you." She turned her palms up. "Then we can all sit around like three adults and hash out this little family spat."

His smile returned with a chuckle. "His ego is far too big for there to be two of us."

"Two of you?"

"Yes. Only one of us can be king of the vampires, the one to call all the shots. Since he has a few years of this blood-sucking life over me, not to mention the fact he turned me and not the other way around, that makes him superior. Everyone listens to him as if he's a god. That is until I take his head."

"If you plan on killing him, then why am I here?"

He tapped his finger to his temple. "Because what fun would there be in simply ending his life? I'd rather take what's his and watch him go ballistic. And you, sweetheart, are what I think he holds dear."

"Back to that." Janelle groaned, the headache not subsiding in the least. "I don't belong to Vlad or anyone for that matter."

"No, but you will."

Her gaze snapped back to his, recalling her vision. Dear Lord in Heaven, this man thought to make her his by turning her. She would rather die before becoming one of his blood-drinkers. Janelle hadn't asked for immortality, nor did she want it.

"You can't think to keep me. That's kidnapping. I'm a DEA special agent. If I go missing, they'll come looking for me."

He laughed maniacally, proving his insanity. No wonder Vlad wanted him dead. Mircea was beyond saving. "They'll never find you. Another statistic, another unsolved missing person."

"You can't keep me forever."

He rolled his eyes. At least she thought he did. It was hard to tell with his black orbs. "I wouldn't dream of eternity. Christ, you'd drive me batty. I only plan to make Vlad believe it right before I kill him. Then, when I tire of you, I'll bury you right alongside my dear brother."

"That will be a blessing."

Janelle didn't see the second slap coming either. Much more and her lips would be the size of Grandpa Simpson's. She really did need to curb the sarcasm. Her only chance in survival was Vlad finding them before her vision played out. If she kept this up, her brain would be scrambled long before the big guy arrived. Mircea obviously didn't care what shape he left her in.

Shaking her head, she attempted to clear the bit of fog trying to take residence in her skull. The last thing she needed was to black out. Mircea returned to the window. "What are you looking for? Do you expect your brother to find us so quickly?"

"He already knows I favor these out of the way cabins."

"Surely, there are hundreds more like this in these woods."

He turned back around, his grin returning as if the last burst of anger hadn't happened at all. "I let one of my vampires know where to find us. He's already spoken with one of Vlad's grandsons. Kane will believe he's making a deal with my little vamp."

Holy shit! Vlad was being set up and walking right into Mircea's trap.

"He's to let Vlad know where we are when I give him the okay. I'm keeping an eye out to make sure things aren't expedited by him finding us on his own. I'd be a fool to let down my guard even a moment where my brother is concerned."

Janelle tested her balance as she slowly got to her feet and wobbly knees, using the chair to steady herself. She needed to find a way to escape, and soon. If fleeing no longer seemed like an option, she'd take her own life rather than become one of his minions. Death would be preferable over becoming his mate and spending any lengthy time with this psychotic.

Grabbing an old rusty knife from the counter that looked as if it had been there for years, she aimed it at Mircea.

His answering laugh mocked her. "Surely, you aren't dumb enough to think you can kill me."

She had hoped he'd take the knife and end her instead. "Not at all."

Without her as leverage, Janelle was giving Vlad the advantage. His anger over her death would aid him in his mission to end this motherfucker's life. Janelle had no doubt he'd be the victor. She turned the knife around and offered him the handle. "Why not just kill me and get it over with?"

"Because I have other plans for you."

Her vision played through her head again. Janelle wasn't about to give Mircea the chance to turn her. Taking the knife to her own throat, she said, "Like hell," and meant to slice through the flesh and arteries, doing the damn job herself. Except … she hadn't factored in Mircea moving faster than she could slice, not managing more than a hairline cut.

The knife clattered to the wooden floor. Mircea stood precariously close, all fangs and crazy-eyed. Within the blink of an eye, he had her turned around with an arm banded over her chest. Janelle fought his hold to no avail. And just like in her vision, it was mere seconds before he had forced open her mouth and his blood flowed down her throat.

"What the fuck have you done?" she cried.

WHAT FELT LIKE HOURS LATER, but could have been mere minutes for all she knew, Janelle lay curled into a ball atop a grungy mattress, unable to care about the filth and dirt beneath her. The strong stench of must carried to her nose, causing bile to rise in her esophagus. Never had she experienced such physical suffering, draining her of the energy to move. The cramping of her muscles had made her limbs useless.

Fire coursed through her veins.

Mircea had forced his blood down her throat, his bitter blood still coating her tongue. Lord help her, Mircea had just sealed her to him for eternity when she was desperately in love with his brother. Mircea's blood now flowed through her.

The son of a bitch had won.

Vlad's image swam through her fever-induced brain, soothing her. The pain-driven hallucination was her only respite from the fact she had become Mircea's mate. Vlad would no doubt be gutted from the knowledge…

…making Janelle wish she had succeeded in taking her own life.

CHAPTER TWENTY-ONE

"WHERE IS SHE?"

Vlad strode past the broken doorframe. His heart dipped to his stomach, because he already knew the answer. The damage alone would've told him that his brother had been in his penthouse, even if his scent hadn't been stamped all over the damn place. The *nenorocitule* knew how to mask his trail but he hadn't bothered this time. No, he wanted Vlad to know he had been there, loud and clear.

"I should have your fucking head!" he barked, wanting to destroy everything in his path. Right now that was his great-nephew, for having lost Janelle when Vlad trusted she was in his care for safe-keeping.

"She was gone before I got here." Ryder squared his shoulders, anger turning his gaze black. Long white fangs punched through his gums as he dared to snarl. He jabbed a finger at Vlad. "You're the one who left her alone before I arrived, so don't you put this on me, old man. This is the way I found your penthouse and I called you straight away."

Vlad jammed both hands through his hair, fear and frustration climbing up his spine, bringing out the asshole in him. Damn, but he wanted someone else to blame, as shouldering it meant he had been the one to majorly fuck up, putting

249

Janelle in grave danger. He should have never listened to her when she told him to go, that she'd be fine.

Jesus, she was anything but.

Ryder was right, this was his own fault. He should have never left her alone, even for a second. In his haste to get to Kane and his obsession to find his brother he had failed Janelle in the worst way.

The steel entry door lay in the center of the room, having flown a good twenty feet. Vlad knelt on his haunches, scenting blood—her blood. He flipped the metal panel to inspect the other side where a small crimson stain marred the pristine surface, right about the height of Janelle. Anguish and guilt washed over him, nearly crippling him. Vlad pictured Janelle hearing the ding of the elevator, expecting the arrival of Ryder, before she approached the entry and Mircea blew the damn thing inward.

Vlad let go of the door, dropping it to the floor with a clatter. As he stood, his attention caught on the glint of glass shards scattered about the tiles near the kitchen island. A tray of meat and cheeses that had been brought up on his request from the lobby's restaurant sat on the marble counter, alongside a jug of milk. Janelle had no doubt been preparing a bite when something startled her, causing her to drop the glass.

"You haven't touched anything?" he asked Ryder, not bothering to apologize for his gruff behavior.

The biker shook his head, still in vampire form, apparently yet miffed by Vlad's accusations. "As soon as I got here, I called. Did you even make it to Kane and Kaleb?"

Vlad shook his head. Christ, his precautions in his attempt to keep Janelle safe had all been in vain. "After I heard from you, I called Kane and told him to handle it. He and Kaleb are taking care of the situation."

"So, what's the plan now?"

Vlad growled. "My brother won't surface until he's ready. Until then, I want everyone combing the fucking woods for abandoned cabins. He'll be in one of them, I'm sure of it. Mircea is, if nothing else, a creature of habit."

One of Ryder's dark brows shot up. "You're sure? Maybe we've been playing into his hands all along, looking where he wants us to. Mircea could be holding her right under our noses, here in the city."

Vlad hoped Ryder was wrong in his assessment. The state of Oregon was over ninety-eight thousand square miles and he couldn't bear the thought of combing every fucking mile. No, Mircea would be hiding out in an abandoned cabin; he was sure of it. No one knew his brother's behavior better than he. And yet Mircea had managed to carry out the one deed Vlad vowed he wouldn't let happen. The son of a bitch had gotten his hands on Janelle.

Agony and grief weighed heavily on him. His damn heart felt battered and bruised. Vlad tilted his head to the heavens and bellowed. If anything happened to Janelle, he wouldn't want to go on. He didn't even want to think of his future without Janelle. Should he … no, when he got her back, no more secrets, he'd tell her just how damn much he loved her.

This failing was on his shoulders, no one else's. Kane'd had the opportunity to take Mircea's head months ago, but Vlad had forbidden him from doing so. It could have ended there and then. Hell, Vlad should have taken his brother's head himself instead of foolishly hoping to redeem his brother and incarcerating him. And now this! Damn it, he should have stayed with Janelle until Ryder's arrival.

Ironically, Mircea had been the reason Vlad had met her. That he might have lost her to his brother's evil now was like a slap in the face from fate. He looked at Ryder, who had returned to his human form.

"She's it for you, isn't she?"

Vlad wanted to scoff at the idea, but couldn't. Not with the truth mocking him. "She can't be."

"Why?"

Vlad hung his head, feeling the futility of his words. Because he did love Janelle. "She doesn't belong in my world. It's too dangerous."

"I'm pretty sure with her job she's been in a lot of dangerous situations."

Vlad rocked back on his heels. "If my brother decides to kill her, there's not a damn thing I can do unless I can get to them first."

"It's not her he wants." Ryder rubbed his callused hands together. "She's only good to him if she's alive."

"I hope you're right." Vlad didn't want to think of the alternative.

"Kane get one of those asswipes talking?"

Vlad nodded. "There were about five of them when they arrived. Two had to be dealt with. Kane thought one of the remaining three might help lure Mircea out of hiding in exchange for their lives."

The pressure in Vlad's chest built. While they were frittering time chit-chatting, it was hard telling what his brother was doing to Janelle. Every second counted. Sitting here wasted precious time.

"We need to get the hell out of here. I can force one of those sons of a bitches into telling me what I need to know. I'll make them wish for death."

"I'll call Kane." Ryder pulled out his phone and slid his finger over the glass. When Kane answered, Ryder placed him on speaker. "What's the scoop, Viper? Janelle is still MIA."

"Mircea's vampires have no way to get a hold of him. Mircea is always the one to make the connection."

"So you're telling me we have nothing," Vlad grumbled.

"More than we did," Kane replied, seemingly unfazed.

"We're on our way. I'll make them tell me my brother's location if I have to kill every last one of them."

Kane's sigh came through the speaker. Vlad was being unreasonable. "Look, Vlad, I'll bring them to the clubhouse where you can grill them. I've offered them immunity in exchange for Mircea. As soon as the motherfucker calls, they'll lure him to us. It's all we've got, other than scouring thousands of miles of forest. Regardless, I'll have the Sons combing the woods, looking for out-of-the-way abandoned cabins. Diablo believes it's likely where Mircea is holding out."

"Who the fuck is Diablo?"

"The vampire who's likely going to be your fucking savior," Kane growled. "He was Mircea's first turned. I like him, but yes, we're still working on trust issues going both ways. He's a self-professed loner, left the Devils back when their empire came tumbling down thanks to Spike."

"Diablo's his real name?" Great, they were putting their trust in someone who probably thought of himself as evil incarnate.

"No. It's his biker name. He has history, and no doubt earned the moniker. But that's neither here nor there. We need him, so play nice. Without Diablo, the others won't budge on helping us. They're looking to him for leadership."

Vlad's voice rose. "This is all we have?"

"You have something better?"

"*Nenorocitule*!" Vlad nearly came unglued. He had no other choice than to trust a guy named after the devil. "Bring them in. I'll meet you at the clubhouse."

JUST SHY OF YANKING THE heavy door off its hinges, Vlad strode into the clubhouse with Ryder close on his heels. The short fuse on his temper was ready to blow, the scene before him not helping. Kane, Kaleb, and three other men stood around the bar tossing back shots of whiskey. Vlad wanted to tear some heads from newly turned vampires' necks. But if he were to have a chance in hell at finding Janelle, he needed these vampires alive.

Too much time had already been wasted, making him dread he might find her too late. Never in all of his time on this earth had he felt so powerless and out of control. He had failed to keep his promise to keep her from harm's way. If anything happened to Janelle, he'd never forgive himself for walking out and leaving her alone, even for a second. Mircea must have been lying in wait and pounced on the given opportunity.

Looking for the one Kane called Diablo, Vlad zeroed in on the taller of the three. The man's black T-shirt stretched taut over muscles honed from years of working out, no doubt some of those done on the inside of a prison like San Quentin. He looked as though he had seen the inside of a cell, and not because of his appearance but by the way he held himself, alert, vigilant, and wary of those around him. Normally, Vlad could respect a man who instilled fear in others.

But not today.

Diablo was on the wrong side of the equation, having been allied with his brother. Lucky for him, though, Kane had offered him immunity. Otherwise, Vlad would have offered him nothing but death.

Diablo had some black tribal art, not unlike many of the Sons. A black sleeve tattoo started on his hand and traveled up his arm, but it wasn't the one catching Vlad's attention. His neck tattoo was particularly telling of Diablo's dark character, matching that of his moniker. A devil's skull centered in his throat with glowing red eyes, nose, and mouth. Tribal black tattoos fanned from the skull like fingers of black fire, nearly wrapping his thick throat. His hair was military short, his beard cut much the same way. Vlad bet most men would take one look and not want to fuck with this one, but not him.

Vlad saw Diablo as the one standing in the way of life or death for Janelle and he meant to get the son of a bitch's cooperation, one way or another. Moving at the speed of light, he clasped the *nenorocitule* by his neck and shoved him against the back wall of cupboards, Diablo's head bouncing off the wood.

"Son of a bitch," the man snarled, his fangs punching through his gums, eyes blackening.

Diablo's hands clasped Vlad's wrists and damn near succeeded in loosening the grip. Vlad was pleasantly surprised by the strength of this one. What fun was a fight if it wasn't fair?

"What the fuck, man?" His voice wasn't the least affected by Vlad's tight grip around his tree-trunk throat.

"I take it you're the king of this ragtag group."

"Vlad," Kane warned, keeping him from crushing the man's windpipe.

Vlad bared his fangs at the *nenorocitule*, feeling anything but friendly. "Where the fuck is my brother?"

"Let go and we'll talk. Otherwise, go fuck yourself, man."

Vlad growled, tightening his grip, causing the man to grimace. Had Kane not laid a hand on his forearm, Vlad might have just taken Diablo out. Instead, he dropped his hold. If Kane didn't get a handle on Diablo, Vlad might just send the condescending asshole to an early grave once he outlived his usefulness.

"What do we know about Mircea's whereabouts?"

"That we have no fucking idea where he is. When Mircea wants something, he calls." Reaching into his pocket, Diablo laid a cell phone on the counter. He rubbed the tattooed skull on his throat. "I haven't heard from him in a couple of days."

Kane picked up the phone, aimed it at Diablo's face to unlock it, then scrolled through the incoming calls. "All unknowns. Not surprised. Anyone have an idea?"

No one spoke up. Vlad couldn't help but wonder if they weren't going about this all wrong. If these vampires had no way of getting a hold of Mircea, they were worthless to him. He walked away from the crew and began pacing the floor. Sooner or later, his brother had to contact him. Mircea didn't take Janelle for his own entertainment. If he so much as harmed a hair on her head, he'd make Mircea suffer long and hard before he finally ended his degenerate life. In the end, there would be room for only one of them on this earth. His brother's days were numbered.

The men chatted behind him about the different hideouts Mircea had used. If they were correct, then Kane and Kaleb had the Sons in the right vicinity scouring the woods. It was only a matter of time before they found him.

A cell phone rang. Vlad whirled on his heel and strode back to the bar. Diablo's phone vibrated before it rang a second time. Kane nodded for him to pick it up. Diablo answered the phone, putting it on speaker.

"What took you so fucking long?" his brother's voice hissed through the speaker.

"I was taking a leak," Diablo said.

"I need you to do something for me."

"Name it."

"I need you to find the Sons of Sangue's clubhouse—"

"Already know of it."

"Good. Go there and tell them I'm looking for my brother."

"And how is he supposed to get a hold of you?" Diablo baited him.

Mircea gave him the phone number. "Tell him to call me. I have something that may be of interest to him. Where are you?"

"None of your concern."

"Mind telling me what that is in case he asks?"

A soft cry was heard in the background causing Vlad's heart to clench. Jesus, it was all he could do not to grab the phone from Diablo's hand. "Just tell him it's something he's going to want back."

The call went dead. Vlad had already pulled his phone out and was about to dial when Kaleb stopped him. "Wait a few hours."

"You're fucking kidding, right?" Vlad snarled.

"Think about it, Grandpa. He doesn't expect his vampires to be standing next to you. Give them a bit of time to … arrive."

"Hawk's right, Vlad," Kane said. "Two hours and you'll call."

"Fuck that shit." Vlad dialed the number and his brother picked up.

"Wow, that was fast." Mircea chuckled. "I take it you must have already found Diablo."

"And a couple more. We left two for dead."

"Ah, well I suppose it couldn't be helped."

"Where the fuck are you, brother?"

"My, my, such haste. I was correct in assuming this little woman you've been safeguarding means something to you."

"She better be uninjured." Vlad heard another cry in the distance, causing him to fist his free hand. "What the fuck did you do to her?"

"Nothing she can't sustain, I assure you. Your little love bug will be better than new when you come to get her."

"Where the hell are you, Mircea?"

"You'll come alone? Leave the calvary or she dies."

Vlad clamped his teeth, causing an ache clear to his ear. "I don't need anyone else to fight you. Where?"

"Good. But please, bring Diablo with you."

"Why?"

"An exchange, of course."

Vlad looked at the large vampire who nodded. "I'll bring him."

"Good." Mircea rattled off the coordinates of the cabin. "See you in about ten minutes, big brother."

The phone went dead in Vlad's hand. He glanced at the Diablo again. "You know he'll kill you when this is over. I trust you won't side with him to try and save your hide?"

"You'll get to him first." The large vampire shrugged. "Besides, I never liked the son of a bitch anyway."

"What do you want us to do?" Kane asked.

"Give me twenty minutes, then you follow, bring the rest of the Sons. If something goes south and there are more of his turned vampires in the area, take them all out."

CHAPTER TWENTY-TWO

*T*EN MINUTES, MY ASS.

Six and a half minutes to be exact. That's the amount of time it took Vlad to locate the cabin where his brother held Janelle. To his surprise, Diablo had easily kept up, no doubt due to Mircea's primordial blood coursing through him. If the vampire even so much as made one move in the wrong direction, he'd send him to hell with his brother.

They stopped a few hundred yards from the dwelling. Mircea unquestionably had scented their arrival; knew they were in the vicinity. But Vlad hadn't planned to sneak up on the cagey bastard. Hell, no. He was going in guns blazing. The Grim Reaper had come calling and Vlad was more than happy to hand over his brother.

Vlad tilted his nose to the breeze. Something was amiss. Although he could scent Janelle within the cabin, her aroma had changed. Christ, had he already arrived too late?

"*Nenorocitule.*"

Diablo raised a brow. "Something I should know?"

Janelle's soft cries of anguish carried to Vlad's ears, giving him the answer to his question. Mircea had more than stepped over the line. The son of a bitch had managed to damn near cripple him, fueling his fury to take his life. He'd no longer find pain in doing so.

Janelle no longer smelled wholly human.

Mircea had given her his damn blood and for that Vlad would show no mercy. Death was too good for him. This century-long feud ended now. But first, he needed to see to Janelle, that she would be far away from the bloodshed. Vlad couldn't chance Mircea harming her further. She needed to be his first priority, even if it killed him to hand her safekeeping over to a man he barely knew.

"Tell me now who you're siding with."

Diablo narrowed his gaze. "I don't understand."

"When I go in there, I'm ripping Mircea's head from his shoulders. No mercy. I need to know I'm not facing two enemies when I enter that cabin. If I am, Diablo, it's my promise you'll suffer the same fate."

"I gave you my word."

"Then your word better be gold." Vlad gritted his teeth. Every muscle tautened, ready for the kill. Christ, she hadn't asked for this life.

"What do you need me to do?"

"Protect Janelle with your life. Get her the hell out of there and away from any danger. Wait with her at the clubhouse for my return."

"What if I encounter other vampires coming to his rescue?"

Vlad glared at him. "Are there more of you that I should know about?"

"Not that I'm aware of. Those I knew banded together at the cabin where Viper and Hawk found us. But that doesn't mean he didn't create more."

"Presently, I only smell Mircea, so be damn fast about getting her out of there. Should more vampires arrive, I'll handle them." Vlad turned his attention back to the cabin, hearing Janelle's whimper. "You go through the front. I'll take the back. Get Janelle the hell out of there, and let me deal with whatever comes my way. The Sons won't be far behind should I be ambushed."

"Got it."

"On the count of—fuck that. Go."

THE BACKDOOR SPLINTERED FROM the force of his fist, tinder raining down around him. Vlad stormed into the cabin, fury nipping at the booted heels clomping against the scarred-wood decking. His gaze searched out and found the reason for his rage standing across the room. From the corner of his vision, he saw Janelle thrashing about in agony on a filthy mattress along an adjacent wall, cutting him straight to the heart. Jesus, he wanted to go to her, comfort her and absorb her pain. Tell her that he fucking loved her. She belonged to him, damn it, regardless of who's blood ran through her veins.

Vlad had no choice but to trust Diablo's word that he'd get her the hell out of there. Her whimper of pain nearly unmanned him. Christ, he wished he could leave his brother to Diablo, and protect Janelle himself. To do so, though, would likely leave his brother alive while Diablo's head was the one to roll to the trash-littered floor. The young vampire was no match for one of Mircea's maturity, regardless of his brother's primordial blood running through him.

Vlad needed to be the one to end Mircea's life.

Standing smugly against the farthest wall, arms crossed over his chest, his brother was all but two steps from the cabin's second exit. Easy access for the coward to flee should things go south. And they would. Vlad would make sure of it. The old wood door imploded to Mircea's immediate left as Diablo forced his way into the cabin. To his brother's credit, he didn't so much as flinch at the newly-turned vampire's explosive arrival.

"Glad to see you could make it, Diablo," Mircea greeted the younger vampire, baring his teeth, though his black gaze never wavered from Vlad. "Who has your loyalty, boy? You best think long and hard or follow this one to a certain death."

"Go fuck yourself, Mircea." Diablo strode to the mattress and scooped Janelle into the cradle of his arms. "I owe you nothing, certainly not my loyalty."

"Take her and you're dead," Mircea said, spittle flying from his mouth. He took a step in Diablo's direction.

Vlad moved at the speed of light, coming between Mircea and Janelle. He wouldn't allow Mircea to put his hands on Janelle a second time. Failing her again wasn't an option. "Over my dead body, *nenorocitule*."

"That will be my pleasure, brother."

Vlad's gaze heated. He could feel Janelle close behind him, felt her pain to the marrow of his bones. She had been his weakness, but also his strength. His love for her empowered him.

 "Get her the hell out of here," Vlad bellowed.

Mircea's gaze turned ugly. "When I'm finished here with my brother, Diablo, mark my words, I'll hunt you both down. For certain, you'll lose your head while she becomes my bitch."

"Like hell, she will," Vlad growled but stayed his position, not giving Mircea a chance to get to Janelle, not without going through him first. He reined in the fury his brother's words evoked, needing Janelle free from danger before he squared off against his brother.

"Good luck with that, asshole." Diablo smirked, tightening his hold on Janelle.

Vlad couldn't help but steal a look behind him, see with his own eyes that she was okay. She curled into the vampire's hold. To Vlad's relief, it didn't appear she had been battered or bruised. Her lids lifted, her eyes now nearly black in color as she was at the very beginning stages of being turned. Her gaze found and held Vlad's for a brief second before she drifted back into unconsciousness. Lord, he hoped to hell she didn't hold his brother's actions against him, even if it was her right.

Fear and anxiety over losing her nearly robbed him of breath.

Diablo gave Vlad a brief nod before turning and hightailing it from the rear of the cabin. Their scent dissipated, telling Vlad the two were no doubt a safe distance away. Tension eased from his shoulders. Kane and Kaleb, along with the Sons of Sangue, were no doubt close behind his and Diablo's arrival. He had to put his trust in Diablo, his only choice, that he'd get her to safety. Once he rid the earth of the scourge that was his brother, he'd hightail it back to the clubhouse and see where he stood. Lord, she had every right to hate him. He had been the one to bring her into this life.

Becoming a vampire should've been her choice.

Janelle had captured his heart and soul. If she could find it in her heart to forgive him, he'd spend his life making up for his mistakes and the sins of his brother.

Vlad's heated gaze turned to the object of his antipathy.

Mircea stood across from him, unfazed by the fact Vlad had come to take the life he should have forfeited months ago. His smile widened, telling Vlad he had not only expected this confrontation, but counted on it. Mircea wouldn't have allowed Diablo to leave with Janelle, not without having a plan to turn the tides in his favor. He was too much of a coward to take on Vlad one-on-one. Vlad had already anticipated more turned vampires ready to do his brother's bidding, which was why Kane and Kaleb would soon be his backup.

As if on cue, the scent of unfamiliar vampires drifted to his nose as they closed in to outnumber him. The question was, how many?

If Kane, Kaleb, and the Sons didn't arrive shortly, he was prepared to take every one of them out. His only fear was Mircea escaping while he battled the others. Janelle continued to be in danger as long as his brother drew breath.

He flew across the room, knocking Mircea against the far wall just as five vampires entered the cabin, with more no doubt outside.

"The only one of us dying today is you, my dear brother."

Vlad snarled. "Not likely."

His brother steepled his hands and brought them up swiftly with great force between Vlad's arms, tearing his grip loose. Mircea quickly spun away as five minions pounced on Vlad. Fangs bit and tore chunks of flesh from his arms, neck, and shoulders. Vlad easily whipped the vampires to the side, sending them flying against the cabin walls, the foundation shaking from the impacts. With quick work, he easily tore off three of the five's heads while two more opponents entered the fray. Rushing him before he could shake off the other two motherfuckers, Vlad spun quickly, sending two of them crashing against Mircea and knocking him to the floor. Within seconds, he had ripped two more heads off. Five down, leaving two more minions in the cabin to go.

Vlad dove at Mircea and the other two vampires as they scrambled to their feet. Before they could sink in their fangs and do him more damage, both heads hung from his fists. He flung them to the floor, leaving them to roll across the filth. Snagging Mircea by his shirt just before he could reach the door, Vlad pulled him up short.

Beyond the scent of splattered and spent blood, Vlad caught a whiff of Kane and Kaleb. The cavalry had arrived. Vlad threw his brother against the old creaking wood. The walls shook and termite-eaten boards tumbled to the ground. He saw Kane taking the last of the vampires' heads just outside the dilapidated cabin walls, the sickening crunch of vertebrae separating from the neck carrying to Vlad's ears.

Mircea scrambled back to his feet and lunged, his claw-like hands aiming for Vlad's neck. He couldn't move aside fast enough as Mircea shoved him against one of the cabin's studs. It cracked beneath his weight, the roof threatening to cave in. Mircea reared his ugly head, fangs drawn, and sank them into Vlad's shoulder, tearing another large chunk of flesh.

Gripping Mircea by the biceps, he sank his thumbs through flesh and muscle until his brother was forced to release his hold with an anguished cry. The sounds of battle outside the walls died, telling Vlad that Mircea was the last of his crew. His heart panged as he looked at his defeated brother, no longer looking like the crazed monster he had become.

Mircea was beaten. He dropped to his knees before Vlad, his gaze beseeching him for mercy … mercy Vlad didn't have to give. For too long he had allowed his brother's crimes to go unpunished, all for the sake of his love. But no longer. This ended here.

"You've won, brother." Mircea raised his hands together as if expecting Vlad to tether them. "Take me back to your island and put me back in my cell. I promise to adhere to your rules."

Vlad frowned, his heart already aching with the coming loss. "That's more than you deserve."

"You name my punishment—"

"Death."

Without allowing for a response, Vlad grabbed his brother's head and gave a mighty twist. Every evil deed his brother had been guilty of flashed through his mind like a horror flick, only worse because it had been real life. As deserved as Mircea's execution was, Vlad's own cry of anguish traveled through the forest as he completed what he'd come to do, sending birds and animals to flight. Mircea's body dropped to his feet while his head still dangled from Vlad's fist. Vlad tossed it away in distaste as he turned and left the cabin. He wasn't even aware of the tears dropping from his lashes, tears his brother didn't deserve, until Kaleb gripped his shoulder and stopped him.

"You okay, Grandpa?" Kaleb asked, the term of endearment no longer unpleasant. The twins were the last of his immediate family.

"I will be." Vlad cleared his throat. "Clean this mess and torch the cabin."

Kane nodded. "Go back to the clubhouse. We'll meet you there once we finish here. Diablo is there with Janelle."

He rubbed his beard, feeling the filth left from the battle. His wounds had already begun to heal. "I think maybe first I should shower."

"Yeah." Kane chuckled. "We could all use one."

Vlad glanced around at the brave men, the Sons of Sangue, who stood beside him, battle-scarred and bloodied. His heart swelled. These vampires were men of honor. Not only were they Kane and Kaleb's brethren, but they were now also his family.

CHAPTER TWENTY-THREE

A WEEK OF HELL. JENELLE REMEMBERED VERY LITTLE, OTHer than the excruciating pain and the comfort of Vlad's arms. Thankfully, the arduous effects of her turning had mostly alleviated. Lord, there were times she had prayed for the Grim Reaper. Had it not been for Vlad holding her through most of it, taking away some of the agonies, she might've pleaded for the black-cloaked ghoul with the scythe to take her.

Janelle was now immortal, a heady notion.

Not that she had asked for it, of course, but thrilling nonetheless.

The idea of drinking blood was no longer repulsive as she had once speculated. After all, Vlad tapping her vein had been downright pleasurable. But drinking blood herself? Janelle needed a little more time to get used to the concept. Her entire existence had been transformed due to a psycho's need for revenge. She had been more than a little elated to overhear that Vlad had ended the son of a bitch's life. Janelle couldn't imagine how difficult it must have been for him to do, no matter that Mircea got the justice he was due.

Melancholy settled in at the notion she might not be able to return to her job. She loved being a special agent and had been damn good at it. But being a vampire, one who craved

271

red blood cells for lunch, might not fit into her career at the DEA. What if the scent of blood at a crime scene made her accidentally transform?

Her gaze traveled to Cara Brahnam who sat across the room on a barstool talking quietly with Suzi Stevens, neither woman aware she had awakened judging by their whispering. Although, due to her newly gained vampire hearing, Janelle easily picked up every word said. She sniffed the air. Her sense of smell had also improved, detecting the different pheromones of the two women and the child napping across from her.

Where was Vlad?

Janelle wasn't sure what she would have said had he been here, other than to thank him for his care over the past week. What must he think of her? Killing his brother couldn't have been easy. Surely, he mourned Mircea's death, even if it was well-deserved. But had Janelle not come snooping into his life, Vlad might've had a shot at redeeming the bastard, or at the very least imprisoning him again.

Did he blame her … even the tiniest bit?

Sitting, she tested her legs. The wobbliness was gone, her body now feeling stronger than ever. Recalling the speed with which Vlad and Ryder had traveled when they each had carried her, Janelle wondered if she too could run as fast. Lord, she hoped her vampirism would curb the damn motion sickness that had come with it. Otherwise, she was opting to trek by car.

"You're awake," Cara said, rising and waddling over to her. "How do you feel?"

"Fantastic actually." Janelle stood and stretched. No aches or any pain remained. In fact, she had never felt better. "Maybe a little hungry."

"I'm not surprised." Suzi chuckled, walking over and joining them. "It's been a week since you've had anything."

"You'll need blood to complete the turn," Cara said.

Could she do this? "I'm hoping one of you will teach me the ropes."

"Absolutely." Cara smiled. "As a matter of fact, Viper and Hawk went to the Blood 'n' Rave to secure you a donor."

"A donor?"

"A human who knows about vampires and is a willing host," Suzi said. "Draven created a secret society of donors who make sure we get the sustenance we need. Feeding is easy. The scent of human blood will help aid you in turning into your vampire form the first time. After that, it will become second nature."

Steak and lobster, a burger and fries.

Would she ever be able to enjoy human food again? Janelle fidgeted. Food was the least of her worries. She couldn't help wondering where Vlad had disappeared to again. Maybe she was too painful of a reminder of the brother he had been forced to kill. Not to mention, said psycho brother's blood now ran through her veins.

Janelle took in a shaky breath. She needed to know where she'd now stand with him "Viper and Hawk gave you their blood, making you their mates. That makes you a mate for life, correct?"

Suzi nodded. "There is no such thing as divorcing a vampire."

Cara swatted Suzi's arm with the back of her hand. "Janelle is not mated to Mircea."

The short brunette's eyes widened in understanding. "Oh, no. You may have ingested Mircea's blood, but he's dead. That means you're open to mate yet with someone else."

"If he were still alive?"

Cara grimaced. "Then yes, you would be his mate."

"Even though I didn't ask for his blood?"

"There are times it can be set aside." Cara recounted the story of Rosalee and Kane's dissolved mating and how her actions had caused the death of their son, Ion. "Viper had asked Mircea to set aside his mating to Rosalee so Kane and I could be mated."

"Why ask Mircea and not Vlad?"

"At the time, no one knew where Vlad was. He tends to disappear for long periods of time."

"Don't forget Brea," Suzi added. "She was Kinky's mate before he was killed. Now, she's mated to Draven. Death negates a mating if the living mate chooses."

"But am I still considered Mircea's mate?"

Cara laid her hand on Janelle's forearm. "Technically, but only until you decide to take another."

Janelle frowned. "And how does that happen?"

"Someone, like Vlad, can give you his blood."

Janelle quickly blinked away the moisture gathering in her eyes. Vlad would never want her as a mate, not with Mircea's blood running through her. "I would be nothing but a bad reminder of his brother. I can't … I won't do that to him."

"You can stay here at the clubhouse for as long as you want."

"I can take care of myself." Janelle couldn't take Cara up on her generous offer, not with Vlad coming and going as he pleased. She couldn't take the heartache of seeing him and not being able to be with him. "I have a place."

"Viper would insist. He'll want to see you're taken care of. You're now part of our family."

"Thank you, Cara. I appreciate that but I prefer to stay at my own place." Janelle would be damned before she became someone's pity mate, least of all Vlad's. "Speaking of Vlad, where is he?"

Stefan picked that moment to wake up from his nap. He rubbed his little eyes, then ran up and circled Suzi's legs. She scooped him up and placed him on her cocked hip. "He's back at the penthouse. He said he needed to have the door fixed, clear his things, and turn in the keycards."

An ache shot through her heart, not all that different from the agony of her past week. The news debilitated her, though his leaving shouldn't have been a surprise. Of course, he'd think his job here was finished with his brother being dead. Janelle didn't want to be more of a burden, the reason Vlad stayed if moving on was what he truly wanted. Vlad owed her nothing.

"How soon is he leaving?" Janelle masked the pain of him not telling her his plans.

"Viper wasn't sure." Cara rubbed her distended belly, grimacing. "Ooooh…"

"Are you okay?" Janelle asked, concerned. As large as Cara was, surely the babies were due at any moment.

"Just a couple of restless boys. I'm only eight months along." She took in a deep breath, licking her lips before continuing, "I think Vlad is more comfortable hiding away on his island. We never know when he's going to pop up in the States."

"I can't imagine he'd leave you behind," Suzi quickly added. "He seems pretty protective when it comes to you."

"Because he felt responsible for putting me in danger."

"Maybe…" Suzi drifted off with her response, saying nothing more.

Janelle looked at Cara, eager to get the conversation off of her and Vlad. "You're in law enforcement. How do you handle that, being a vampire?"

"We're still human." Cara shrugged. "You separate your two selves. In my case, the sheriff knows about us, but the rest of the force doesn't. It might be a bit tricky once he retires the first of the year and my partner, Joe Hernandez, takes over. But I'm sure not much will change. I'll still go to work and fight the bad guys."

"So, I can continue doing my job?"

"Heck, yes, girlfriend." Cara smiled. "It might even be beneficial. Never hurts to have someone on the inside looking out for our interests. Please know, Janelle, we will always be here for you. As I said, we're family."

The door opened and Ryder and Gabriela strolled into the room. "We have a problem."

"What's going on?" Cara asked.

Gabby's eyes were red and swollen, obviously fresh from tears. "I got a text from Adriana. She's gone."

"To where?"

"Mexico with her asshole of a fiancé."

Suzi gasped. "With Mateo?"

"Adri said she missed him. Oh, and he's sorry for burning down our house." Ryder rolled his eyes. "My ass."

"Adri wired my bank account enough money to rebuild," Gabby said. "No doubt, Mateo's money. She doesn't have that kind of funds."

"You think she did this of her free will?" Cara asked.

"She made her decision," Ryder grumbled.

"How can you be so damn cynical?" Gabby's voice raised.

"She could've come to us for help and she chose not to."

"Because she didn't want to involve the Sons, not after costing us our house. Regardless, she's my best friend, Ryder."

"And the fiancée of the kingpin for the La Paz cartel." Ryder took in a calming breath before running a knuckle down Gabby's cheek. "Look, sweetheart, I love you, but you have to know we can't make decisions for Adri. She's an adult. Even Gunner agrees."

"What's Gunner have to do with this?" Cara asked.

"They've become friends, talked on the phone quite often when he wasn't in Oregon," Gabby said. "When he was, they either hung out at the house or the Blood 'n' Rave. I think Gunner might've even liked Adri as more than a friend, but she'd closed herself off to relationships following Mateo. In the back of her mind, I believe she feared Mateo would come after her, and go through anyone standing in his way."

"Which is exactly what he did, Gabs," Ryder said. "He wasn't even quiet about it."

The door opened again. Viper, Kaleb, and a young woman Janelle didn't recognize, entered the clubhouse. Janelle assumed her to be the donor they had retrieved for her.

"What's going on?" Kane asked.

"Adri texted Gabby, said she was going back to Mexico with Mateo, supposedly on her own," Cara filled him in. "She also wired Gabby money to rebuild."

"What do you think, Gabby?" Kane asked.

"Adri said she loves Mateo and that leaving him was a mistake. But I believe she's lying and just trying to protect us."

"Should we take it to the table? Put it to a vote whether the Sons should go after her?"

Ryder placed an arm over Gabby's shoulder. "You should know, Viper, I'm against it. We already lost enough men due to the La Paz cartel. However, what Gab's wants is most important to me. I'll go along with what needs to be done."

Gabby shook her head. "There are too many of them. I couldn't live with myself if more of you died."

"Did you try talking to Adri in person?" Kane asked.

"Her phone is no longer in service."

Kane glanced at Ryder. "We could call in the Washington chapter."

"We won't get their help," Ryder said. "I talked to Gunner. Whatever she said to him, he's washed his hands of her. If we do this, Viper, we're on our own."

"Gabriela?" Kane gripped one of her hands. "Your call."

A tear slipped past her lashes. "It's too risky. Even if you are vampires, you're far outnumbered."

Kane squeezed her hand before dropping his hold. "I'm sorry, Gabby. If an opportunity comes up to get Adri back, we will do our best."

"Thank you."

Kane turned to Janelle. "You ready to feed?"

Blood seemed to have drained from her head, leaving her lightheaded and no doubt white as a sheet. Instead of saying anything that would give way to her apprehension, she nodded and squared her shoulders. She had this. She was no longer just a grown-ass woman, but a badass vampire. Passing out wouldn't do. Kane led her and the young woman to the meeting room. Cara and Suzi followed, leaving everyone else in the main room.

"Cara and Suzi will take good care of you." Kane smiled, then left them to their privacy, closing the heavy doors behind him.

Janelle's eyes heated as her gaze trained on the young woman's neck. She could actually hear the rushing of her blood through her veins, smell the bouquet of it. The bones in her face cracked and shifted, uncomfortable yes, but not in a painful way. Her gums ached as her newly gained fangs punched through. Suzi had been correct, the woman's blood alone brought out the fiend in her. Her animalistic nature had taken over, and good God, she was hungry. At this point, Janelle doubted she'd need guidance. Having had Vlad feed from her was probably instruction enough.

The young blonde walked over to where Janelle stood and pulled her hair to one side, exposing her neck. Janelle looked at Suzi and Cara, who both nodded. Janelle cradled the young woman's head, then leaned forward and sank her fangs deep into her slender throat. Blood flowed. The warm metallic-flavored fluid warmed her, much like a good shot of whiskey, only ten times better. Euphoria set in. Janelle's stomach no longer ached.

Janelle's name drifted through her subconscious as someone in the room called to her, but she ignored the summons and continued to suckle. A gentle hand to her shoulder, though, had her withdrawing her fangs and stepping away from the young woman.

"Lick the twin holes," Cara urged. "Your saliva will help heal the wounds."

Janelle did as asked, feeling as though she were in some sort of mental fog. Cara eased her into a chair as the young woman left the room.

"Did I hurt her?" Janelle asked.

"No." Cara smiled. "I stopped you well before that could happen. You'll learn to know when you've taken enough. We never harm our donors."

"How will I know?"

"The hunger pains subside. That's when you stop."

Suzi gripped Janelle's hand. "Welcome to the family. I think Cara is right, you should stay here, even if it's just for a bit. Your boss still believes you're undercover with Vlad anyway. Why not take the time to come to terms with all of this?"

"Who's your boss?" Cara asked. "Maybe I've heard of him."

"Captain Robbie Melchor—"

Cara cursed. "Better yet, quit that damn job."

Janelle shook her head, clearing the remaining the fog. "Why?"

"Come to work for the sheriff's office. I'll get you a job as my partner when Joe takes over for sheriff."

Her brow furrowed. "But I like my job."

Cara told Janelle about her time in the Eugene Police Department, before Kane. Robbie and she had been dating when he had taken advantage of her, raping her. Cara knew no one would believe her story due to his position and power within the department. He had even threatened to ruin her if she told. So Cara quit, moved to Pleasant, and took a position as a detective for the Lane County Sheriff.

"Jesus, Cara! I'm sorry." Janelle thought about her boss, believing he was capable of the acts Cara described. The rumor mill around the office had been correct. Captain Melchor was indeed guilty of raping an old girlfriend. "That egotistical ass."

"You don't have to leave your job because of me. I just thought maybe you should watch out for him. But the offer for a job still stands."

Janelle mulled over what Cara had said. She loved her job, but Melchor had always rubbed her the wrong way. Man, she was glad she hadn't taken him up on any of his blatant offers. Maybe working side-by-side Cara would be the perfect solution to help ease her into her new life.

"You know what?" Janelle smiled, feeling right about her decision to quit the DEA. "You get me that job with the Lane County Sheriff and you got a deal."

"Joe takes office in a couple of months." Cara's grin lit up her face. Janelle knew she would like working alongside this woman. "I'll make sure you get his position when he becomes sheriff."

"I'll call Captain Melchor tomorrow and tender my resignation."

Janelle stood and Cara drew her into a hug, her large belly bump between them. "The Lane County Sheriff's Office will be lucky to have you."

"I'm sure I'll be more than happy there…" Her voice trailed off.

Vlad was near. His scent was damn near a calling, making it all she could do to stay put. How would he perceive her, scenting his brother's blood on her every time she came near? Cara and Suzi stole glances at each other, telling Janelle they were also aware of his arrival. Seconds later, one of the large doors opened and he strode in.

"Out," Vlad said, his pointed finger indicating Cara and Suzi should leave.

Cara looked to Janelle. "Do you need me to stay?"

She shook her head. "I'll be fine."

Once the door was closed behind them, Janelle placed her fists on her hips. "Were you even going to tell me?"

His dark brows gathered over the bridge of his nose. "Tell you what?"

Janelle wasn't about to let him know how much his departing hurt, not when she knew his leaving was probably for the best. She didn't want to be a daily reminder of the brother he had to kill with his own bare hands. Or the fact she was Mircea's mate. She may have fallen hard for Vlad, but having him look upon her disgust one day would only tear her up inside.

"That you're leaving."

VLAD THREADED BOTH HANDS over the top of his head, brushing his hair back from his face. What the hell had her so fired up? He had just left the penthouse, having packed everything up and readying it to ship home. The only thing left to retrieve was her. He supposed he should have explained himself earlier, but this certainly was not the response he was expecting when he returned. She looked as if she was ready to do battle.

His nostrils flared, taking in her unique aroma, now slightly different than before, tinged with a bit of Mircea's essence. Had she also inherited his brother's stubborn streak?

"I was on my way here to tell you. You were asleep when I left."

Janelle crossed her arms beneath her chest, pushing her cleavage above the V-neck of her sweater. Lord, even now she made him hard enough he could drive through concrete blocks. But now was not the time.

"Well then, I guess I should tell you to have a safe trip."

His gaze lifted from her cleavage to her crystal blue eyes. They reminded him of the ocean surrounding his home, what he was hoping to be their home. Lord, she was killing him. Letting her go wasn't something he was prepared to do. He raised a brow. "I take it you're staying."

Janelle's brow furrowed. "I was never asked to do otherwise."

He reached inside his jacket pocket and withdrew a travel itinerary and tossed it to the table. "You didn't give me the chance. I planned to take you—"

"No."

Vlad inhaled sharply. Her denial felt like a blade had been driven straight through his heart. "You aren't coming?"

"No. And the fact you assumed I would, frankly, pisses me off."

"I expect you have a good reason to stay. Care to share?"

Tears filled Janelle's sad eyes. She quickly looked away. What was she hiding? He reached for her hand but she pulled it from his reach. "Don't."

"You're not being straight with me." Christ, his chest hurt. Tell her you love her. *What difference would it even make?* "What's going on, Janelle?"

"Please." Her voice trembled. She took a step back. "You've done enough."

Vlad swallowed the lump threatening to choke the life from him. Enough? Although he had been the one put her in danger, he had also been the one hold her over the past week. To cherish the very blood that ran through her veins, even if some of it belonged to his damn brother.

"You blame me for all of this?"

"Damn it." A tear slipped past her lashes but she swatted it away, looking to the floor. "Enough, as in holding me all of this past week. I meant that as a compliment."

"Then what the hell is wrong?"

Janelle was walking away from him and there wasn't a damn thing he could do. Christ, he could envision spending the rest of his life with her. And she was rejecting him? He wasn't above begging if necessary. He, the eldest of all vampires, was ready to get on one knee.

He stepped forward, closed the gap between them, and reached out to touch her cheek. She jerked from his contact, turning her head to the side.

"I have to go," her voice cracked.

Didn't she know how much he loved her? So much so that it hurt? "You belong with me."

"If I understand this whole mating thing correctly, then" — her haunted gaze rose to his, chilling him— "I belong to your brother."

And with that, she skirted him and ran to the door, yanking it open. Vlad stood there momentarily stunned, before dropping heavily onto a chair. It wasn't long before he could no longer scent her. She was gone. His gaze dropped to the itinerary. Well, that hadn't gone as planned. Vlad rubbed his palm over his sternum in an effort to ease the pain her words had caused—fucking words. Jesus, had he been so wrong about her? No, he knew she loved him, had seen it in her eyes, felt it when they made love.

Just as he stood and was about to go after her, Kane entered the room and shut the door. "What the fuck do you want, Kane? I'm a little busy."

Pacing over to him, Kane gently pushed him back into the chair. It hadn't taken much effort as Vlad's energy was spent. Janelle walking out had depleted him.

Kane's gaze took in the paper lying on the table. "You planned to take her with you?"

He nodded but said nothing. There were no words. Her rejection stung more than anything had in his centuries on this hell-stricken earth. She had been the one to give his life hope again.

"You love her. I get that," Kane said. "But you have to let her go."

"I can't."

His great-grandson sat in the chair next to him and placed a hand on Vlad's knee. "She's not a possession, Vlad. She has to make her own decisions."

Vlad clasped his hands between his spread knees and looked to the floor. He cleared his clogged throat. "She told me that she belongs to Mircea, for God's sake. My brother." His voice broke on the last word.

Kane retracted his hand and sat back, looking at him in pity. Vlad, a broken man, had been brought to his fucking knees. "I failed her, and because of that, Mircea gave her life. I could even smell the son of a bitch on her."

"All the more reason to let her go," Kane repeated. "She's not yours, at least not at the moment. Give her time; she'll come around."

Vlad couldn't even fathom life without her. "And if she doesn't?"

"Then she was never yours to begin with." Kane picked up the itinerary and handed it to him. "Go home, Vlad. You also need time to heal."

Kane left the room. Vlad left out a breath, deflated, crumbling the itinerary in his fist.

"I belong to your brother."

Vlad bowed his head, tears falling to his fisted hands. He should leave, walk away, but Christ, it killed him to do so.

"...you have to let her go."

Did he have any choice? Dropping the crumpled paper to the floor, Vlad stood and left the room. If she didn't want him, then Kane was correct and there wasn't a damn thing he could do to change her mind. He glanced around the living area at his descendants, all of them. The Sons of Sangue were now just as much his family.

"I'll be flying out."

Not waiting for a response, he left behind the clubhouse and his Aston Martin sitting in the parking lot, taking to the woods and walking away.

CHAPTER TWENTY-FOUR

W EEKS LATER, JANELLE FOUND HERSELF 35,000 FEET over the ocean, hoping she had made the right decision. Nerves fluttered like butterflies in her stomach, hoping Vlad would be happy to see her.

"Lord, I hate flying in these things. A large plane is bad enough, but a small jet?" Kaleb said, catching Janelle's attention as he leaned against the headrest of the airplane's seat. Other than the pilot, they were the only two onboard, the small aisle between them. "I'd much rather travel by land. But no, Grandpa has to live on some damn remote island in the middle of fucking nowhere."

Janelle stifled a giggle, finding it funny that a badass vampire had an aversion to planes. Flying, she thought, was better than moving at the speed of light when you suffered from motion sickness. It had gotten marginally better now that she was a vampire, but she still preferred conventional methods of traveling. Thankfully, the small plane wasn't bothering her motion issues at all.

"You could have sent someone else to babysit me."

Kaleb lifted his head and looked at her. "You're kidding, right? And miss the chance to see where the old guy lives? All this time he's never invited any of us to his home. I wouldn't have missed this for the world."

"You're his great-grandson. Why haven't you been to his home?"

He shrugged. "Grandpa's extremely private. I suppose he feels if he told us where he lives, we'll just drop by."

Janelle smiled. "Like now?"

"Yeah, like now. It's my good luck Cara's close enough to delivering that Viper had no choice but to send me to accompany you."

"Not to mention our luck at Vlad leaving that itinerary behind."

"The icing on the cake. He knows I'm coming because we had to get permission to land, but you" —he winked— "you're his surprise."

She sure hoped Vlad liked his surprise or the flight home promised to be a miserable one. With the help of the Sons and their mates, Janelle had finally come to terms with who she had become. It was time to see if Vlad could come to terms with it too.

After nearly a month of wallowing in self-pity, she realized she needed to tell him just how she felt. If he loved her as well, then everything else would find a way of working out. Her job was in the States, a job she wasn't willing to give up. Janelle hoped he'd be open to compromise and live part-time in Oregon with her.

Come the first of the year, thanks to Cara, she would be a detective for Lane County Sheriff's Office. A new career she was excited about. Janelle had called Robbie Melchor and told him she was resigning, that she would hand in the paperwork when she returned to collect her things. When it became obvious he couldn't change her mind, his reply became quite colorful. Kane had taken the phone. His veiled threats left Robbie telling Janelle she could mail in that resignation and he'd see to it her things were packed and sent to her new office. Janelle got the impression Kane enjoyed every second of his conversation with Robbie, due to their history.

"You okay?" Kaleb asked.

Janelle looked from the window back to Vlad's handsome great-grandson. It was easy to see where Kane and he had gotten their good looks. "Sorry. I guess my nerves are getting to me a bit."

"You know, down deep he's just a big ol' pussycat."

Janelle laughed. She had seen Vlad at his worst. A big lovable pussycat wouldn't come close to describing him. Lion maybe, tiger definitely, but pussycat not at all.

"Are you guys going to let this thing with Adriana go?" Janelle asked, eager to get her nerves off landing shortly and seeing Vlad for the first time in nearly a month.

"For now." Kaleb scratched the scruff on his chin. "The truth is, without the support of the Washington chapter, we'd likely get slaughtered down there in La Paz territory. They know us and what we look like, so infiltrating them a second time would be nearly impossible. But should Adri ask for our help, then damn straight we will. We were able to take out the kingpin once; we can take out Mateo if necessary."

"Do you think she might want your help but is afraid to ask?"

"Who knows? Gabby would be the best one to answer that. Adriana is her best friend. She was there when Adri was first engaged to that piece of shit. If she wants him back, then who are we to say otherwise?"

Being in law enforcement, Janelle had seen the ugly side of domestic abuse. And being that Mateo was the head of the La Paz cartel, he topped the list of bad guys. She sure hoped Adriana knew what she was in for with men like that.

Diablo came to mind. If she were to profile him, he was textbook bad guy. And yet he was careful in handling her, also instrumental in helping her get to safety.

"What happened to Diablo? Where'd he go after taking me back to the clubhouse? I seem to remember he left after Vlad returned."

"Viper talked him into sticking around. He and the other two vampires left alive but turned by Mircea will become part of the Washington chapter. Viper called Gunner, who was more than happy to welcome them into the fold. So, you'll still see him from time-to-time."

"Good. I never got to thank him." Janelle cleared her throat, uneasy about what she was about to ask. "There's something I need you to do for me."

Kaleb looked at her, his gaze studying her. "What is it?"

"The lab where the DEA takes their evidence?"

"What about it?"

"They have something of Vlad's."

His gaze darkened. "Like what?"

"A hair. DNA." Janelle proceeded to tell him about her blunder, her stomach sinking from her colossal mistake. "At the time, I didn't know what Vlad was. You have to know I would have never told them about him had I known."

"What was their reaction"

"They don't know what they have, only that the DNA isn't wholly human." She swallowed, attempting to dislodge the lump that had taken up residence. "Is there anything I can do to fix this?"

Kaleb winked at her. "You fix things with Grandpa. Viper and I will make sure this disappears along with the lab and the technician's memory of it."

"And the open case dealing with the murders of the priest and nun? Detective Barker from the Eugene PD is working that case."

He shrugged. "Nothing to find. A couple of cold cases."

Janelle supposed he was correct. There would be nothing to go on. "Thank you, Hawk. Again, I'm so sorry."

"You didn't know."

What felt like a two-ton brick lifted from her shoulders. She was extremely thankful Kaleb hadn't been furious with her. Looking out the plane window, a small island came into view, setting her nerves back into action.

What if Vlad didn't want to see her?

"Looks like we're almost there," she said, right before the pilot came over the intercom and announced the plane would be landing soon. Janelle refastened the seatbelt over her lap and worried her bottom lip. Was it too late to turn around?

Kaleb snapped his belt, then no doubt detecting her nerves, said, "It'll be all right, Janelle. Never have I seen Vlad so distraught as the day you walked out. He's going to be ecstatic when he sees you disembark."

She hoped Kaleb was right. The plane tilted, taking a wide turn, before Janelle could feel their descent in the pit of her stomach. If everything went according to her best hope, she'd be staying on the island for a lot of catching up, while Kaleb made the trip back home alone. She had a good month before she would be due back in the States to start her new job. Working with Cara Brahnam was preferable to Robbie Melchor any day of the week. Maybe being a vampire wasn't going to be so bad after all, especially if her new life included Vlad.

Janelle gripped the arms of her seat as the plane landed with a soft bounce. Within minutes, they rolled to a stop near a small hangar. She took in a deep breath and blew it out slowly before she unhooked her belt.

"You stay here a couple of minutes," Kaleb said. "Let me talk to Grandpa. I should probably soften the reason for my arrival."

Janelle nodded and watched as Kaleb exited the plane. He walked swiftly toward the hangar, just as Vlad stepped out of it. Her heart squeezed at the sight of him. It felt like a lifetime and it was all she could do to stay put. Janelle couldn't tell from her position whether Vlad was pissed at

Kaleb's arrival. He seemed to hold himself stiffly, while his lips slashed a straight line across his handsome face.

Oh, boy. He didn't look happy at all. Kaleb laughed at whatever Vlad had said, only further annoying his great-grandfather. With the plane's engines vibrating, Janelle couldn't pick up their conversation even with her vampire hearing. She thought to go out and rescue Kaleb, but he seemed to be enjoying himself, unruffled by Vlad's current mood. Staying her position, though, was making her antsy. She had given Kaleb enough time, hoping her arrival was more welcomed than Kaleb's seemed to be.

Walking to the front of the plane, she ducked her head, then descended the stairs, her gaze glued to the man who owned her heart. Vlad caught sight of her. The harsh lines of his face softened, but she couldn't judge by his reaction if he was happy to see her. Ignoring Kaleb, Vlad headed in her direction.

He stopped just short of touching her, his expression masked. "Was it my great-grandson's idea to drag you along?"

Janelle shook her head.

"Then why are you here?"

His question nearly had her turning around and running for the plane, but she would not cry. If he meant to send her on her way, then she'd damn well do it with her dignity intact. Janelle squared her shoulders. She had not come all this way to tuck her tail and run.

She took a deep breath, crossed her arms beneath her breasts, and glared at him. "I came to tell you I love you, you big oaf. Not that you deserve it."

One of his dark brows arched. "You love me?"

"Against my better judgment."

Janelle didn't know what to expect, but surely not his laughter. A large smile curved his lips, telling her she hadn't misjudged. "An old vampire like me?"

"Yes."

"I don't deserve you."

Her nerves finally alleviating, she said, "No, you don't."

Vlad picked her up in a bear hug, earning him a squeal. "Christ, I love you, too."

Her legs dangled a half-foot off the ground. Tilting his head, he sealed his lips to hers, kissing her soundly. Maybe he had yet to say the words, but she certainly felt his love in the possession of the kiss. Janelle's heart swelled as he lowered to her feet.

She tried to hide the smile tickling her lips. "That's a hell of a greeting."

"You think?" Vlad didn't attempt to hide his good humor. His thumb indicated Kaleb still standing behind them. "Just wait until I get his sorry ass back on that plane."

WHATEVER KALEB HAD BEEN in the process of saying the minute she appeared in the plane's door had been lost on Vlad. His cock had instantly hardened, making his pants extremely uncomfortable. He had watched her descend the stairs, one step after the other, mesmerized by her beauty. The jeans hugged her curves and long legs like a second skin. On top, she wore a low-cut, pink tank that showcased her full breasts. He already knew they fit his mouth quite perfectly. Christ, he couldn't wait to get her naked.

Now, Vlad followed her toward the front door, anxious to see what she thought of his home, hoping to make it hers as well. But the tour would have to wait. A dry month of no sex? Not usually his style. Janelle, he had no doubt though, would make it worth every agonizing minute.

"How did you get rid of Kaleb so quickly?" Janelle asked before she turned and headed for the house, her ass sashaying nicely in a pair of skinny jeans.

"I had to promise that he and Kane could teach me to ride a motorcycle upon my return to the States."

Janelle turned and smiled. "You've never ridden one before?"

He shook his head.

"Oh, this I can't wait to see."

Vlad opened the door, then followed her through, swatting her on the ass. "I swear you, Kane, and Kaleb live to find my faults."

"Well, when you don't have many..." Backing down the entryway into the living area, she stopped right next to his master suite. "That armor you wear is pretty damn thick. Nice to see you have a human side like the rest of us."

"Blame the years I've spent on this earth. It tends to make one cynical."

"That's right." Her eyes turned up in merriment. "You're older than dirt."

"Old?" He harrumphed. "I believe that's called more experienced."

Vlad scented the rise in her desire, making his own go off the charts. If she kept this up, they wouldn't make it the several yards to his large bed, waiting just beyond the opened door behind her.

Janelle smiled. "I can certainly attest to your experience."

"I'm of the mind to give you a repeat performance."

"Just one?"

Lord, he loved this woman. Vlad wasn't about to let her get away this time. He planned on living his years out making up for all the ways he had failed her.

"Trust me, you're about to lose count." Her laughter warmed his cold heart, one he thought dead years ago until she had come into his life. "In fact, if you'd cross through that door behind you, I'd be more than happy to show you just how glad I am to see you."

Janelle placed her hand over his heavily beating heart before sliding her palm south and cupping his erection. "Oh, I plan to make good on that promise, but first we need to talk."

Vlad groaned. "Talking is way overrated."

"Maybe." Janelle removed her hand from his crotch, much to his disappointment. "I had a vision when I was disembarking from the plane."

"Something bad happen?"

"No." She smiled. "Quite the opposite. You're a great-great-grandfather again."

"Cara had the twins?"

"Arrived safely. Did you know their names were going to be Kade and Kalen? Apparently, they wanted to continue the K&K theme for the motorcycle shop they'll one day inherit."

"I'll look forward to meeting them our next trip back to the States." He raised a brow. "Are we done talking yet?"

"There is something else I need to get off my chest."

"Like that tank?"

Janelle swatted his arm. "I'm being serious here."

"So am I." Vlad chuckled. "There is nothing more serious than my need to get you out of those clothes."

Janelle raised a brow.

He gripped her by the shoulders. "Look, *iubi*, I want you to stay here. This could be your home."

"Not that you don't have a beautiful house, but would you mind moving to Oregon?"

"What on God's earth for?"

She grimaced. "I start my new job come first of the year."

Vlad looked into her black gaze. "Your new job?"

He could see in her hopeful eyes how important this was to her. "I left the DEA and took a position as a detective with the Lane County Sheriff's Office. I'm Cara's new partner."

God, help him, he was going to have to live close to family. "I'd follow you halfway across the world if need be, *iubi*. I'd give you my life. Providing we can come here when the family thing gets to be a bit too much."

She laughed, her dark gaze twinkling. Janelle then raised her hands and framed his face, her expression growing serious. "As much as I'd love to get on to the showing part, we really need to clear the air between us. When we make love again, I don't want your brother in that room with us."

Vlad blasphemed, his face heating in anger. There certainly was no room in his bed for that son of a bitch. He gritted his teeth. "Talk."

Janelle dropped her hands and licked her lips, obviously nervous about whatever she had on her mind. "I'm sorry about your brother. Killing him couldn't have been easy."

"No." He smiled cynically. "That was the easy part. I hold no regrets over taking my brother's head. Not after what he took from me. What he also took from you. Christ, Janelle, he turned you into what I am—against your will."

Tears welled in her eyes. "He didn't take me from you. I'm standing right here. I'm yours."

"Yet his blood, damn it, not mine, runs through you. I can scent him even now."

"There must have been a time when you loved him." She worried her lower lip. "He wasn't always bad, or you wouldn't have given him your blood and turned him in the first place."

"Years ago, I had hoped he was worth redeeming. He proved me wrong."

Janelle gripped his hand and placed it over her heart. "Whatever good Mircea had lives here, in me. Whatever bad there was died with him when you took his head. What you scent in me is the brother you tried to redeem. He may have forced me to drink his blood, but he did you a favor, Vlad."

He cleared his throat, his emotions clogging it. "How so?"

"Would you have ever given me your blood? Made me your mate?"

"Christ, Janelle." Vlad considered what life with her as a mate could be, and damn if he didn't want that. "I'm a monster. I have a long history of violence and death."

"And you don't think you're deserving of my love because of all you have done. Because you don't love yourself. How close am I?" She tipped his chin up, made him look her in the eyes. "You're the man I want. Damn it, Vlad, I love you. That is never going to change, no matter whose blood runs through my veins. But you can fix this."

His brow creased. "How?"

"By giving me your blood. Let me be your mate."

"You have no idea what you are asking for." His heart thudded, hope blossoming in his chest. Lord, he wanted to do as she asked. "You'll one day live to regret this, find out the unlovable bastard I really am."

"You said that you loved me, Vlad," she challenged.

"That's not in question." His jaw ached from tension, his fangs erupting from his gums. Every part of him wanted to comply. "I love you so damn much, I never want to let you go again."

"Then don't."

"It would be selfish—"

"It's not selfish when it's what we both want. Please don't turn me away."

"Never." He gripped her ass and pulled her flush against the erection plaguing him. "You belong with me."

"I do." The smile he loved so returned to her lips. He'd make it his life's mission to see it every damn day. "I'm going to enjoy having you around in my life."

"Not half as much as I will. I love you, *iubi*." He placed a kiss on her lips. "Now, can you please be quiet, so I can show you just how much?"

"I need something from you first."

"You have to know I'd give you anything."

"Then give me your blood, Vlad. Do I need to beg?"

Janelle belonged there, with him. If he didn't do as she asked, then he knew she'd leave. Dear Lord, he needed to trust that she'd not resent him, regardless of his demons. But if he gave her his blood, she had to know there would be no turning back.

And right now, he didn't want to turn back.

Vlad scooped her up and carried her through the door to his bed and laid her upon it. He looked down on her, her dark hair fanning across his sheets.

"You'll be stuck with me," he whispered.

Janelle reached out. Vlad crawled onto the bed, the mattress dipping beneath him as he lay between her spread thighs. Pure fucking torture.

"I want to be stuck with you, Vlad, so much so that my chest aches."

Vlad knew the feeling. It echoed in his own heart too. Lifting his wrist to his lips, he tore a hole in his vein. Dark blood ran down his arm. "Are you sure?"

Her smile was his answer as she grabbed his wrist and drew it to her lips. Opening her mouth, two-razor-sharp fangs appeared. And he thought her hot before? The vampire in her turned his blood to lava. Her fangs sank deep into his wrist, suckling his blood into her own veins.

Her scent changed, his mingling with hers to the point he could no longer detect his brother. Good versus evil. His blood had eclipsed Mircea's. Janelle was now his mate. His heart swelled with every red blood cell she ingested, feeling her heart beat in his own damn chest. She had saved him, not the other way around. What good had he ever done for fate to be so kind?

Sealing the wounds at his wrist with her tongue, she smiled up at him, his blood staining her pretty fangs. "Make love to me?"

"Christ, I thought you'd never ask."

Clothes quickly dropped to the floor and he entered her swiftly. Never had his home ever been so complete.

His. There was no question.

This woman belonged to him for now and forever.

ABOUT THE AUTHOR

A daydreamer at heart, Patricia A. Rasey, resides in her native town in Northwest Ohio with her husband, Mark, and her two lovable Cavalier King Charles Spaniels, Todd and Buckeye. A graduate of Long Ridge Writer's School, Patricia has seen publication of some her short stories in magazines as well as several of her novels.

When not behind her computer, you can find Patricia working, reading, watching movies or MMA. She also enjoys spending her free time at the river camping and boating with her husband and two sons. Ms. Rasey is a retired third degree Black Belt in American Freestyle Karate.

Printed in Great Britain
by Amazon